DEBBIE MACOMBER

Kisses in the Snow

mira

mira

ISBN-13: 978-0-7783-0821-8

Recycling programs for this product may not exist in your area.

Kisses in the Snow

Copyright © 2019 by Harlequin Books S.A.

The Christmas Basket
First published in 2002. This edition published in 2019.
Copyright © 2002 by Debbie Macomber

Let It Snow
First published in 1986. This edition published in 2019.
Copyright © 1986 by Debbie Macomber

For questions and comments about the quality of this book, please contact us at CustomerService@Harlequin.com.

Harlequin.com

Printed in U.S.A.

Also available from Debbie Macomber and MIRA Books

Blossom Street

The Shop on Blossom Street
A Good Yarn
Susannah's Garden
Back on Blossom Street
Twenty Wishes
Summer on Blossom Street
Hannah's List
"The Twenty-First Wish"
  (in *The Knitting Diaries*)
A Turn in the Road

Cedar Cove

16 Lighthouse Road
204 Rosewood Lane
311 Pelican Court
44 Cranberry Point
50 Harbor Street
6 Rainier Drive
74 Seaside Avenue
8 Sandpiper Way
92 Pacific Boulevard
1022 Evergreen Place
Christmas in Cedar Cove
  (*5-B Poppy Lane* and
  A Cedar Cove Christmas)
1105 Yakima Street
1225 Christmas Tree Lane

The Dakota Series

Dakota Born
Dakota Home
Always Dakota
Buffalo Valley

The Manning Family

The Manning Sisters
  (*The Cowboy's Lady* and
  The Sheriff Takes a Wife)

The Manning Brides
  (*Marriage of Inconvenience* and
  Stand-In Wife)
The Manning Grooms
  (*Bride on the Loose* and
  Same Time, Next Year)

Christmas Books

A Gift to Last
On a Snowy Night
Home for the Holidays
Glad Tidings
Christmas Wishes
Small Town Christmas
When Christmas Comes
  (now retitled *Trading
  Christmas*)
There's Something About Christmas
Christmas Letters
The Perfect Christmas
Choir of Angels
  (*Shirley, Goodness and Mercy,
  Those Christmas Angels* and
  Where Angels Go)
Call Me Mrs. Miracle

Heart of Texas

Texas Skies
  (*Lonesome Cowboy* and
  Texas Two-Step)
Texas Nights
  (*Caroline's Child* and
  Dr. Texas)
Texas Home
  (*Nell's Cowboy* and
  Lone Star Baby)
Promise, Texas
Return to Promise

Midnight Sons

Alaska Skies
   (*Brides for Brothers* and
   The Marriage Risk)
Alaska Nights
   (*Daddy's Little Helper* and
   Because of the Baby)
Alaska Home
   (*Falling for Him,*
   Ending in Marriage and
   Midnight Sons and Daughters)

This Matter of Marriage
Montana
Thursdays at Eight
Between Friends
Changing Habits
Married in Seattle
   (*First Comes Marriage* and
   Wanted: Perfect Partner)
Right Next Door
   (*Father's Day* and
   The Courtship of Carol Sommars)
Wyoming Brides
   (*Denim and Diamonds* and
   The Wyoming Kid)
Fairy Tale Weddings
   (*Cindy and the Prince* and
   Some Kind of Wonderful)
The Man You'll Marry
   (*The First Man You Meet* and
   The Man You'll Marry)
Orchard Valley Grooms
   (*Valerie* and *Stephanie*)
Orchard Valley Brides
   (*Norah* and *Lone Star Lovin'*)
The Sooner the Better
An Engagement in Seattle
   (*Groom Wanted* and
   Bride Wanted)
Out of the Rain
   (*Marriage Wanted* and
   Laughter in the Rain)
Learning to Love
   (*Sugar and Spice* and
   Love by Degree)

You…Again
   (*Baby Blessed* and
   Yesterday Once More)
The Unexpected Husband
   (*Jury of His Peers* and
   Any Sunday)
Three Brides, No Groom
Love in Plain Sight
   (*Love 'n' Marriage* and
   Almost an Angel)
I Left My Heart
   (*A Friend or Two* and
   No Competition)
Marriage Between Friends
   (*White Lace and Promises* and
   Friends—And Then Some)
A Man's Heart
   (*The Way to a Man's Heart* and
   Hasty Wedding)
North to Alaska
   (*That Wintry Feeling* and
   Borrowed Dreams)
On a Clear Day
   (*Starlight* and
   Promise Me Forever)
To Love and Protect
   (*Shadow Chasing* and
   For All My Tomorrows)
Home in Seattle
   (*The Playboy and the Widow*
   and *Fallen Angel*)
Together Again
   (*The Trouble with Caasi* and
   Reflections of Yesterday)
The Reluctant Groom
   (*All Things Considered* and
   Almost Paradise)
A Real Prince
   (*The Bachelor Prince* and
   Yesterday's Hero)
Private Paradise
   (in *That Summer Place*)

Debbie Macomber's
   Cedar Cove Cookbook
Debbie Macomber's
   Christmas Cookbook

CONTENTS

THE CHRISTMAS BASKET   9

LET IT SNOW   199

THE CHRISTMAS BASKET

To
Laurie and Jaxon Macomber
and
in memory of our son Dale

NOELLE MCDOWELL'S
JOURNAL

December 1

I did it. I broke down and actually booked the flight to Rose. I have a ticket for December 18—Dallas to San Francisco to Portland and then the commuter flight to Rose.

All my excuses are used up. I always figured there was no going back, and yet that's exactly what I'm doing. I'm going home when I swore I never would. Not after what happened... Not after Thom Sutton betrayed me. I know, I know, I've always been dramatic. I can't help that—it's part of my nature.

When I was a teenager I made this vow never to return. I spoke it in the heat of passion, and no one believed me. For that matter, I didn't believe me, not really. But it proved to be so easy to stay away.... I hardly had to invent excuses. While I was in college I had an opportunity to travel to Europe two years in a row. Then in my junior year I had a summer job and was a bridesmaid in a Christmas wedding. And when my senior year rolled around, I was working as an in-

tern for the software company, and it was impossible to get time off. After that...well, it was just simpler to stay away. Without meaning to, my family made it convenient. I didn't need to visit them; they seemed willing enough to come to Dallas.

All of that is about to end. I'm prepared to face my past. I joined Weight Watchers. If I happen to see Thom Sutton, I want him to know exactly what he's missing. I've already lost five of the ten pounds I need to get rid of, and by next week he'll hardly recognize me—if we even run into each other. We won't, of course, but just on the offchance, I plan to be prepared.

Good ol' Thom Sutton. I wonder what he's doing now. Naturally I could ask, but no one dares mention the name Sutton to my family. It's the Hatfields and Mc-Coys or the Montagues and Capulets all over again. Except that it's our mothers who started this ridiculous feud.

If I really wanted to know about Thom, I could ask Megan or Stephanie. They're the only two girls out of my entire high school class who still live in Rose. But I wouldn't do that. Inquiring about Thom would only invite questions from them about what happened between the two of us. As far as I'm concerned, the fewer people who know, the better.

He's bound to be married, anyway. Good. I want him to be happy.

No, I don't.

If I can't be honest in my journal, then I shouldn't keep one. Okay, I admit it—what I really want is for him to have suffered guilt and regret all these years. He should have pined for me. His life should be a bleak series of endless days filled with haunting memories of me. It's what he deserves.

On a brighter note, I'm thrilled for Kristen. I'll return home, help her plan her wedding, hold my head high and pray that Thom Sutton has the opportunity to see me from afar, gorgeous and thin. Then I want him to agonize over all the might-have-beens.

One

It would be the wedding of the year. No—the wedding of the century.

Sarah McDowell intended to create the most exquisite event possible, a wedding worthy of *Vogue* magazine (or at least a two-page spread in the Rose, Oregon, *Gazette*). The entire town would talk about her daughter's wedding.

The foundation for Sarah's plans rested squarely on booking the Women's Century Club for the reception. It was why she'd maintained her association with the club after *that* woman had been granted membership. She was outraged that such a fine institution would lower itself to welcome the likes of Mary Sutton.

Sarah refused to dwell on the sordid details. She couldn't allow herself to get upset over something that had happened almost twenty years ago. Although it didn't hurt any to imagine Mary hearing—second- or third-hand, of course—about Kristen's wedding. As Sarah understood it, Mary's daughter had eloped. Eloped, mind you, with some riffraff hazelnut farmer.

Sarah didn't know that for sure because it was her Christian duty not to gossip or think ill of others. However, sometimes information just happened to come one's way....

Pulling into the parking lot of the Women's Century Club, Sarah surveyed the grounds. Even this late in the year, the rose garden was breathtaking. Many of the carefully tended bushes still wore their blooms, and next June, when the wedding was scheduled, the garden would be stunning. The antique roses with their intoxicating scents and the more recent hybrids with their gorgeous shapes and colors would make a fitting backdrop for the beautiful bride and her handsome groom. It would be *perfect,* she thought with satisfaction. Absolutely perfect.

Sarah had stopped attending the Women's Century Club meetings three years ago. Well, there wasn't any need to obsess over the membership committee's sorry lapse in judgment. For many years Sarah had chaired that committee herself. The instant she stepped down, Mary Sutton had applied for membership to the prestigious club—and received it. Now the only social event Sarah participated in was the annual Christmas dance. Mary Sutton had robbed her of so much already, but Sarah wasn't letting her ruin that, too.

Sarah did continue to meet with other friends from the club and managed to keep up with the news. She understood that Mary had become quite active in the association. Fine. Good for her. It gave the woman something to write about in her column for the weekly *Rose Gazette.* Not that Sarah read "About Town." Someone had told her it was fairly popular, though. Which didn't bother her in the least. Mary was a good writer; Sarah would acknowledge that much. But then, what one lacked in certain areas was often compensated in others. And Mary was definitely lacking in the areas of generosity, fairness, ethics.... She could go on.

With a click of her key chain, Sarah locked her car and headed toward the large, two-story stone structure. There was a cold wind blowing in from the ocean, and she hurried up the steps of the large veranda that surrounded the house. A blast of warm air greeted her as she walked inside. Immediately in front of her was the curved stairway leading to the ballroom on the second floor. She could already picture Kristen moving elegantly down those stairs, her dress sweeping grandly behind her. Today, evergreen garlands were hung along the mahogany railing, with huge red velvet bows tied at regular intervals. Gigantic potted poinsettias lined both sides of the stairway. The effect was both festive and tasteful.

"Oh, how lovely," she said to Melody Darrington, the club's longtime secretary.

"Yes, we're very pleased with this year's Christmas decorations." Melody glanced up from her desk behind the half wall that overlooked the entry. The door to the office was open and Sarah heard the fax machine humming behind her. "Are you here to pick up your tickets for the Christmas dance?"

"I am," Sarah confirmed. "And I'd like to book the club for June seventh for a reception." She paused dramatically. "Kristen's getting married."

"Sarah, that's just wonderful!"

"Yes, Jake and I are pleased." This seriously understated her emotions. Kristen was the first of her three daughters to marry, and Sarah felt as if the wedding was the culmination of all her years as a caring, involved mother. She highly approved of Kristen's fiancé. Jonathan Clark was not only a charming and considerate young man, he held a promising position at an investment firm and had a degree in business. His parents were college professors who lived in Eugene; he was their only son. Whenever she'd spoken with Jonathan's mother, Louise Clark had sounded equally delighted.

Melody flipped the pages of the appointment book to June. "It's a good idea to book the club early."

Holding her breath, Sarah leaned over the half wall and stared down at the schedule. She relaxed the instant she saw that particular Saturday was free. The wedding date could remain unchanged.

"It looks like June seventh is open," Melody said.

"Fabulous." Sarah's cell phone rang, and she reached inside her purse to retrieve it. She sold real estate, but since entering her fifties, she'd scaled back her hours on the job. Jake, who was head of the X-ray department at Rose Hospital, enjoyed traveling. Sarah no longer had the energy to accompany Jake and also maintain her status as a top-selling agent. The number displayed on her phone was that of her husband's office. She'd call him back shortly. He was probably asking about the time of their eldest daughter's flight. Jake and Sarah were going to meet Noelle at the small commuter airport later in the day. What a joy it would be to have all three of their girls home for Christmas, not to mention Noelle's birthday, which was December twenty-fifth. This would be the first time in ten years that Noelle had returned to celebrate *anything* with her family. Sarah blamed Mary Sutton and her son for that, too.

"Should I give you a deposit now?" she asked, removing her checkbook.

"Since you're a member of the club, that won't be necessary."

"Great. Then that's settled and I can get busy with my day. I've got a couple of houses to show. Plus Jake and I are driving to the airport this afternoon to pick up Noelle. You remember our daughter Noelle, don't you?"

"Of course."

"She's living in Dallas these days, and has a high-powered job with one of the big computer companies." What Sarah didn't add was the Noelle had become a workaholic. Getting her twenty-eight-year-old daughter to take time off work was nearly impossible. Sarah and Jake made a point of visiting her once a year and sometimes twice, but this couldn't go on. Noelle had to get over her phobia about returning to Rose—and the risk of seeing Thom Sutton. Oh, yes, those Suttons had done a lot of damage to the McDowells.

With Kristen announcing her engagement and inviting the Clarks to share their Christmas festivities, Sarah had strongly urged Noelle to come home for the celebration. This was an important year for their family, and it was absolutely necessary that Noelle be there with them. After some back-and-forth discussion, she'd finally capitulated.

"Before you leave, there's something you should know," Melody said hesitantly. "There's been a rule change about members using the building."

"Yes?" Sarah tensed, anticipating a roadblock.

"The new rule states that only members who have completed a minimum of ten hours' community service approved by the club will be permitted to lease our facilities."

"But I'm an active part of our community already," Sarah complained. She provided plenty of services to others.

"I realize that. Unfortunately, the service project in question must be determined by the club and it must be completed by the end of December to qualify for the following year."

Sarah gaped at her. "Do you mean to say that in addition to everything else I'm doing in the next two weeks, I have to complete some club project?"

"You haven't been reading the newsletters, have you?" Melody asked, frowning.

Obviously not. Sarah refused to read about Mary Sutton, whose name seemed to appear in every issue these days.

"If you attended the meetings, you'd know it, too." Melody added insult to injury by pointing out Sarah's intentional absence.

Despite her irritation, Sarah managed a weak smile. "All right," she muttered. "What can I do?"

"Actually, you've come at an opportune moment. We need someone who's willing to pitch in on the Christmas baskets."

Sarah was trying to figure out how she could squeeze in one more task before the holidays. "Exactly what would that entail?"

"Oh, it'll be great fun. The ladies pooled the money

they raised from the cookbook sale to buy gifts for these baskets. They've made up lists, and what you'd need to do is get everything on your list, arrange all the stuff inside the baskets and then deliver them to the Salvation Army by December twenty-third."

That didn't sound unreasonable. "I think I can do that."

"Wonderful." A smile lit up Melody's face. "The woman who's heading up the project will be grateful for some help."

"The woman?" That sounded better already. At least she wouldn't be stuck doing this alone.

"Mary Sutton."

Sarah felt as though Melody had punched her. "Excuse me. For a moment I thought you said *Mary Sutton*."

"I did."

"I don't mean to be catty here, but Mary and I have... a history."

"I'm sure you'll be able to work something out. You're both adults."

Sarah was stunned by the woman's lack of sensitivity. She wanted to argue, to explain that this was unacceptable, but she couldn't think of exactly what to say.

"You did want the club for June seventh, didn't you?"

"Well, yes, of course, but—"

"Then be here tomorrow morning at ten to meet with Mary."

Numb and speechless, Sarah slowly turned and trudged toward the door.

"Sarah," Melody called. "Don't forget the dance tickets."

Dance. How could she think about the dance when

she was being forced to confront a woman who detested her? The feeling might be mutual but that didn't make it any less awkward.

One across. A four-letter word for fragrant flower. Rose, naturally. Noelle McDowell penciled in the answer and moved to the next clue. A prickly feeling crawled up her spine and she raised her head. She disliked the short commuter flights. This one, out of Portland, carried twenty-four passengers. It saved having to rent a vehicle or asking her parents to make the long drive into the big city to pick her up.

The feeling persisted and she glanced over her shoulder. She instantly jerked back and slid down in her seat as far as the constraints of the seat belt allowed. It couldn't be. *No, please,* she muttered, closing her eyes. *Not Thom.* Not after all these years. Not now. But it was, it had to be. No one else would look at her with such complete, unadulterated antagonism. He had some nerve after what he'd done to her.

Long before she was ready, the pilot announced that the plane was preparing to land in Rose. On these flights, no carry-on bags were permitted, and Noelle hadn't taken anything more than her purse on board. Her magazines would normally go in her briefcase, but that didn't fit in the compact space beneath her seat, so the flight attendant had stowed it. She had a *Weight Watchers* magazine and a crossword puzzle book marked *EASY* in large letters across the top. She wasn't going to let Thom see her with either and stuffed them in the outside pocket of her purse, folding one magazine over the other.

Her pulse thundered like crazy. The man who'd broken her heart sat only two rows behind her, looking as sophisticated as if he'd stepped off the pages of *GQ*. He'd always been tall, dark and handsome—like a twenty-first-century Cary Grant. Classic features that were just rugged enough to be interesting and very, very masculine. Dark eyes, glossy dark hair. An impeccable sense of style. Surely he was married. But finding out would mean asking her sister or one of her friends who still lived in Rose. Coward that she was, Noelle didn't want to know. Okay, she did, but not if it meant having to ask.

The plane touched down and Noelle braced herself against the jolt of the wheels bouncing on tarmac. As soon as they'd coasted to a stop, the Unfasten Seat Belt sign went off, and the people around her instantly leaped to their feet. Noelle took her time. Her hair was a fright. Up at three that morning to catch the 6:00 a.m. out of Dallas/Ft. Worth, she'd run a brush through the dark tangles, forgoing the usual routine of fussing with mousse. As a result, large ringlets fell like bedsprings about her face. Normally, her hair was shaped and controlled and coerced into gentle waves. But today she had the misfortune of looking like Shirley Temple in one of her 1930s movies—and in front of Thom Sutton, no less.

When it was her turn to leave her seat, she stood, looking staunchly ahead. If luck was with her, she could slip away unnoticed and pretend she hadn't seen him. Luck, however, was on vacation and the instant she stepped into the aisle, the handle of her purse caught on the seat arm. Both magazines popped out of the outside pocket and flew into the air, only to be caught by none other than Thom Sutton. The crossword puzzle magazine tumbled to the floor and he was left holding the *Weight Watchers* December issue. As his gaze slid over her, she immediately sucked in her stomach.

"I read it for the fiction," she announced, then added, "Don't I know you?" She tried to sound indifferent— and to look thin. "It's Tim, isn't it?" she asked, frowning as though she couldn't quite place him.

"Thom," he corrected. "Good to see you again, Nadine."

"Noelle," she said bitterly.

He glared at her until someone from the back of the line called, "Would you two mind having your reunion when you get off the plane?"

"Sorry," Thom said over his shoulder.

"I barely know this man." Noelle wanted her fellow passengers to hear the truth. "I once thought I did, but I was wrong," she explained, walking backward toward the exit.

"Whatever," the guy behind them said loudly.

"You're a fine one to talk," Thom said. His eyes were as dark and cold as those of the snowman they'd built in Lions' Park their senior year of high school—like glittering chips of coal.

"You have your nerve," she muttered, whirling around just in time to avoid crashing into the open cockpit. She smiled sweetly at the pilot. "Thank you for a most pleasant flight."

He returned the smile. "I hope you'll fly with us again."

"I will."

"Good to see you, Thom," the pilot said next.

Placing her hand on the railing of the steep stairs that led to the ground, Noelle did her best to keep her head high, her shoulders square—and her eyes front. The last thing she wanted to do was trip and make an even worse fool of herself by falling flat on her face.

She was shocked by a blast of cold air. After living in Texas for the last ten years, she'd forgotten how cold it could get in the Pacific Northwest. Her thin cashmere wrap was completely inadequate.

"One would think you'd know better than to wear a sweater here in December," Thom said, coming down the steps directly behind her.

"I forgot."

"If you came home more often, you'd have remembered."

"You keep track of my visits?" She scowled at him. A thick strand of curly hair slapped her in the face and she tossed it back with a jerk of her head. Unfortunately she nearly put out her neck in the process.

"No, I don't keep track of your visits. Frankly, I couldn't care less."

"That's fine by me." Having the last word was important, no matter how inane it was.

The luggage cart came around and she grabbed her briefcase from the top and made for the interior of the small airport. Her flight had landed early, which meant that her parents probably hadn't arrived yet. At least her luck was consistent—all bad. One thing was certain: the instant Thom caught sight of her mother and father, he'd make himself scarce.

He removed his own briefcase and started into the

terminal less than two feet behind her. Because of his long legs, he quickly outdistanced her. Refusing to let him pass her, Noelle hurried ahead, practically trotting.

"Don't you think you're being a little silly?" he asked.

"About what?" She blinked, hoping to convey a look of innocence.

"Never mind." He smiled, which infuriated her further.

"No, I'm serious," she insisted. "What do you mean?"

He simply shook his head and turned toward the baggage claim area. They were the first passengers to get there. Noelle stood on one side of the conveyor belt and Thom on the other. He ignored her and she tried to pretend he'd never been born.

That proved to be impossible because ten years ago Thom Sutton had ripped her heart right out.

For most of their senior year of high school, Thom and Noelle had been in love; they'd also managed to hide that fact from their parents. Sneaking out of her room at night, meeting him after school and passing notes to each other had worked quite effectively.

Then they'd argued about their mothers and the ongoing feud between Sarah and Mary. They'd soon made up, however, realizing that what really mattered was their love. Because they were both eighteen and legally entitled to marry without parental consent, they'd decided to elope. It'd been Thom's suggestion. According to him, it was the only way they could get married, since the parents on both sides would oppose their wishes and try to put obstacles in their path. But once they were married, he said, they could bring their families together.

Noelle felt mortified now to remember how much she'd trusted Thom. But their whole "engagement" had turned out to be a ploy to humiliate and embarrass her. It seemed Thom was his mother's son, after all.

She'd been proud of her love for Thom, and before she left to meet him that fateful evening, she'd boldly announced her intentions to her family. Her stomach twisted at the memory. Her parents were shocked as well as appalled; she and Thom had kept their secret well. Her mother had burst into tears, her father had shouted and her two younger sisters had wailed in protest. Undeterred, Noelle had marched out the door, suitcase in hand, to meet the man she loved. The man she'd defied her family to marry. Except that he didn't show up.

At first she'd assumed it was a misunderstanding—that she'd mistaken the agreed-upon time. Then, throwing caution to the wind, she'd phoned his house and asked to speak to him, only to learn that Thom had gone bowling.

He'd gone *bowling?* Apparently some friends from school had phoned and off he'd gone, leaving her to wait in doubt and misery. The parking lot at the bowling alley confirmed his father's words. There was Thom's car—and inside the Bowlerama was Thom, carousing with his friends. Noelle had peered through the window and seen the waitress sitting on his lap and the other guys gathered around, joking and teasing. Before she went home, Noelle had placed a nasty note on his windshield, in which she described him as a scumof-the-earth bastard. Their supposed elopement, their so-called love had all been a fraud, a cruel joke. She figured it was revenge what for her mother had done, losing Thom's grandmother's precious tea service. Not *losing* it, actually. She'd borrowed it to display at an open house for another real estate agent—and someone had taken it. That was how the feud started and it had escalated steadily after that.

To make matters worse, she'd had to return home in humiliation and admit that Thom had stood her up. Like the heroine of an old-fashioned melodrama, she'd been jilted, abandoned and forsaken.

For days she'd moped around the house, weeping and miserable. Thom hadn't phoned or contacted her again. It was difficult to believe he could be so heartless, but she had all the evidence she needed. She hadn't seen or talked to him since. For ten years she'd avoided returning to the scene of her shame.

The grinding sound of the conveyor belt gearing up broke Noelle from her reverie. Luggage started to roll out from the black hole behind the rubber curtain. Thom stepped forward, in a hurry to claim his suitcase and leave, or so it seemed. Noelle was no less eager to escape. She'd rather wait in the damp cold outside the terminal than stand five feet across from Thomas Sutton.

The very attractive Thomas Sutton. Even better-looking than he'd been ten years ago. Life just wasn't fair.

"I would've thought your wife would be here to pick you up," she said without looking at him. She shouldn't have spoken at all, but suddenly she had to know.

"Is that your unsubtle way of asking if I'm married?"

She ground her teeth. "Stood up any other girls in the last ten years?" she asked.

His eyes narrowed. "Don't do it, Noelle."

"You're the one who shouldn't have done it."

The man from the back of the plane waltzed past Noelle and reached for his suitcase. "Why don't you two just kiss and make up," he suggested, winking at Thom.

"I don't think so," Noelle said, sending Thom a contemptuous glare. She was astonished to see his anger, as though *he* had something to be angry about. *She* was the injured party here.

"On that I'll agree with you," Thom said. He caught hold of a suitcase and yanked it off the belt with enough force to topple a second suitcase. Without another word, he turned and walked out the door.

No sooner had he disappeared than the glass doors opened and in walked Noelle's parents.

Noelle's youngest sister held a special place in her heart. Carley Sue was an unexpected surprise, born when Noelle was fifteen and Kristen twelve. She'd only been three when Noelle left for college. Nevertheless, all three sisters remained close. Or as close as email, phone calls and the occasional visit to Dallas allowed.

Sitting on Noelle's bed, Carley rested her chin on one hand as Noelle unpacked her suitcase. "You don't mind that I have your old room, do you?" she asked anxiously.

"Heavens, no. It's only right that you do."

Some of the worry disappeared from Carley's eyes. "Are you really going to be home for two whole weeks?"

"I am." Noelle had tentatively planned a discounted cruise with a couple of friends. Instead, she was vacationing with her parents, planning her sister's wedding and trying not to think about Thom Sutton.

"You're going to the Christmas dance, aren't you?"

"Not if I can get out of it." Her mother was the one who insisted on these social outings, but Noelle would live the rest of her life content if she never attended another dance. They reminded her to much of those long-ago evenings with Thom....

"Mom says you're going."

Noelle sat down on the end of the bed and sighed. "I'll tell her I don't have anything to wear."

"Don't do that," Carley advised. "She'll buy you a pink dress. Mom loves pink. Not just any old pink, either, but something that looks exactly like Pepto-Bismol. She actually wanted Kristen to choose pink for her wedding colors." She grimaced. Reaching down for her feet, Carley curled her fingers over her bare toes and nodded vigorously. "You'd better come to the dance."

This was one of the reasons Noelle found excuse after excuse to stay away from Rose. Admittedly it wasn't the primary reason—Thom Sutton and his mother were responsible for that. But as much as she loved her family, she dreaded being dragged from one social event to the next. She could see her mother putting her on display—in Pepto-Bismol pink, according to Carley. If that wasn't bad enough, Sarah had an embarrassing tendency to speak as though Noelle wasn't in the room, bragging outrageously over every little accomplishment.

"Hey, you want to go to the movies tomorrow?" Noelle asked her sister.

Carley's eyes brightened. "Sure! I was hoping we'd get to do things together."

The doorbell chimed and Carley rolled onto her stomach. "That's Kristen. She's coming over without Jonathan tonight."

"You like Jonathan?" Noelle asked.

"Yeah." Carley grinned happily. "He danced with me once and no one asked him to or anything."

This was encouraging. Maybe he'd dance with her, too.

"Noelle!" Kristen called from the far end of the hallway. She burst into the room, full of energy and spirit. Instantly Noelle was wrapped in a tight embrace. "I can't believe you're here—oh, sis, it's so good to see you."

Noelle hugged her back. She missed the chats they used to have; discussions over the phone just weren't the same as hugs and smiles. "Guess who I ran into on the plane?" Noelle had been dying to talk about the chance encounter with Thom.

Some of the excitement faded from Kristen's eyes. "Don't tell me. Thom Sutton?"

Noelle nodded.

"Who's Thom Sutton?" Carley asked, glancing from one sister to the other.

"A guy I once dated."

"Were you lovers?"

"Carley!"

"Just curious." She shrugged as if this was information she was somehow entitled to.

"Where?" Kristen demanded.

"He was on the same flight as me."

"He still lives here, you know. He's some kind of

executive for a mail-order company that's really taken off in the last few years. Apparently he does a lot of traveling."

"How'd you know that?" They'd always avoided the topic of Thom Sutton in their telephone and email communications.

"Jon told me about him. I think Thom might be one of his clients."

"Oh." Not only was Thom Sutton gorgeous, he was successful, too. "I suppose he's engaged to someone stunningly beautiful." That was to be expected.

"I hear—again from Jon—that he dates quite a bit, but there's no one serious."

Noelle shouldn't be pleased, but she couldn't help it. She didn't want to examine that reaction too closely.

"I want to know what happened," Carley demanded, rising to her knees. "I'm not a kid anymore. Tell me!"

"He was Noelle's high school sweetheart," Kirsten explained.

"The guy who left you at the altar?"

"Who told you that?" Noelle asked, although the answer was obvious. "And he didn't leave me at the altar." *Just being accurate,* she told herself. *I'm not defending him.*

"Mom told me 'cause she wants me to keep away from those Suttons. When I asked her why, she said you learned your lesson the hard way. She said a Sutton broke your heart and jilted you."

"There's more to it than that," Kristen told her.

"I want to know *everything,*" Carley pleaded. "How can I hate them if I don't know what they did that was so awful?"

"You shouldn't hate anyone."

"I don't, not really, but if our family doesn't like their family, then I should know why."

"It's a long story."

Carley sat back on her heels. "That's what Mom said."

"God help me," Kristen murmured, covering her eyes with one hand. "Don't tell me I already sound like Mom. I didn't think this would happen until I turned thirty."

Noelle laughed, although she wasn't sure how funny it was, since she herself was only days from her twenty-ninth birthday.

"Did you love him terribly?" Carley asked with a faraway look in her eyes.

Noelle wasn't sure how to respond. She felt a distant and remembered pain but refused to let it take hold. "I thought I did."

"It was wildly romantic," Kristen added. "They were madly in love, but then they had a falling-out—"

"That's one way to put it," Noelle said, interrupting her sister. Thom had apparently fallen out of love with her. He'd certainly fallen out of their plans to elope.

"This is all so sad," Carley said with an exaggerated sigh.

"Our parents not getting along is what started this in the first place."

"At least you and Thom didn't kill yourselves, like Romeo and Juliet—"

"No." Noelle shook her head. "I've always been the sane, sensible sister. Remember?" But even as she spoke, she recognized her words for the lie they were. Staying away for ten years was a pretty extreme and hardly "sensible" reaction. Even she knew that. The fact was, though, something that had begun as a protest had simply become habit.

"Oh, sure," Kristen teased. "Very sensible. You work too hard, you don't date nearly enough and you avoid Rose as though we've got an epidemic of the plague."

"Guilty, guilty, not guilty." She wasn't *purposely* avoiding Rose, she told herself, at least not anymore and not to the extent that Kristen implied. Noelle's job was demanding and it was difficult to take off four or five days in a row.

"I've never met Thom, and already I don't like him," Carley announced. "Anyone who broke your heart is a dweeb. Besides, if he married you the way he said he would, you'd be living in Rose now and I could see you anytime I wanted."

"Well put, little sister," Kristen said. She shrugged off her coat, then joined Carley at the foot of the bed.

Noelle smiled at her two sisters and realized with a pang how much she missed them. Back in Texas it was all too easy to let work consume her life—to relegate these important relationships to fifteen-minute conversations on the phone.

"Look," Kristen said and stretched out her arm so Noelle could see her engagement ring. It was a solitaire diamond, virtually flawless, in a classic setting. A perfect choice for Kristen. "Jon and I shopped for weeks. He wanted the highest-quality stone for the best price." Her eyes softened as she studied the ring.

"It's beautiful," Noelle whispered, overcome for a moment by the sheer joy she saw in her sister's face.

"You'll be my maid of honor, won't you?"

"As long as I don't have to wear a dress the color of Pepto-Bismol."

"You're safe on that account."

"If you ask me to be the flower girl, I think I'll scream," Carley muttered. "Why won't anyone believe me when I tell them I'm not a little kid anymore? I'm almost fourteen!"

"Not for ten months," Noelle reminded her.

"But, I'm *going* to be fourteen."

Kristen brushed the hair away from Carley's face. "Actually, I intended to ask you to be a bridesmaid."

"You did?" Carley shrieked with happiness. "Well, then, I'll tell you what I overheard Mom tell Dad." Her voice dropped to a whisper as she detailed a conversation between their parents regarding Christmas baskets.

"Mom's meeting with *Mrs. Sutton* tomorrow morning?" Noelle repeated incredulously.

"That's what she said. She didn't sound happy about it, either."

"I'll just bet she didn't."

"This should be interesting," Kristen murmured.

Yes, it should, Noelle silently agreed. *It should be very interesting, indeed.*

NOELLE McDOWELL'S
JOURNAL

December 19
(2:00 a.m.)

So I saw him before I even got back to town. Of all the flights I could've taken...

Seeing Thom after all these years was probably the most humbling experience of my life, except for the last time I was with him. Correction. Wasn't with him. Why did this have to happen to me? Or did I bring it on myself because of my obsession over seeing him again?

Okay, the thing to do is look at the positive aspect of this. It's over. I saw him, it was worse than I could have imagined, but now I don't need to worry about it anymore. Thom made it clear that he wasn't any happier to see me than I was about running into him. At least the feeling's mutual. Although I'm kind of confused by that, since I'm the offended one. He jilted me. Unfortunately, after this latest run-in, he doesn't have any reason to regret that. I behaved like an idiot.

On a brighter note—and I'm always looking for brighter notes!—it's good to be home. I shouldn't have

*stayed away for ten years. That was foolish and I'm
sorry about it. I walked all through the house, stopping in each room. After a while, I got all teary as I
looked around. Nothing's really changed and yet everything's different. I didn't realize how much I've missed
my home. Mom's got the house all decorated for Christmas, including those funny-looking cotton-ball snow-
men I made at camp a thousand years ago. When I
commented on that, she told me it was tradition. She
puts them out every Christmas. She got all choked up
and I did, too. We hugged, and I promised I'd never
stay away this long again. And I won't.*

*Carley Sue (she hates it when I use her middle name)
is so much fun. Seeing her here, in her own space (even
if it is my old room), is like discovering an entirely different side of her. She's freer, more relaxed, and so
eager to share the camaraderie between me and Kristen.*

*Speaking of Kristen—she's on cloud nine. We sat up
and talked for hours, and she told me all about meeting
and falling in love with Jonathan. I'd heard it before,
but the story felt brand-new as I listened to her tell it
in person. It's so romantic, meeting her future husband
in a flower shop when he's there to pick up a dozen red
roses for another woman. I give him credit, though;
Jonathan knew a real flower when he saw one. It was
Kristen who walked out with those roses.*

*Carley warned me that Mom's going to be looking
for company when she has to meet Mrs. Sutton in the
morning. We've already thwarted her. We sisters have
our ways....*

Two

Sarah would have preferred a root canal to meeting with Mary Sutton. A root canal without anaesthetic.

Her husband lingered over his morning coffee before leaving for the hospital. "You're really stressed about this, aren't you?"

"Yes!" Sarah wasn't afraid to admit it. "The last time I spoke to Mary was the day she wrote that dreadful article about me in her column."

"You think that article was only about you," Jake said. "But it could've been about any real estate agent. Maybe even a bunch of different ones." His voice drifted off.

Sarah didn't understand why her husband was arguing when they both knew the entire dreadful piece titled *The Nightmare Real Estate Agent,* was directed solely at *her.* Although she hadn't committed any of sins Mary had described, she'd been guilty of the one crime Mary hadn't mentioned. Never once had she misrepresented a home or hidden a defect. Nor had she ever low-balled a client. But Sarah had borrowed something she couldn't return.

"Was that *before* or *after* you planted the OPEN HOUSE sign in her front yard?" Jake asked.

"Before, and she deserved it."

Her husband chuckled. "Go on, meet with her and don't for a moment let her know you're upset."

"You sound like a commercial for deodorant."

"Yes, dear." He kissed her cheek and headed out the door to work.

Tightening the belt of her housecoat, Sarah gazed out the front window as he drove away. *Meet with her...* Easy for him to say. He wasn't the one coming face-to-face with Mary after all these years.

Yawning, Noelle wandered into the kitchen and poured a cup of coffee. Sarah's spirits lifted immediately. It was so good to have her daughter home—and even better that she'd arrived at such an opportune moment. Noelle could act as a buffer between her and that demented newspaper writer who'd once been her friend. True, there was the business with the Sutton boy, but if nothing else, that unfortunate bit of history would distract them all from this current awkwardness. She felt a twinge of guilt at the idea of involving her daughter. Still, she needed reinforcements, and surely Noelle was long over her infatuation with Thom.

"Good morning, dear," Sarah said, mustering a cheerful greeting. "I was wondering if you'd like to come with me this morning." Try as she might, she couldn't keep the plea out of her voice.

Her daughter leaned against the kitchen counter, holding the mug with both hands. "I promised to take Carley shopping and to the movies."

"Oh. That won't be until later, will it?"

"Mom," Noelle said, sighing loudly. "I'm *not* going to let you use me as a buffer when you meet Mrs. Sutton."

"Who told you I was meeting…" She didn't bother to finish the question, since the answer was obvious. Jake! Dumping the rest of her coffee down the sink, she reluctantly went to her room to dress. She'd be entering the lion's den alone, so she wanted to look her best.

"I don't think she's nearly the monster you make her out to be," Noelle called after her.

That her own daughter, her oldest child—the very one who'd been jilted by Thom Sutton—could say such a thing was beyond Sarah. As far as she was concerned, there was too much forgiveness going on here. And if Noelle thought Mary was so wonderful, then she should be willing to come along.

Didn't Noelle grasp the unpleasantness of this situation? Clearly not. Even Jake didn't take it seriously. He seemed to think this was some kind of joke! Well, she, for one, wasn't laughing.

Despite her bad feelings about the meeting with Mary Sutton, Sarah arrived at the Women's Century Club twenty minutes early. This was the way she'd planned it. As she recalled, Mary possessed a number of irritating habits, one of which was an inability to ever show up on time. Therefore, Sarah considered it advantageous to be early, as though that would highlight Mary's lack of responsibility and basic courtesy.

"Good morning, Melody," she said as she stepped briskly into the entry.

"Morning," came Melody's reply. The phone rang just then, and she reached for it, still standing in front of the copy machine.

While she waited, Sarah checked her appearance in the lobby restroom. She'd taken an inordinate amount of time with her makeup that morning. Her hair was impeccably styled, if she did say so herself, and her clothes looked both businesslike and feminine. Choosing the right outfit was of the utmost importance; in the end, after three complete changes, she'd chosen navy-blue wool slacks, a white cashmere sweater and a silk scarf with a pattern of holly and red berries.

Melody finished with the phone. "Sorry, it's crazy around here this morning. Everyone's getting ready for the dance."

Of course. In her dread, she'd nearly forgotten about the annual dance.

The door opened, and with a dramatic flair—all swirling scarves and large gestures—Mary Sutton entered the building. Did the woman think she was on stage, for heaven's sake? "Hello, Melody," she said, her voice light and breezy. Then—as if she'd only now noticed Sarah—she turned in her direction, frowned slightly and then acknowledged her with a curt nod.

"Good to see you, too," Sarah muttered.

"I'm here for the list. The Christmas basket list," Mary said, walking over to the half wall behind which Melody stood.

"That's why I'm here," Sarah said and forced herself into the space between Mary and the wall.

The two jockeyed for position, elbowing each other until Melody stared at them aghast. "What's *wrong* with you two?" she asked.

"As I explained earlier, we have a *history,*" Sarah said, as though that should account for everything.

"A very long and *difficult* history," Mary added.

"You'll have to work together on this." Melody frowned at them both. "I'd hate to see these needy families deprived because you two can't get along." The phone rang again and Melody scooped up the receiver.

"You're impossible to work with," Mary said, practically shoving Sarah aside.

"I won't stand here and be insulted by the likes of you," Sarah insisted. Talk about impossible!

"This isn't going to work."

"You're telling me!" She was ready to walk out the door. But then she realized that was exactly what Mary wanted her to do. She'd been provoking Sarah from the moment she'd made that stagy entrance. This was a low, underhanded attempt to prevent her from holding Kristen's wedding reception at the club. Somehow Mary had found out about the wedding and hoped to thwart the McDowells' plans. That had to be it. But Sarah refused to let a Sutton—especially *this* Sutton—manipulate her.

"There are ways of doing what needs to be done without tripping over each other's feet," Sarah murmured, trying to sound conciliatory. She could only hope that Kristen truly appreciated the sacrifice she was making on her behalf. If it wasn't for the wedding, she wouldn't be caught dead working on a project with Mary Sutton, charity or not!

"What do you mean?"

"There *must* be a way." She personally didn't have any ideas, but perhaps the club secretary could think of something. "Melody?"

Another line rang, and Melody put the first caller on hold in order to answer the second. She placed her palm over the mouthpiece and said, "Why don't you two go talk this out in the lobby?" She waved them impatiently away. "I'll be with you as soon as I can."

Sarah took a few steps back, unwilling to voluntarily give up hard-won territory. This was more of a problem than she'd expected. For her part, she was willing to make the best of it, but she could already tell that Mary had her own agenda.

"The Christmas decorations are lovely this year, aren't they?" Sarah said, making an effort to start again. After all, she was stuck with the woman.

"Yes," came Mary's stilted reply. "I'm the chair of the decorating committee."

"Oh." She studied the staircase again and noticed a number of flaws apparent on closer inspection. Walking to the bottom step, she straightened a bow.

"Leave my bows alone!"

"A little possessive, are we?" Sarah murmured.

"You would be, too, if you'd spent twenty minutes making each of those velvet bows."

"I could have done it in ten."

"Next year, I'll let you." Then, as if she was bored with the subject, Mary said, "I understand Noelle's in town."

"Yes, and I'd appreciate if you'd keep your son away from her."

"My son!" Mary cried. "You don't need to worry about *that*. Thom learned his lesson as far as your daughter's concerned a long time ago."

"On the contrary, I believe your son broke my daughter's heart."

"Ladies!" Melody came out from behind the counter, shaking her head. "I thought we were discussing ways you two can work together to fill those Christmas baskets."

"I don't think I *can* work with her," Mary said, crossing her arms. She presented Sarah with a view of her back.

"Then divide the list," Melody suggested. "One of you can shop for the gifts and the other can buy the groceries. Arrange a day to meet and assemble the baskets, and then you'll be done with it."

Sarah didn't know why she hadn't thought of that earlier. It made perfect sense and would allow them to maintain a healthy distance from each other.

"Divide the list," Mary instructed with a dramatic wave of her hand.

"By all means, divide the list," Sarah said and mimicked Mary's gesture.

"All right," Melody said. She went back to her office, with the two women following, and slipped the list into the photocopier. The phone rang again, and she answered it, holding the receiver between her shoulder and ear. Melody retrieved the original and the copy, reached for the scissors and cut both lists in two. Still talking, she dropped the papers, then picked them up and handed half of the original list to Mary and half to Sarah. The copies of each woman's list went into a file on her desk.

Sarah glanced over her list and tucked it inside her purse. "When do you suggest we meet to assemble the baskets?"

"The twenty-third before noon. That way, we'll be

able to drop them off at the Salvation Army in plenty of time. They'll distribute the baskets on Christmas Eve."

"Fine." That settled, Sarah charged out the door without a backward glance. This wasn't the best solution, but it was manageable. She'd do her share of the work, and she wasn't about to let anyone suggest otherwise.

"This is so cool," Carley said as they left the mall late Thursday afternoon, their arms loaded with bags and packages. Noelle smiled fondly at her youngest sister. That summer, Carley had spent two weeks with her in Texas while their parents were on a cruise. She'd matured noticeably in the six months since then.

"Mom's not selling much real estate anymore," her sister told her as they climbed into the car. "I think she's bored with it, but she won't admit it."

"Really?"

"She's totally involved in Kristen's wedding. It's all she thinks about. She's read a whole bunch of books and magazine articles and has everything set in her mind. Just the other day, she said that what this town really needs is a wedding planner."

"And you think Mom would enjoy that?"

"Are you kidding?" Carley said. "She'd *love* it."

Their mother was extremely sociable, which was one of the reasons she was such a successful real estate agent, Noelle mused. Sarah knew nearly everyone in town and had wonderful connections. Perhaps Carley was right.

"The Admiral really hasn't changed," Noelle murmured. She'd spent a lot of time at the old downtown theater, back in high school. It was there, in the balcony, that Thom had first kissed her. To this day—as much as she wanted to forget it—she remembered the thrill of that kiss.

The Admiral was a classic theater built sixty years earlier. The screen was huge and the second-floor balcony held the plush loge seats—always Noelle's favorite place to sit.

They purchased the tickets, a large bucket of popcorn and drinks.

"Do you want to go up to the balcony?" Carley asked.

"Where else would we sit?" Noelle was already halfway up the winding staircase that led to the second floor. She went straight to the front row and plopped down on a cushioned seat. Carley plopped down beside her. The main feature was a Christmas release, an animated film starring the voices of Billy Crystal and Nathan Lane.

"I'm not a kid anymore, but I'm glad you wanted to see this movie, too," her sister confided.

Noelle placed the bucket of popcorn between them. "Thanks for giving me the excuse." She leaned forward and looked at the audience below. The theater was only half-full and she wondered if she'd recognize anyone.

"Oh, my goodness," she whispered. This couldn't be happening! Thom Sutton sat almost directly below her. If that wasn't bad enough, a blonde sat in the seat beside him and—to Noelle's disgust—had her hands all over him.

"What?" Carley demanded.

"It's Thom." Heaven help her, Noelle couldn't keep from watching. The blonde's hand lingered at the base of his neck; she was stroking his hair with all the tenderness of a longtime lover.

"Not Thom Sutton? The son of the enemy?" Carley asked.

Noelle nodded. Sad and shocking though it was, he obviously still had the power to hurt her. No, not hurt her—infuriate her!

Carley reached for a kernel of popcorn and tossed it down.

Noelle gasped, grabbing her sister's hand. The last thing she wanted was to call attention to the balcony. "Don't do that!"

"Why not? He jilted you and now he's here with another woman." She hurled another kernel in his direction.

Noelle glanced down and saw the blonde nibbling on his earlobe. That did it. She scooped out a handful of popcorn and threw it over the balcony railing. Noelle and her sister leaned back and smothered their giggles. A few minutes later, unable to resist, Noelle looked down again.

"Oh, no," Carley muttered under her breath as she sent a fresh shower of popcorn over the edge. She jerked back instantly.

"What?" Noelle asked.

"I think we're in trouble. He just turned around and looked up here and I don't think he's pleased."

Fine, the management could throw her out of the theater if he complained. Noelle didn't care.

"I want to know about you and him," Carley said. "I wasn't even born when his mom and our mom had their big fight."

Noelle was reluctant to describe all this old history, but she supposed her sister had a right to know. "Well, Mom had just started selling real estate and was making new friends. She claims Mary was jealous of those friends, especially one whose name was Cheryl. Cheryl had been working at the agency for a while and was kind of showing Mom the ropes. She was holding an open house and wanted something elegant to set off the dining room. Mom knew that Mary had this exquisite silver tea service—the perfect thing. But Mom also knew that if she asked Mary to lend it to Cheryl, Mrs. Sutton would turn her down. Instead, Mom asked to borrow it for herself, which was a fib."

Carley frowned. "So that's why Mrs. Sutton blamed Mom? Because Mom lied—I mean fibbed—and then the expensive silver tea service got stolen? Oh, I bet Mom was just sick about it."

"She felt awful. According to Mrs. Sutton, the tea service had belonged to her grandmother and was a family heirloom. It was irreplaceable."

"What did Mom do?"

"She called the police and offered a reward for its return, but the tea service didn't turn up. She went to every antiques store in the area, looking for something similar. Finally there was nothing more she could do. She tried to repair the damage to the friendship, but Mrs. Sutton was angry—and really, you can't blame her. She was hurt because Mom had misled her. They got into this big argument about it and everything escalated from there. Mrs. Sutton did some petty things and Mom retaliated. Next thing you know, a grudge developed that's gone on to this day."

"Retaliated?" Carley asked. "How?"

"When it became clear that Mrs. Sutton wasn't going to forgive and forget, Mom tried another tactic. She thought she'd be funny." Noelle smiled at the memory. "Mrs. Sutton got her hair cut, and Mom sent her flowers and a sympathy card. Then Mrs. Sutton ordered pizza with double anchovies and had it delivered to Mom. You know how Mom hates anchovies—and furthermore she had to pay for it." She shook her head. "It's sad, isn't it? That a good friendship should fall apart for such a silly reason."

"Yeah," Carley agreed. "They acted pretty childish."

"And my relationship with Thom was one of the casualties."

"When did you fall in love with him?" Carley wanted to know.

"We became good friends when we were kids. For a long time, our families got along really well. We often went on picnics and outings together. Thom and I were the closest in age, and we were constant companions—until the argument."

"What happened after the argument?"

"Mrs. Sutton sent Thom and his older sister to a private school, and I didn't see him again for about six years. He came back to public school when we were sophomores. We didn't have a lot in common anymore and hardly had anything to do with each other until we both were assigned to the same English class in our senior year."

"That was when you fell in love?" Carley's voice rose wistfully.

Noelle nodded, and the familiar pain tightened her stomach. "Apparently I fell harder than Thom."

Noelle carefully glanced down again. Talking about Thom and her romance—especially while she was sitting in this theater—brought up memories she'd prefer to forget. Why wouldn't the stupid movie start? It was two minutes past the scheduled time.

The boy who'd rung up the popcorn order marched down the side aisle toward Noelle and Carley. He wore a bored but determined look. "There's been a complaint from the people down below about you throwing popcorn," he said accusingly.

Noelle could feel the heat build up in her cheeks. "I'm sorry—that was, uh, an accident."

The kid's expression said he'd heard it all before. "Make sure it doesn't happen again, okay?"

"It won't," Noelle promised him.

"Sorry," Carley said in a small voice as the boy left. "It was my fault. I encouraged you."

"But I started it."

"You think you're the one who invented throwing popcorn? Hey, I've got fifteen years on you."

"I want to fall in love one day, too," Carley said, leaning back in her seat, which rocked slightly.

"You will," Noelle said, hoping her sister had better luck in that department than she'd had.

The lights dimmed then and with a grand, sweeping motion the huge velvet curtains hanging over the screen slowly parted. Soon, they were watching previews for upcoming features. Noelle absently nibbled on popcorn and let her mind wander.

Thom had changed if the blonde down below was the

type of woman he found attractive. That shouldn't surprise her, though. Time changed a lot of things in life. Some days, when she felt lonely and especially sorry for herself, she tried to imagine what would've happened if she *had* married Thom all those years ago. Getting married that young rarely worked out. They might've been divorced, she might've ended up a single mother, she might never have completed her education.... All kinds of difficult outcomes were possible. In all honesty, she told herself, it was for the best that they hadn't run off together.

Carley slid forward and peeked over the railing. Almost immediately she flopped back. "You wouldn't *believe* what they're doing now."

"Probably not."

"They're—"

Noelle gripped her sister's elbow. "I don't want to know."

Carley's eyes were huge. "You don't want me to tell you?"

"No."

Her sister stared at her in utter amazement. "You really don't care?"

Noelle shook her head. That wasn't the whole truth— or even part of it. But she didn't want to know if Thom had his arm around the blonde or if he was kissing her—or anything else. It was a lot less painful to keep her head buried in a popcorn bucket. Forget Weight Watchers. Sometimes fat grams were the only source of comfort.

"Are you going to confront him after the movie?" Carley asked excitedly.

Noelle snickered. "Hardly."

"Why not?"

"Just watch the movie," she advised.

Carley settled in her seat and and began to rock back and forth. Another time, the action might have annoyed Noelle, but just then she found it oddly comforting. She wanted a special someone to put his arm around her and gently rock her. To create a private world for the two of them, the way Thom had once done in this very theater, on this very balcony. He'd kissed her here and claimed her heart. It'd been a pivotal moment in their fledgling romance. From that point onward, they knew—or at least Noelle had known. She was in love and willing to make whatever sacrifices love demanded.

All too soon, the feature had ended and the lights came back on. "That was great," Carley announced.

Caught up in wistful memories, Noelle got to her feet, gathering her coat and purse. She took pains not to glance below, although her curiosity was almost overwhelming.

"We meet again," an all-too-familiar voice said from behind her.

"Thom?" She turned to see him two rows back, with a four-or five-year-old boy at his side.

Noelle's reaction was instantaneous. She looked below and discovered the blonde beauty with her male friend, who just happened *not* to be Thom Sutton. "I thought—"

"*You're* Thom?" Carley asked, glowering with righteous indignation.

"Don't tell me you're Carley," he returned, ignoring the girl's outrage. "My goodness, you've grown into a regular beauty."

Carley's anger died a quick death. "Do you really think so?"

"I sure do. Oh, this is my nephew Cameron."

"Hello, Cameron," Noelle said. "Did you enjoy the movie?"

The boy nodded. "Yeah, but the best part was when the man came up and told you not to throw any more popcorn. Uncle Thom said you got in trouble." The kid sounded far too smug for Noelle's liking.

So Thom had heard and seen the whole thing.

Oh, great.

Friday morning, Sarah dressed for her Christmas basket shopping adventure. She felt as though she was suiting up for an ordeal, some test or rite of passage. The hordes of shoppers were definitely going to try her patience; she'd finished her own shopping months ago and failed to see why people waited until the very last week. Well, the sooner she purchased the things on her half of the list, the better. With Christmas only five days away, she didn't have a minute to waste.

She wasn't getting any help from her family—not that she'd really expected it. Jake was at work, and Noelle was driving Carley to her friend's house and then meeting Kristen for lunch.

She was on her own.

Wanting to get the most for her buying dollar, Sarah drove to the biggest discount store in Rose. The Value-X parking lot was already filled. After driving around repeatedly, she finally found a space. She locked her car and hunched her shoulders against the wind as she hurried toward the building. The sound of the Salvation

Army bell-ringer guided her to the front entrance. She paused long enough to stick a dollar bill in his bucket, then walked into the store.

Sarah grabbed a cart and used the booster seat to prop up her purse. The list was in the side pocket of her bag, and she searched for the paper as she walked. She hadn't gone more than a few feet from the entrance when she nearly collided with another woman obtaining a cart.

"I'm sorry," she said automatically. "I—" The words froze on her lips.

"I should've known anyone that rude must be you," Mary Sutton muttered sarcastically.

Although her heart was pounding, Sarah made a relatively dignified escape and steered the cart around Mary. With purpose filling every step, she pushed her cart toward the toy department. Her list was gifts, which meant Mary had the grocery half. Hmph. It didn't surprise her that Mary Sutton bought her family's Christmas gifts at a discount store—or that she waited until the last minute.

The first part of the list directed her to purchase gifts for two girls, ages six and seven. The younger girl had requested a doll. Having raised three daughters, Sarah knew that every little girl loved Barbie. This late in the season, she'd be fortunate to find the current Barbie.

Almost right away she saw that the supplies were depleted, just as she'd suspected. But one lone Firefighter Barbie stood on the once-crowded shelf. Sarah reached for it at the precise moment someone else did.

"I believe I was first," she insisted. Far be it from her

to allow some other person to deprive a poor little girl longing for a Barbie on Christmas morning.

"I believe you're wrong."

Mary Sutton. Sarah glared at her with such intensity that Mary must have realized she was not about to be dissuaded.

"Fine," Mary said after a moment and released her death grip on the Barbie.

"Thank you." Sarah could be gracious when called upon.

With her nose so high in the air she was in danger of hitting a light fixture, Mary stomped off in the opposite direction. Feeling satisfied with herself, Sarah studied the list again and noticed the name of a three-year-old boy. A small riding toy would do nicely, she decided and headed for that section of the department.

As she turned the corner she ran into Mary Sutton a third time. Mary stopped abruptly, her eyes narrowed. "Are you following me?" she demanded.

"Following *you?*" Sarah faked a short, derisive laugh. "You've got to be joking. I have no desire to be within ten feet of you."

"Then I suggest you vacate this aisle."

"You can't tell me where to shop or in what aisle!"

"Wanna bet?" Mary leaned forward and, intentionally or not, her cart rammed Sarah's.

Refusing to allow such an outrage to go unanswered, Sarah retaliated by banging her cart into Mary's.

Mary pulled back and hit her again, harder this time.

Soon they were throwing stuffed French poodles at each other, hurling them off the shelves. A German shepherd sailed over Sarah's head. That was when she reached for the golden retriever, the largest of the stuffed animals.

"Ladies, ladies." A man in a red jacket hurried toward them, his arms outstretched. His name badge read Michael and identified him as the store manager.

"I'm so sorry, Michael," Sarah said, pretending to recognize him. "This little, uh, misunderstanding got completely out of hand."

"You're telling me!" Mary yelled.

"This woman is following me."

"Oh, puh-leeze." Mary groaned audibly. "This woman followed *me*."

"I don't think it's important to know who followed whom," the manager said in a conciliatory voice. "But we need to—"

"She took the last Barbie," Mary broke in, pointing an accusing finger at Sarah. "I got it first—the doll was *mine*. Any jury in the land would rule in my favor. But I kindly offered it to her."

"Kindly, nothing. I had that Barbie and you know it!"

"Ladies, please…." The manager stood between them in an effort to keep them apart.

"There's only so much of this I can take," Mary said, sounding close to tears. "I'm here—"

"It isn't important why you're here," Sarah interrupted. She wasn't about to let Mary Sutton come off looking like the injured party. The woman had purposely rammed her cart. "She assaulted me."

"I most certainly did not!"

"You should check the front of my cart for damage, and if there is any, I suggest that you, as manager, charge this woman," Sarah said.

Two security officers arrived then, dressed in blue uniforms.

"Officer, officer…"

Mary turned soft and gentle. "Thank you for coming."

"Oh, give me a break," Sarah muttered. "Is it within your power to arrest this woman?" she demanded.

"Ladies," the manager said, trying once more, it seemed, to appeal to their better natures. "This is the season of goodwill toward men—and women. Would it be possible for you to apologize to each other and go about your business?"

Mary crossed her arms and looked away.

Sarah gestured toward the other woman as if to say Mary's action spoke for itself. "I believe you have your answer."

"Then you leave me no choice," the manager said. "Officers, please escort these two ladies from the store."

"What?" Mary cried.

"I beg your pardon?" Sarah said, hands on hips. "What is this about?"

The larger of the two security guards answered. "You're being kicked out of the store."

Sarah's mouth fell open.

The only person more shocked was Mary Sutton. "You're evicting me from Value-X?"

"You heard the manager, lady," the second officer said. "Now, come this way."

"Could I pay for the Barbie doll first?" Sarah asked, clutching the package to her chest. "It's for a little girl and it's all she wants for Christmas."

"You should've thought of that before you threw the first poodle," the manager said.

"But—"

Dramatically, he pointed toward the front doors. "Out."

Mortified to the marrow of her bones, Sarah turned, taking her cart with her. One wheel was now loose and it squeaked and squealed. Just when she figured things couldn't get any worse, she discovered that a crowd had gathered in the aisle to witness her humiliation.

"Merry Christmas," she said with as much bravado as she could manage.

The officer at her side raised his hand. "We're asking that everyone return to their shopping. What happened here is over."

With her dignity intact but her pride in shreds, Sarah made her way to the parking lot, still accompanied by the officer.

She could see the "About Town" headline already. *Manager Expels Sarah McDowell From Value-X After Cat Fight.* Although technically, she supposed, it should be Dog Fight.

She had no doubt that Mary Sutton would use the power of the press to complete her embarrassment.

NOELLE MCDOWELL'S
JOURNAL

December 19
11:30 p.m.

I can't believe it! Even now, when it's long past time for bed, I'm wide-awake and so furious, any chance of falling asleep is impossible. I doubt if anyone could do a better job of looking like a world-class idiot. Right there in the theater, with my little sister at my side, I behaved like a juvenile.

I've worked hard to be a positive influence on Carley. I take my role as oldest sister very seriously. Then I go and pull a stunt like this. Adding insult to injury is the fact that I then had to face Thom, knowing he was completely aware of what a fool I'd made of myself.

Speaking of Thom...no, I don't want to think about him. First the airplane and now this! I'd sincerely hoped he'd be married with a passel of kids. I wanted him to be so completely out of the picture that I'd never need to think about him again. Instead—just my luck— he's single, eligible and drop-dead handsome. Life can be brutally unfair.

One good thing that came from all this is the long conversation I had with Carley after the movie. She's young and idealistic, much the same way I was at her age. We talked some more about Mom and Mrs. Sutton. It's really a very sad feud. I told her what good friends our two families used to be. The telling brought up a lot of memories. At one time, our families did everything together.

Thom was the first boy ever to kiss me. We were both sixteen. Wow! I still remember how good it felt. I don't remember what movie was playing and I doubt Thom does, either. That kiss was really something, even though we had no idea what we were doing. There was a purity to it, an innocence. His lips stayed on mine for mere seconds, but somehow we knew. I certainly did, and I thought Thom did, too.

It's funny how much it hurts to think about the way he deceived me. I try not to dwell on it. But I can't help myself, especially now....

Three

"I've never been so humiliated in my life!" Thom's mother sagged into the chair across from his desk as if she were experiencing a fainting spell. The back of her hand went to her forehead and she closed her eyes. "I'll never be able to look those people in the eye again," she wailed. "Never!"

"Mother, I'm sure no one recognized you," Thom said, hoping to calm her down before she caused a second scene by retelling the first. He hadn't really appreciated his mother's flair for drama until now. This was quite a performance, and he could only imagine the show she'd put on at the store.

"Of *course* I was recognized," Mary insisted, springing to life. "My picture's right there by my news column each and every week. Why, I could be fired from the newspaper once the editor gets wind of this." She swooned again and slumped back in the chair. "Where's your father, anyway? He should've known something like this was bound to happen. It seems every time I need him, he's conveniently in court." Greg Sutton was the senior partner in a local law firm.

Thom managed to hold back a smile. As far as he was concerned, his father possessed impeccable timing. Unfortunately, that meant his mother had sought solace from him.

"I'll sue Sarah McDowell," his mother said, as if she'd suddenly come to that decision. "Assault and besmirching my reputation and…and—"

"Mother," Thom pleaded. He stood and leaned forward, his hands on the edge of his desk. "Take a couple of deep breaths and try to calm down." Dragging a lawyer—most likely someone from his father's firm—into the middle of this feud would only complicate things.

"Do you believe it's remotely possible to calm down after this kind of humiliation?"

Perhaps she was right. "Why don't I take you to lunch and we can talk about it," Thom suggested. It was the Friday before Christmas and he could spare the time.

"The Rose Garden?" His mother raised pleading eyes to him. The Rose Garden was the most elegant dining room in town.

"If you like." It was more a "ladies who lunch" kind of place, but if that was what it took to make his mother listen to reason, then he'd go there.

"At least the day won't be completely ruined," she mumbled, opening her purse. "Let me put on some lipstick and I'll be ready to go." She took out her compact and gasped when she saw her reflection in the mirror.

"What?" Thom asked.

"My hair." Her fingers worked feverishly to repair the damage. "Why didn't you say something?"

Mainly because he hadn't been able to get a word in edgewise from the moment she'd stormed into his office. At first, Thom had assumed she'd been in some kind of accident. His mother had spoken so fast it was hard to understand what she was saying—other than the fact that she'd been kicked out of the Value-X because of Sarah McDowell.

"This must have happened when she hurled a French poodle at me."

"Mrs. McDowell threw a dog at you?" He gazed at her in horror.

"A stuffed one," she qualified. "It hit me on the head." Her hand went back to her hair, which she'd more or less managed to straighten.

Thom could picture the scene—two grown women acting like five-year-olds fighting in a schoolyard. Once again, he struggled to hide his amusement. His mother had tried to give him the impression that she was an innocent victim in all this, but he strongly suspected she'd played an equal role.

"I think I might be getting a bruise on my cheek," she said, peering closely into the small compact mirror. She lowered it and angled her face for him to get a better look.

"I don't see anything," he told her.

"Look harder," she said.

To appease her, he did but saw nothing. "Sorry," he said and reached for his overcoat. "Ready for lunch?"

"I'm starving," his mother told him. "You know how hungry I get when I'm angry."

He didn't, and felt this was information he could live without. The Rose Garden was only a block from his office, so they decided to walk. His mother chattered the whole way, reliving the incident and her outrage all over again, embellishing it in the retelling. Thom listened politely and wondered what Noelle would think when she heard *her* mother's version of the incident. He quickly pulled himself up. He didn't want to think about Noelle; that was something his self-esteem could do without.

As he'd expected, The Rose Garden bustled with activity. Christmas was only a few days away, and shoppers taking a welcome lunch break now filled the restaurant. Thom glanced about the room as they were waiting to be seated. He recognized a few associates, who acknowledged him with nods. Two women sitting by the window gave him an appreciative glance and he warmed to the attention. That was when he caught sight of another pair of women.

Noelle and her younger sister Kristen. Wouldn't you know it? He nearly groaned aloud. He hadn't seen or heard from her in ten years and yet in the last three days she seemed to turn up every place he went.

This wasn't good. In fact, if his mother were to see them, she might very well consider it her duty to create a scene and walk out of the restaurant. Worse yet, she might find it necessary to make some loud and slanderous comment about their mother. Staring in their direction was a dead giveaway, but for the life of him, he couldn't stop. Noelle. The years had matured her beauty. He'd been in love with her as a teenager and she'd become the greatest source of pain in his life. For a long time, he'd convinced himself that he hated her. Eventually he'd realized it wasn't true. If anything, he was as strongly drawn to her now as he had been back then. More so, and he detested his own weakness. The woman had damn near destroyed him. In spite of that, he couldn't look away.

"I can seat you now," the hostess said.

Thom hesitated.

"Thom," his mother said, nudging him, "we can be seated now."

"Yes, sorry." He could only hope it wouldn't be anywhere close to Noelle.

The hostess escorted them to a table by the window. He pulled out his mother's chair, making sure her back was to Noelle and Kristen. Unfortunately, that meant *he* was facing them. Kristen had her back to him, which left him with an excellent view of Noelle. She apparently noticed him for the first time because her fork froze halfway to her mouth. For the longest moment, she stared at him, then caught herself and averted her eyes.

"Do you see someone you know, dear?" his mother asked, scrutinizing the menu.

"Yes...no," he corrected. He lifted the rather large menu and pretended to read over the offerings. The strategy of entertaining his mother in order to get her mind off the events of that morning was about to backfire.

In the years since Noelle, Thom had been in several relationships, two of which had grown serious. Both times he'd come close to suggesting marriage and then panicked. It was little wonder after what Noelle had done to him, but he couldn't blame her entirely.

When the moment came to make a commitment, he couldn't. He simply couldn't. And he knew why—although the reason baffled and frustrated him. He didn't love either Caroline or Brenda with the same intensity he'd loved Noelle. Perhaps it was impossible to recapture the emotional passion of that youthful episode; he didn't know. What he did know was that the feelings he'd had for other women hadn't been enough. He'd found them attractive, enjoyed their company...but he needed more than that.

He needed what he'd had with Noelle.

As he thought about the scene at the theater, he started to grin. It couldn't have worked out better had he planned it. Just thinking about her tossing popcorn at some poor, unsuspecting moviegoer's head was enough to keep him laughing for years. He'd listened in while she talked about their mothers—and about them. But the most priceless part of all was the astonished look on her face when she'd realized he was sitting right behind her and had heard every word.

"What is so amusing?" his mother asked.

"Oh, I was just thinking about something that happened recently."

"What? Trust me, after the morning I've had, I could use a good laugh."

Thom shook his head. "It'll lose something in the translation."

"Oh." She sounded disappointed, then sighed. "I do feel better. This was an excellent idea."

The waitress came by and his mother ordered a glass of wine. "For my nerves," she explained to the woman. "Ordinarily I don't drink during the day, but...well, suffice it to say I've had a very difficult morning."

"I understand," the waitress told her in a sympathetic voice. She glanced at Thom and gave him a small coy smile.

"What a nice young woman," his mother commented as the waitress walked off.

"I suppose so," he said with little interest. He looked up, straight into Noelle's steady gaze.

"Perhaps now isn't the right moment to broach the subject, but both your father and I think it's time you considered settling down."

She was right; the timing could be better. However, a little appeasement seemed in order. "I've been thinking the same thing myself," he said, forcing himself to focus on his mother.

"Really?" Her face lit up. "Is there someone special?"

"Not yet." Involuntarily he stared at Noelle again. As if against her will, her eyes met his and held. Then she looked away—but she quickly looked back.

Kristen turned around and glanced at him over her shoulder.

"Did you know Kristen McDowell is getting married?" his mother said.

Thom nearly choked on his glass of water. "Now that you mention it, I remember hearing something about that." It also explained why his mother had brought up the subject of his settling down. She didn't want Sarah McDowell to outdo her in the married children department.

"Now," his mother said, eagerly leaning forward, "tell me about your lady friend."

"What lady friend?"

"The one you're going to propose to."

"Propose?" He'd only proposed to one woman, the

one watching him from two tables away. "I told you already—I'm not seeing anyone."

"You were never able to keep a secret from me, Thomas. I'm your mother."

He stared at her blankly, not knowing how to respond. "What makes you think I've met someone?"

"It isn't *think,* Thom, I know. I told your father, too. Ask him if you don't believe me. I noticed it the day you came home from your business trip to California. It was the sparkle in your eyes."

"California?" Thom tried to recall the trip. It had been a quick one, and strictly business. But on the return flight, he'd bumped into Noelle McDowell.

Noelle got home after lunch with Kristen to discover her mother sitting in the family room, stocking feet propped up on the ottoman. She leaned back against the sofa cushion and held an icepack to her forehead.

"Mom?" Noelle whispered. "Are you ill?"

"Thank goodness someone's finally home," her mother said, lowering the bag of ice.

"What's wrong?"

"Never in all your life could you guess the kind of morning I had." She clutched Noelle's arm as she spoke.

"What happened?"

Sarah closed her eyes. "I can't even tell you about it. I have never been more humiliated."

"Does this have something to do with Mrs. Sutton?"

Her mother's eyes sprang open in sheer terror. "You heard about it? Who told you?"

"Ah…"

"She's going to report it in the newspaper, I just know

she is. I wouldn't put it past her to use her news column to smear my good name. It was *her* fault, you know. She followed me, and then purposely rammed her cart into mine. And that was only the beginning."

An ugly picture began to take shape in Noelle's mind. A Sutton/McDowell confrontation would explain the fierce looks Thom had sent her way during lunch. The fact that he'd showed up at The Rose Garden—with his mother in tow—was a coincidence she could have done without.

Kristen had invited her to lunch, and then after a few minutes of small talk, her sister had immediately turned to the subject that happened to be on Noelle's mind: Thom Sutton. Noelle had described the disaster at the movies the day before and reluctantly confessed her part. To her consternation, Kristen had thought the incident downright hilarious. Noelle, however, had yet to recover from the embarrassment of knowing that Thom had seen her resort to such childish behavior.

Now their mother had been involved in another confrontation with Mary Sutton. If her present state of mind was anything to go by, Sarah had come out of it badly. Judging by what Noelle had seen of Mrs. Sutton at the restaurant, *she* wasn't the least bit disturbed.

"The police took down our names and—"

"The *police?*"

"Value-X Security, but they wear those cute blue uniforms and look just like regular policemen."

"They took your names? What for?"

Her mother covered her face with both hands. "I can't talk about it."

The door off the garage opened and in walked Noelle's father. "Dad," she said, hoping to prepare him. "Something happened to Mom this morning."

"Oh, Jake…" Her mother languished in her seat as though she lacked the energy to even lift her head.

"Sarah?"

"Apparently Mom and Mrs. Sutton tangled with security at the Value-X this morning."

"We more than tangled," her mother insisted, her voice rising, "we were…banished. The officer who escorted me out told me I won't be allowed inside the store for three months." She bit her lip and swallowed a loud sob. "I don't know if I misunderstood him, but I think I might be permanently banned from all blue-light specials."

"No!" Her father feigned outrage.

"Jake, this is serious."

"Of course it is," he agreed. "I take it this is Mary's doing?"

Her mother's fist hit the sofa arm. "I swear to you she started it!"

"You don't need to tell me what happened," Jake said. "I can guess."

So could Noelle.

"From here on out, I absolutely refuse to be in the same room as that woman." She sat straighter, jaw firm, head back. "For years I've had to deal with her…her malice, and I won't put up with it anymore!"

Jake reached for Sarah's hand and gently patted it. "You're absolutely right—you shouldn't."

Her mother's eyes narrowed suspiciously. "How do you mean? Are you being sarcastic?"

"Of course not, dear," he said reassuringly. "But there's no need to rehash old history, is there?"

"No-o-o." Noelle heard her mother's hesitation.

"Not going to the Christmas dance will show Mary Sutton that she won't have you to kick around anymore."

As far as Noelle was concerned, missing the Century Club Christmas dance was far from a tragedy. The only reason she'd agreed to attend was to placate her mother. This mysterious incident at the Value-X was a blessing in disguise; it seemed her father saw it in the same light. She just hoped he hadn't overplayed his hand with that last ringing pronouncement.

"Who said anything about not going to the dance?" her mother demanded.

"You did." Her father turned to Noelle for agreement, which she offered with a solemn nod.

"Yes, Mom, you just said you won't be in the same room with that woman ever again."

"I did?"

"Yes, sweetheart," Noelle's father said. "And I agree wholeheartedly. Missing the dance is a small price to pay if it means protecting your peace of mind."

"We aren't going to the dance?" Carley asked, entering the room. She looked disappointed, but then Noelle's little sister was too young to understand what a lucky escape she'd just had.

"No," Jake said. "We're going to skip the dance this year, and perhaps every year from now on. We won't let Mary Sutton hurt your mother's feelings or her reputation again!"

"We're going," her mother insisted.

"But, sweetheart—"

"You're absolutely right, Jake, Mary Sutton's done enough to me. I refuse to allow her to ruin my Christmas—and Noelle's birthday—too. We're going to show up at the dance and hold our heads high. We have nothing to be ashamed of."

"But…" Her father cleared his throat. "What if Mary mentions the incident at the Value-X?" He lowered his voice, sounding as though that would be a horrible embarrassment to them all. Noelle had to give her father credit; he was good at this.

"She won't say a word," her mother said with complete confidence. "Mary wouldn't dare bring up the subject, seeing that she was tossed out on her ear, right along with me."

Her resolve clearly renewed, Sarah stood and placed her hands on her hips. Nothing would thwart her now. "We're attending the dance tomorrow night, and that's all there is to it."

Her father made a small protesting noise that echoed Noelle's sentiments. She was stuck going to this dance when it was the very last thing she wanted.

Dressed in a floor-length pink formal that had once been worn by Kristen in high school, Noelle felt like last year's prom queen. Her enthusiasm for this dance was on a par with filing her income tax return.

"You look positively lovely," her mother told her as they headed out the door.

How Noelle looked had little to do with how she felt. Her father brought the car out of the garage and held open the doors for Noelle and Carley, then helped their mother into the front seat beside him.

"How did I get so lucky—escorting three beautiful women to the biggest dance of the year?"

"Clean living," Noelle's mother said with authority.

"And a clear conscience." Noelle didn't know whether to laugh at that remark or shrug in bewilderment. Leaning forward in order to look out the front window, Sarah added, "I think it's going to snow."

Hearing "Jingle Bells" on the car radio, Noelle suspected her mother was being influenced by the words of the song.

"We're more prone to ice storms than snow this time of year," her father said mildly.

Noelle had forgotten about the treacherous storms, although she'd experienced a number of them during the years she'd lived in Rose. They created astonishing beauty—and terrible dangers.

"Kristen and Jonathan are meeting us at the dance, aren't they?" Carley asked.

"That's what she said," Noelle answered. Carley was dressed in a full-length pale blue dress with cap sleeves and she wore matching low-heeled shoes. She looked lovely and so mature it was all Noelle could do not to cry. Her baby sister was growing up.

"Do you think *she'll* be there?" her mother asked, lowering her voice.

"Mrs. Sutton's probably asking the same thing about you," Noelle said.

Her mother gave an exaggerated sigh. "I'll say one thing about Mary Sutton—she never did lack nerve."

The Century Club was festive, with Christmas music and evergreen swags and large red bows. The ballroom was on the second floor, the cloakroom, a bar and buffet on the first. Couples lingered on the wide staircase, chatting and sipping champagne.

Noelle glanced toward the upstairs, and her stomach

tensed. Thom was there. She didn't need to see him to feel his presence. Why did he have to show up everywhere she did? Was this some kind of cosmic joke?

"Kristen!" her mother called. "Yoo hoo!" Anyone might think it'd been weeks since she'd last spoken to her daughter. "Hello, Jonathan." She hugged her soon-to-be son-in-law.

"Hi, Mom. Hi, Dad." Kristen paused in front of Carley, feigning shock. "This isn't my little sister, is it? It can't be."

Carley rolled her eyes, but couldn't hide her pleasure. "Of course it's me. Don't be ridiculous."

"Shall we go upstairs?" her mother suggested.

Noelle recognized the order disguised as a request. They were to mount the stairs on guard, as a family, in case they ran into the dreaded Mary Sutton.

Kristen cozied up to Noelle. "He's here," she whispered in her ear.

"I know."

"Who told you?"

"No one." She couldn't explain how she'd recognized Thom's presence. She just did. Like it or not.

The ballroom was crowded, and although this wasn't the kind of social activity Noelle would have attended on her own, she couldn't help getting caught up in the spirit of the evening. A six-piece orchestra was playing a waltz, the chandeliers glittered and she saw that it had indeed begun to snow; flakes drifted gently past the dark windows. On the polished dance floor, the women in their long shimmery gowns whirled around in the arms of their dashing partners. The scene reminded her of a Victorian Christmas card.

"Would you care to dance?" Jonathan asked.

Surprised, Noelle nodded. She'd only spoken once or twice to this man who was marrying her sister, and was anxious to know him better. "Thank you. That would be very nice."

Just as Noelle and Jonathan stepped onto the dance floor, Kristen's gaze met her fiancé's. Noelle could have sworn some unspoken message passed between them. She didn't have time to question her sister before Jonathan loosely wrapped her in his arms.

"I assume you heard what happened at the Value-X store," she said, searching for a subject of conversation.

"Did you have as much trouble not laughing as I did?"

"More," Noelle confessed with a grin.

"I've done business with the Suttons. They're good people."

"This feud between our mothers is ridiculous." Out of the corner of her eye, she noticed Kristen, who was dancing, too—her partner none other than Thom Sutton. It didn't take a genius to put two and two together, especially when she noticed that Kristen was steering Thom in her direction. Noelle marveled at her sister's courage in asking Thom to dance with her. And of course she had. Thom would never have sought Kristen out, especially for a dance in the Women's Century Club Ballroom with both mothers present.

The two couples made their way toward the center of the polished floor. When they were side by side, Jonathan stopped.

"I believe you're dancing with the wrong partner," he said.

Noelle didn't need to look over her shoulder to guess Jonathan was speaking to Thom.

"I believe you're with the wrong woman," Noelle heard Kristen tell her partner.

Jonathan released Noelle, and Kristen stepped out of Thom's embrace and sailed into her fiancé's waiting arms, leaving Thom and Noelle standing alone in the middle of the crowded dance floor.

Slowly, dread dictating every move, Noelle turned and came face-to-face with Thom. He didn't look any happier than she felt at this sudden turn of events. "I didn't plan this," she said in clear, even tones.

His expression implied that he didn't consider her comment worthy of a response.

"Are you two going to dance or are you just going to stand there and stare at each other all night?" Jonathan asked.

Thom shrugged, implying that he could do this if he had to. Reluctantly Noelle stepped into his arms. She wasn't sure what to expect. Actually, she hadn't expected to feel anything, certainly not this immediate deluge of emotion. He kept her at arm's length and gazed into the distance.

To Noelle's horror, tears filled her eyes as all the old feelings came flooding back. She was about to turn and walk off the dance floor when his fingers dug into her upper arms.

"You're not running away from me again."

"Me?" she cried, furious at the accusation.

"Yes, you."

His words made no sense, she thought grimly, but said nothing. The dance would be over soon and she could leave him behind. Or try to. Kristen would answer for this.

No, she decided, she had only herself to blame. Over lunch, Noelle had confided in her sister. Kristen, being idealistic and in love, had plotted to bring Noelle and Thom back together. She didn't understand that reconciliation wasn't always possible.

"I'd like to ask you a question," she said when she could tolerate the silence no longer.

"Fine."

"Why'd you do it? Did you want revenge for your mother so badly it was worth using me to get it?"

He stopped dancing and frowned at her. "What?"

"You heard me." She couldn't keep the pain out of her voice.

He continued to frown, as if he still didn't understand the question.

"Don't give me that injured look," she said, clenching her jaw. "Too many years have passed for me to be taken in by that."

"You were the one who stood *me* up."

"Yeah, right," she said with a mocking laugh. "After I made an idiot of myself in front of my parents, too. That must've given you a real kick."

"I don't know what you're talking about."

"Thom, I waited in that park for two miserable hours and you didn't show."

Not an inch separated them now as his icy glare cut into her. Dancing couples swirled around them, but Noelle was barely conscious of anyone else. For all she knew or cared, they were alone on the dance floor.

"I waited hours for you, too."

His lying to her now was almost more than she could stand. "I beg to differ," she said stiffly.

"Noelle, listen to me! I was there."

"You most certainly were not." Then, to prove that she wasn't going to accept a lie, no matter how convenient, she added, "You think I just waited around? I was sure something had gone wrong, sure there was some misunderstanding, so I phoned your home."

"I wasn't there because I was waiting for you!"

He persisted with the lie and that irritated her even more.

"You were gone, all right," she said, spitting out the words. "You were with your buddies bowling."

His eyes narrowed and he began to speak.

But the music stopped just then, which was all the excuse Noelle needed to get away from him. He reached for her hand and pulled her back. "We need to talk."

"No. It happened years ago. Some things are better left alone."

"Not this time," he insisted, unwilling to budge.

"What do you hope to accomplish by going through all of this now? It's too late." They'd gain nothing more than the pain of opening old wounds. Any discussion was futile. It'd been a mistake to let herself get drawn into this silly drama—just one very big mistake.

"I'm not hoping to accomplish one damn thing," he told her coldly.

"I didn't think so."

Thom released her hand. "Just a minute," he said as she turned from him.

Noelle hesitated.

"I *was* there. I stood there for two hours and waited. You were the one who never showed."

"That's not true!"

They stood glowering at each other, both refusing to give in. Noelle wasn't going to let him lie his way out of this, though—not after what his deception had cost her.

"Hey, you two, this is Christmas," someone called out.

The voice ended Noelle's resolve. Whatever had happened in the past didn't matter anymore. Certainly not after all these years.

"If you find comfort in believing a lie, then do so," he said, "but don't involve me." He walked away, his face hard and impassive.

Left alone in the middle of the dance floor, Noelle stared at him in amazement. Of all the nerve! He'd stopped her from leaving and now *he'd* taken off!

Picking up her skirt, she raced after him. "All right! You want to talk this out, then we will."

"When?" He continued walking, tossing the question over his shoulder.

With Christmas so close, her time was booked solid. "I...soon."

"Tonight."

"All right." She swallowed hard. "When and where?"

"After the dance. In the park, same place as before."

That seemed fitting, since it was where they were originally going to meet the day they'd planned to elope.

"What time is the dance over?"

"Midnight." He glanced at his watch. "So make it one."

"I'll be there."

He shot her a look. "That was what you said the *last* time."

NOELLE MCDOWELL'S
JOURNAL

December 21
5:00 p.m.

Everyone's getting ready for the big dance, but my head's still spinning and I've learned that it helps me sort through my emotions if I write everything down. I ran into Thom again. It's as though we're being drawn together, as though we're trapped in some magnetic field and are being pulled toward each other from opposite directions. I can tell he doesn't like it any better than I do.

It happened yesterday when I met Kristen for lunch at The Rose Garden. No sooner had our order arrived when in walked Thom and his mother.

Try as I might, I couldn't keep my eyes off him. He apparently suffered from the same malady. Every time I glanced up, he was staring at me—and frowning. His mother was with him and I could see that he was trying to keep her distracted so she wouldn't notice Kristen and me. I didn't completely understand why until we arrived home and discovered that Mom and Mrs.

Sutton had had another run-in while shopping for the Christmas baskets. That must have been something to see, although I'm grateful I didn't!

After we left the restaurant, Kristen and I had a long talk about Thom. I told her far more than I meant to. I don't think I've thought or talked this much about Thom in years, and I found myself experiencing all those pathetic emotions all over again. Kristen confessed that she's been hurt and upset with me for staying away, and now that I'm home, I can understand her disappointment. It's ironic, because after I told her how devastated I was when Thom and I broke up, she said she could understand why I'd stayed away. She even said she'd probably have done the same thing.

When I got back to the house, Mom was in quite a state. For a moment I thought she might have talked herself out of attending the dance, but our hopes were quickly dashed. Dad and I should've realized Mom has far too much pride to let Mary Sutton get the upper hand.

This Christmas-basket project is driving her nuts, but Mom's determined to make Kristen's wedding one this town will long remember, and she's willing to make whatever sacrifice is necessary. I do admire her determination.

It's time to get ready for the dance. Wouldn't you know it? Mom came up with a dress, and just as Carley predicted, it's pink. Pepto-Bismol pink. I can only hope Thom doesn't show up, but at the rate my luck is running...

Four

The rest of the Christmas dance passed in a blur for Noelle. She danced with a constant stream of attractive men. She greeted longtime family friends and socialized the evening away, but not once did she stop thinking about Thom. They were finally going to settle this. Only she wasn't a naive eighteen-year-old anymore and she wouldn't allow his lies to go unchallenged. Thom claimed he'd been waiting for her in the park, but she knew otherwise.

At the end of the evening, the families trooped down the wide sweeping staircase. Noelle, Carley and their mother waited while Jake stood in line to collect their coats. No more than three feet away from them was Mary Sutton, who also appeared to be waiting for her coat. Noelle had to hand it to the woman; she did a marvelous job of pretending not to see them.

"Good evening, Mrs. Sutton," Noelle greeted her, refusing to ignore Thom's mother.

Sarah's onetime friend opened and then closed her mouth, as if she didn't know how to respond.

"Noelle." Her mother elbowed her sharply in the ribs. "What's the matter with you?"

"Nothing. I'm greeting an old family friend."

"*Former* friend," her mother insisted. "We haven't been friends in almost twenty years."

"But you once were."

Her mother sighed wearily. "I was younger then, and I didn't have the discretion I have now. You see, back then I took friendship at face value. I trusted in good-will and forgiveness."

"Hello, Noelle," Mary Sutton said, moving closer. "I, too, was once young and I, too, believed in the power of friendship. But I was taught a painful lesson when the woman I assumed was my dearest friend lied and deceived me and entrusted a priceless family heirloom to another. But that was a very long time ago. Tell me," she said, turning a cold shoulder to Noelle's mother. "How are *you?*"

"Very well, thank you."

Her mother clasped Carley's arm and stepped back as though to protect her youngest daughter.

"You're looking lovely," Thom's mother said, and her eyes were kind.

"Thank you," Noelle said, although she could feel her mother's gaze burning into her back.

Mary Sutton lowered her voice. "I couldn't help overhearing your mother's comments just now about friendship. I probably should've stayed out of it—but I couldn't."

"It's so sad that the two of you have allowed this nonsense to go on for all these years."

"Let me assure you, my grandmother's tea service

is not nonsense. It was all I had to remind me of her. Your mother lied to me about using it, and then lost it forever." Her downcast eyes clearly said that the loss of her grandmother's legacy still caused her pain. "You're right, though. It's unfortunate this has dragged on as long as it has."

That sounded encouraging, and Noelle was ready to leap on what she considered a gesture of peace.

"However," Mrs. Sutton continued, "there are certain things no friendship can overcome, and I fear your mother has crossed that line too many times to count. Regrettably, our friendship is unsalvageable."

"But—"

"Another thing," Mrs. Sutton said, cutting Noelle off. "I saw you dancing with Thom this evening. You two were once sweet on each other, but you hurt him badly. I hope for both your sakes that you're not thinking of renewing your acquaintance."

"I… I…" Noelle faltered, not knowing how to answer.

Noelle's mother stepped forward. "I suggest your son stay away from our daughter."

"Mom, keep out of this, please," Noelle cried, afraid of what would happen if the two women started in on each other—particularly after the Value-X incident. This was the town's biggest social event of the year, and a scene was the last thing either family needed.

Mr. Sutton returned with the coats, and Noelle's father followed shortly afterward. The McDowells headed immediately for the parking lot, careful to avoid any and all Suttons. Everyone was silent on the drive home, but Noelle knew she'd upset her mother.

Fifteen minutes later as they walked into the house, she decided she should be the one to compromise. "Mom, I wish now that I hadn't spoken to Mrs. Sutton," she said quietly. And she meant it; she should have restricted her remarks to "Hello" and maybe "Merry Christmas."

"I do, too," her mother said. "I know your intentions were good, but it's best to leave things as they are. I tried for a long time to make up with her, but she refused to accept a replacement set and she refused my apology." Sadness crept into her voice. "Mary did make one good point, though."

Noelle mentally reviewed the conversation.

"She said it's a good idea for you to stay away from Thom, and she's right." She sighed, then briefly placed her palm against Noelle's cheek. Her eyes were warm with love. "The two of you have a history you can't escape."

"Mom, it isn't like that. We—"

"Sweetheart, listen please. I know you once had strong feelings for that young man, and it hurt me deeply."

"It hurt *you?*"

Her mother nodded. "Very much so, because I knew you'd be forced to make a choice between your family and Thom. I couldn't bear the thought of you married to him or sharing my grandchildren with Mary Sutton. You saw for yourself how she feels about me. There's no forgiveness in her. Really, is this the kind of woman you want in your life and the lives of your children? That's the history I mean." She kissed Noelle on the cheek and headed down the hallway to her room. "Good night now."

Noelle shut her eyes and sagged against the wall. She'd been just a moment away from explaining that she was going to meet Thom in order to talk things out. Her mother sounded as though she'd consider it a personal affront if Noelle so much as looked at him. It was like high school all over again.

The only thing left to do now was sneak out the same way she had as a teenager. She couldn't leave him waiting in the cold, that was unthinkable. Besides, this might be her one and only chance to sort out what had really happened, and she wasn't going to throw it away. She didn't intend any disrespect toward her mother or his, but she *had* to be there. If she didn't show up, she'd confirm every negative belief he already had about her.

Carley was in bed asleep as Noelle passed her room. She went in to drop a kiss on her sister's forehead, then softly closed the door. Noelle changed out of her party dress, choosing wool slacks and a thick sweater to wear to the park. Sitting on the edge of the bed, she waited for the minutes to tick past. With luck, her parents would be exhausted and both go directly to bed. Then Noelle could slip away undetected.

Finally the house was dark and quiet. The only illumination came from the flashing Christmas lights that decorated the roofline.

Opening her bedroom door, Noelle was horrified by the way it creaked. On tiptoe, she carefully, silently crept down the narrow corridor.

"Jake." Her mother was instantly awake. "I heard something."

"Go to sleep, honey."

"There's someone in the house," her mother insisted.

Noelle froze. She could hardly breathe. Just imagining what her mother would say was enough to paralyze her.

"Jake, I'm serious."

"I don't hear anything," her father mumbled.

"I did. We could all be murdered in our beds."

"Sarah, for the love of heaven."

"Think of the children."

Noelle nearly groaned aloud. She was trapped. She'd have to pass her parents' bedroom in order to steal back into her own. They were sure to see her. She couldn't go forward and she couldn't go back.

"All right, all right," her father muttered as he climbed out of bed.

"Take something with you," her mother hissed.

"Like what?"

"Here, take a wooden hanger."

"So I can hang him out to dry if I happen on a burglar?"

"Just do it, Jake."

"Yes, dear."

Noelle had made it safely into the kitchen by the time her father came upon her. "Dad," she whispered, hiding in the shadows, "it's me."

"Why didn't you say so?" he whispered back.

"I couldn't. I'm sneaking out of the house."

"This late? Where are you going?"

He wouldn't like the answer, but she refused to lie. "I'm meeting Thom Sutton in the park. We're going to talk."

Her father didn't say anything for a long moment. Then it sounded as if he was weeping.

Noelle felt dreadful. "Dad? I'm sorry if this upsets you."

"Upsets me?" he repeated. "I think it's hilarious."

"You...do?"

"Go ahead and meet your young man and talk all you want. This thing is between Sarah and Mary. Greg and I have been friends for years."

This was news to Noelle. "You're still friends?"

"Of course. He's the best golfing partner I ever had."

"You and Mr. Sutton are golf partners?" Noelle thought perhaps she'd slipped into another dimension.

"Shhh." Her father raised a finger to his lips. "Your mother doesn't know."

"Mom doesn't know." This was more unbelievable by the moment.

"Scoot," her father ordered, and reaching for the keys on the peg outside the garage door, he said, "Here, take my car. It's parked on the street."

Noelle clutched the set of keys and leaned forward to kiss his cheek. "Thanks, Dad."

He coughed loudly as she opened the back door. "You're hearing things, Sarah," he called out. "There's nothing." He gave her a small wave and turned back toward the hallway.

As soon as she was out the door, Noelle sprinted toward her dad's car. It took her a moment to figure out which key she needed and then another to adjust the mirror and the seat. When she glanced at her watch, she was shocked to see the time. It was already ten minutes past one.

Thom would assume she wasn't coming. He'd think she'd stood him up…when nothing could be further from the truth.

Thom expelled his breath into the cold, and it came out looking like the snort of a cartoon bull. An *angry* cartoon bull. That was exactly how he felt. Once again, he'd allowed his heart to rule his head and he'd fallen prey to Noelle McDowell.

He should have known better. Everything he'd learned about heartache, Noelle had taught him. And now, fool that he was, he'd set himself up to be taken again. Noelle McDowell was untrustworthy. He knew it and yet he'd still risked disappointment and worse.

Slapping his hands against his upper arms to ward off the cold, he paced the area beneath the trees across from the pool at Lions' Park. This had been their special meeting place. It was here that Thom had kissed Noelle for the second time. Here, they'd met and talked and shared their secrets. Here, he'd first confessed his love.

A car door slammed in the distance. Probably the police coming to check out his vehicle, which was parked in a lot that was closed to the public at this time of night. He deserved to get a ticket for being enough of an idiot to trust Noelle.

He didn't know why he'd hung around as long as he had. Looking at his watch he saw that it was twenty after one. She'd kept him waiting nineteen minutes too long. Her non-appearance was all the proof he'd ever need.

"Thom… Thom!" Noelle called out as she ran across the lawn.

Angry and defiant, he stepped out from beneath the shadow of the fifty-foot cedar tree.

"Thank goodness you're still here," she cried and to her credit, she did sound relieved. She was breathless when she reached him. "I had to sneak out of the house."

"Sneak out? You're almost thirty years old!"

"I know, I know. Listen, I'm so sorry." She pushed back the sleeve of her coat and squinted at her watch. "You waited—I can't believe you stayed for twenty extra minutes. I prayed you would, but I wouldn't have blamed you if you'd left."

The anger that had burned in him moments earlier evaporated so fast it shocked him.

"When did they turn Walnut into a dead-end street?"

"Years ago." Of course she'd drive down the same street they'd used as teenagers. He'd forgotten the changes made over the last decade; it hadn't occurred to him that she wouldn't know. "You're here now."

"Yes…listen, I know I shouldn't do this, but I can't help myself." Having said that, she slipped her arms around his waist and hugged him hard. His own arms went around her, too, tentatively and then with greater strength.

Closing his eyes and savoring the feel of her was a mistake, the first of many he knew he'd be making. She smelled like Christmas, somehow, and her warmth wrapped itself around him.

"Why'd you do that?" he asked gruffly as she released him and took a step back. He was trying to hide how damn good it'd felt to hold her.

"It's the only way I could think of to thank you for staying, for believing in me enough to wait."

"I wasn't exactly enumerating your good points while I stood here freezing."

"I know, I wouldn't, either—I mean, well, you know what I mean."

He did.

Clearing off a space on the picnic table, Noelle climbed up and sat there just as she had when they were teenagers. "All right," she said, drawing in a deep breath. "Let's talk. Since you were the one to suggest we do this, you should go first."

So she'd become a take-charge sort of woman. That didn't surprise him. She'd displayed leadership qualities in high school, as well, serving on the student council and as president of the French Club. "All right, that's fair enough." She might be able to sit, but Thom couldn't. He had ten years of anger stored inside and that made it impossible to stand still for long. "We argued, remember?"

"Of course I do. The argument had to do with our mothers. You said something derogatory about mine and I defended her."

"As I recall, you had a less-than-flattering attitude toward *my* mother."

"But you were the first…" She paused. "None of that's important now. What we should be discussing is what happened afterward."

Once again she was right. "We made up, or so I thought."

"We made up because we refused to allow the ongoing feud between our mothers to come between us. Later that day, you wrote me a note and suggested we elope."

Her voice caught just a little. He wanted so badly to believe her. It was a struggle not to. "I loved you, Noelle."

She smiled, but he saw pain in her eyes and it shook him. For years he'd assumed that she'd used his love against him. That she'd stood him up just to hurt him. To humiliate him. He'd never really understood why. Was it vindication on behalf of her mother?

"We were going to confront our parents, remember?" Noelle said.

"Yes. I made a big stand, claiming how much I loved you and how I refused to let either of our mothers interfere in our lives. You should've heard me."

"I did, too!" she declared. "I spilled out my guts to them. Can you imagine how humiliating it was to have to go back and confess that you'd tricked me—that you'd jilted me?"

"Me!" he shouted. "You were the one—"

Noelle held up both hands and he let his anger fade. "Something happened. It must have." She pressed one hand to her heart. "I swear by all I consider holy that I've never lied to you."

"You're assuming I did?" he challenged.

"Yes. I mean no," she cried, confused now. "Something *did* happen, but what?"

"I don't know," he said. "I was here at three, just like I wrote you in the note."

She frowned, and he wondered if she was going to try to tell him she hadn't gotten his note. He knew otherwise because he'd personally seen Kristen hand it to her at school.

"The note said eight."

"Three," he insisted. Now it was his turn to look perplexed. "I wrote down three o'clock."

"The note said…" She brought her hand to her mouth. "No, I refuse to believe it."

"You think Kristen changed the time?"

"She wouldn't do that." She shook her head. "I know my sister, and she'd never hurt me like that."

"How do you explain the discrepancy then?"

"I have no idea." She squeezed her eyes shut. "I remember it vividly. You'd sent it to me after your math class."

His defenses were down. Time rolled back, and the events of that day were starting to focus in his mind. The fog of his pain dissipated. Finally he was able to look at the events with a clear head and an analytical eye.

"Kristen spilled soda on it," Noelle said thoughtfully. "Do you think that might have smudged the number?"

"It might explain part of it—but not the nasty note you left on my windshield."

She had the grace to blush at the reminder. "After waiting until after ten o'clock, I didn't know what to do. It was pretty dark by then, and I couldn't believe you'd just abandon me. I was positive something must've happened, so I phoned your house."

He nodded, encouraging her to go on.

"Your father said you were out with your friends bowling. I went to the alley to see for myself." Her voice tightened. "Sure enough, you were in there, boozing it up with your buddies."

"Don't tell me you actually thought I was having a good time?"

"Looked like it to me."

"Noelle, I was practically crying in my beer. I felt… I felt as if I'd just learned about some tragedy that was going to change my whole life."

"Why didn't you call me? How could you believe I'd stand you up? If you loved me as much as you said, wouldn't you make some effort to find out what happened?"

"I did." To be fair, it'd taken him a day, but he had to know, had to discover how he could've been so mistaken about Noelle. "I waited until the following afternoon. Your mother answered the phone and said I'd already done enough damage. She hung up on me."

"She never told me," Noelle whispered. "She never said a word."

"Why would she?" Thom murmured. "Your mother assumed I'd done you wrong, just the way everyone else in your family did."

"I left that horrible note on your car and you still phoned me?"

He nodded.

"I can only imagine what you must have thought."

"And you," he said.

They both grew quiet.

"I'm so sorry, Thom," she finally said. "So very sorry."

"So am I." He was afraid to touch her, afraid of what would happen if she came into his arms.

Noelle brushed the hair back from her face and when he glanced at her, he saw tears glistening in her eyes.

"It all worked out for the best, though, don't you think?" he asked. He had to say *something*.

She nodded. Then after a moment she spoke in a voice so low he had to lean closer to hear. "Do you really believe that?"

"No." He reached for her then, crushing her in his arms, lifting her from the picnic table and holding her as if his very life depended on keeping her close to his heart.

His mouth found hers, and her lips were moist and soft, her body melting against his. Their kisses were filled with hunger and passion, with mingled joy and discovery. This sense of *rightness* was what had been missing from every relationship he'd had since his breakup with Noelle. Nothing had felt right with any other woman. He loved Noelle. He'd always loved her.

She buried her face in his shoulder and he kissed the top of her head. Her arms circled his neck and he ran his fingers through her hair, gathering it in his hands as he closed his eyes and let his emotions run free— from anger to joy. From joy to fear. From fear to relief.

"What happens now?" he asked. They didn't seem to have many options. Each had made a life without the other.

She didn't answer him for a long time, but he knew she'd heard the question.

"Noelle," he said as she raised her head. "What do we do now?"

She blinked back tears. "Do we have to decide this minute? Can't you just kiss me again?"

He smiled and lowered his mouth to hers. "I think that could be arranged."

Fresh from Sunday services—where she'd been inspired by a sermon on giving—Mary Sutton drove to the local Walmart store. She refused to show up the following day and not have the items on her list. No doubt Sarah McDowell assumed she'd arrive at the club empty-handed, but Mary fully intended to prove otherwise.

As soon as Greg had settled in front of the television set watching the Seahawks' play-off game, she was out the door. Shopping this close to Christmas went against every dictate of common sense. Usually she was the organized one. Christmas gifts had been purchased, wrapped and tucked away soon after Thanksgiving. But, with these six Christmas baskets, she had no choice. She had to resort to last-minute shopping.

The parking lot at Walmart was packed. Finding a space at the very rear of the lot, Mary trudged toward the busy store. She dreaded dealing with the mob of shoppers inside. On the off chance she might have a repeat of that horrible scene in Value-X, she surveyed the lot—looking up one row and down the next—in search of Sarah's vehicle. She sighed with relief when she didn't see the other woman's car.

List in hand, Mary grabbed a cart and headed straight for the toy section. She hoped the store would have Barbie dolls left on the shelf. She hated the thought of a single child being disappointed on Christmas morning. Fortunately, the shelves appeared to have been recently restocked.

Reaching for a Firefighter Barbie doll, she set it inside her basket. With a sense of accomplishment, she wheeled the cart around the corner to the riding toys. To her horror and dismay, she discovered Sarah McDowell reading the label on a toddler-sized car. This was her worst nightmare.

"No," she muttered, not realizing Sarah would hear her.

Her bitterest enemy turned and their eyes locked. "What are *you* doing here?" Sarah demanded.

"The same thing you are."

Sarah gripped her cart with both hands, as if she was prepared to engage in a second ramming session. Frankly, Mary had suffered all the humiliation she could stand and had no desire to go a second round.

"Can't you buy your grandson's gifts some other time?"

"How dare you tell me when I can or cannot shop." Mary couldn't believe the gall. She would shop when and where she pleased without any guidance from the likes of Sarah McDowell.

"Mary, hello."

Mary wanted to groan out loud. Janice Newhouse, the pastor's wife, was easing her cart toward them. "This must be Sarah McDowell. I've seen your photo on a real estate brochure." She smiled warmly at the woman who had caused Mary so much pain. "I'm Janice Newhouse."

"Hello." Sarah's return greeting was stiff.

"I've heard so much about you," Janice said, apparently oblivious to the tension between the two women.

"I'll just bet you have." Sarah said this as though to suggest that Mary was a gossipmonger, when nothing could be further from the truth. For years, she'd quietly refused to get drawn into any discussion involving Sarah. It wouldn't do either of them any good. The same could not be said for Sarah McDowell. She'd taken delight in blackballing Mary's membership in the Women's Century Club. She'd dragged Mary's name and reputation through the mud. Mary, on the other hand, had chosen the higher ground—with the exception, perhaps, of that newspaper column on the perfidy of real estate agents, and that certainly hadn't been a personal attack.

"I understand the Willis family bought their home through you," Janice said, making polite conversation.

"You know the Willises?"

"Yes, they're members of our church. So are Mary and her husband."

Sarah's expression was glacial. "Oh."

"Sarah and I are buying gifts for the charity baskets," Mary said.

"We divided the list and now we're each getting half," Sarah went on to explain. "Tomorrow we're assembling the baskets and taking them to Salvation Army headquarters."

That was much more than Janice needed to know, Mary thought irritably. Sarah was just showing off.

"That's wonderfully charitable of you both," Janice murmured.

"Thank you." Sarah added a pull toy to her basket.

Mary reached for one herself.

Next Sarah took down a board game; Mary took two.

Sarah grabbed a skateboard.

"How generous you are," Janice commented, eyes widening as she observed their behavior. "Both of you appear to be very...zealous."

"I believe in giving back to the community," Mary said.

"As do I," Sarah insisted. By now her cart was so full she couldn't possibly cram anything else into it.

"Leave something for me to buy," Mary challenged, doing her best to keep the smile on her face from turning into a scowl.

"I'm the one who has the little girl who wants a Firefighter Barbie on my list," Sarah said, staring pointedly at the doll in Mary's cart.

"*I'm* the one with the gift list," Mary countered. "Besides, there are plenty of Barbie dolls."

"You aren't even supposed to be buying toys. That was *my* job." Sarah's eyes narrowed menacingly.

"Ladies, I don't think there's any reason to squabble here." Janice raised both hands in a calming gesture. "Let me look at your lists."

"Fine," Sarah snapped.

"Good idea," Mary added in a far more congenial tone. She opened her purse and dug out the list Melody Darrington had given her.

Janice examined both pages. She ran down Sarah's first and then Mary's. She frowned. "Here's the problem," she said, handing them back. "You have the same list."

"That's impossible," Mary protested.

"Let me see." Sarah snatched Mary's from her hand with such speed it was a wonder Mary didn't suffer a paper cut.

"That's what I think happened," Janice said. "You were accidentally given one list instead of two."

Sarah glanced over each page. "She's right."

Mary wanted to weep with frustration. "Do you mean to say we're actually working from the same list?" It made sense now that she thought about it. Melody had been so busy that morning, and the phone was ringing off the hook. It was no wonder the secretary had been distracted.

"You were supposed to pick up the grocery items," Mary said.

"I most certainly was not. That was *your* job."

If Sarah was trying to be obtuse and irritating, she was succeeding.

Janice glanced from one to the other. "Ladies, this is for the Christmas baskets, remember?"

Mary smiled benevolently at the pastor's wife, who was new to the area. Janice couldn't know. But then, a twenty-year-old feud wasn't something Mary was inclined to brag about.

"She's right," Sarah said again. "We're both behaving a bit childishly, don't you think?"

Mary was staying away from that question.

"I'll call Melody in the morning and pick up the second half of the list."

"No, you won't," Mary told her. "I'll do it."

"I said I would," Sarah said from between clenched teeth.

"You don't need to, I will."

"Would you ladies prefer that I do it?" Janice volunteered.

"No way," Sarah muttered.

"Thank you, but no," Mary said more politely.

Janice looked doubtful. "You're sure?"

"Yes."

"Yes." Sarah's voice blended with Mary's.

"All right, ladies, I'll leave you to your good works then."

Out of the corner of her eye, Mary watched Janice stroll away.

As soon as the pastor's wife was out of earshot, Sarah said, "You can pick up the list if you want." She made it sound as though she was making a big concession.

Naturally, she'd agree now. Mary sighed; this problem with the list complicated everything. "I'll need time to shop for the groceries."

"And your point is?"

"Shouldn't it be obvious?" Clearly it wasn't. "We'll need to meet on the morning of the twenty-fourth now."

"Christmas Eve?"

"Yes, the twenty-fourth is generally known as Christmas Eve," Mary told her a bit sarcastically.

"Fine. Let's meet at the club at nine and deliver the baskets to the Salvation Army from there."

"Fine."

"In the meantime," Sarah suggested, "let's do the sensible thing and divide up the toys on this list. Why don't I get the girls' stuff and you get the boys'?"

Wordlessly, they each returned half of their purchases. Mary hated to follow Sarah's lead, but for once the woman had come up with a reasonable idea. "I'll see you Tuesday morning at nine," she finally said.

Sarah gave a curt nod.

Mary wheeled her cart to the front of the store. All the cashiers were busy, so she found the shortest line and waited her turn. Not until a few moments later did she notice that Sarah stood in the line beside hers.

Mary took a magazine from the stand, leafed through it and tossed it into her cart.

Sarah placed two magazines in hers.

Mary decided to splurge and buy a candy bar. As she put it in the cart, she glanced at Sarah. The other woman grabbed one of every candy bar on the rack. Refusing to be outdone, Mary reached for two.

Sarah rolled her eyes and then emptied the entire container of candy into her cart.

Mary looked over and saw two men staring at them. A woman was whispering to her companion, pointing in her and Sarah's direction.

Once again, they'd managed to make spectacles of themselves.

NOELLE McDOWELL'S
JOURNAL

December 22

*I just got back from church, and it was lovely to attend
services with Mom and Dad and Carley. The music was
stirring and brought back so many memories of Christmases spent in Rose. I wish I'd paid closer attention to
the sermon, but my mind refused to remain focused on
the pastor's message. All I could think about was Thom.*

*Now that we've talked, I think we've actually created
more problems than we've solved. We're going to get
together again later in the day, but that's not until one.
We both realize we can't leave things as they are, yet
neither one of us knows where to go from here.*

*Still, it's wonderful to know my faith in him was jus-
tified. That makes this decision even harder, though.
I'm afraid I'm falling in love with him again—if I ever
stopped!—but there are so many complications. In fact,
I wonder if our best choice would be simply to call it
quits. But I'm not sure we can, because we made a mistake last night. We kissed.*

If we hadn't done that, I might've found the courage

to shake Thom's hand, claim there were no hard feelings and walk away. But we did kiss and now…well, now we're in a quandary. I wish his kisses didn't affect me, but they do. Big-time. Oh boy, nothing's changed in that department. It's as if I was sixteen all over again, and frankly, that's a scary feeling.

I felt Thom's kisses all the way through me, from head to toe. Thom felt them, too, and I think he's just as confused as I am. Things got intense very quickly, and we both recognized we had to stop. Now it's decision time.

Thom withdrew from me, physically and emotionally, and I did from him, too. We both tried to play it cool— as if this was all very nice and it was good to clear the air. He acted as if we should just get on with our lives. I played along and was halfway back to the car when he stopped me. He wanted to know if we could meet at the mall today to talk again.

God help me, I jumped at the invitation. Maybe I should've been more nonchalant, but I couldn't do it. I was just happy for the chance to see him again.

Five

Shopping was the perfect excuse to get out of the house on Sunday afternoon, and Noelle used it. Her mother was gone, her father was absorbed in some televised football game and Carley was in her room checking *Buffy* websites on her computer.

"I'm going out for a while," Noelle said casually.

Her father's eyes didn't waver from the television screen. "Are you meeting Thom?"

"Ah…"

Her father raised his hand. "Say no more. What do you want me to tell your mother if she asks?"

"That I've gone shopping… We're meeting at the mall."

"That's all she needs to know."

Noelle kissed her father on the cheek. His eyes didn't leave the screen as he reached inside his pants pocket and handed her his car keys. "Why don't you take my car again?"

"Thanks, Dad."

"Don't mention it." Then her father did look away

from the television and his gaze sought hers. "You have feelings for this young man?"

Noelle nodded. It was the truth, much as she hated to acknowledge it, even to herself.

Her father nodded, too. "I was afraid of that."

His words lingered in Noelle's mind as she drove to the Rose Mall on the west side of town. She'd lived for this moment ever since she and Thom had parted the night before. They'd resolved what both had considered a deception, but so many questions were still unanswered. They needed time to think, to consider the consequences of becoming involved a second time. Nothing had changed between their families—or more specifically, their mothers—but other things *were* different. Noelle wasn't the naive eighteen-year-old she'd been ten years ago; neither was Thom.

It took a good twenty minutes to find a parking space, and the mall was equally crowded. Carolers dressed in Victorian costumes stood in front of the JCPenney store, cheerfully singing "Silver Bells." Noelle wished she could listen for a while, but fearing she might be late, she paused only a moment to take in the sights and the sounds of the holiday season.

She hurried through the overheated mall and found Thom at a table in the food court, just the way they'd agreed. He stood as she approached.

"I haven't kept you waiting, have I?" she asked.

"No, no. It occurred to me that with Christmas this close we might have trouble finding a table so I grabbed one early."

He'd always been thoughtful. As he put down his coffee and pulled out her chair, she shrugged out of her coat and threw it on the back of the seat. "Would you like to get some lunch?"

She shook her head. "You should have something, though." Her stomach had been upset all morning.

"Are you ill?"

"No—it's guilt." He might as well know. She'd been anxious since last night, since their first moonlit kiss... All through church services and afterward, she'd repeatedly told herself how ridiculous it was to sneak around behind her mother's back. Her father had apparently been doing it for years, but secretive actions truly bothered Noelle.

"Guilt?"

"I don't like being dishonest."

"Then tell your mother." Thom made it sound so easy, but he didn't need an excuse every time he stepped out the front door. He didn't even live at home, and he wasn't visiting his family for Christmas the way she was. He wasn't accountable to his parents for every minute spent outside their presence.

"Did you let your parents know we were meeting?" she asked.

He half grinned, looking sheepish. "No."

"That's what I thought."

"How about coffee?" he asked in an all-too-obvious effort to change the subject. "I could use a refill."

She gave a quick nod. She'd been counting the minutes until they could talk again. After their meeting in the park, she'd barely slept. She'd relived their conversation—and their kisses—over and over. It seemed a miracle that they'd finally learned what must have happened that day ten years ago. Truly a Christmas miracle. Now, if only their mothers would miraculously reconcile...

Thom left and returned a few minutes later with two steaming cups of coffee.

Noelle held her cup with both hands, letting the heat warm her palms. She hadn't felt chilled before, but she did now. "I—I don't know where to start."

"Why didn't you ever come home?" he asked bluntly. "Start by telling me that."

"It was just too painful to come back here. I made excuses at first and it got easier after a while. Plus, Mom and Dad and my sisters were always willing to visit Texas. It's beautiful in a way that's completely different from the Northwest. Oh, and the shopping is excellent."

He laughed. "Is there anyone special in your life?"

"I have a number of good friends."

"Male or female?"

She hesitated. "Female."

Thom visibly relaxed. "You don't date much, then?"

"Of course I date—I've gone out lots. Well, maybe not as much as I'd like, but I *was* engaged for a while. How about you?"

"I came close to getting engaged. Twice."

Without knowing a single detail, Noelle was instantly jealous. "Who?"

He seemed pleased by her reaction. He leaned back in his chair, stretched out his legs and crossed his ankles. "No one you know. Besides, I'm the one asking the questions here. You can drill me later."

"No way! In other words, you became some kind of ladies' man after you dumped me?"

His face suddenly grew serious and he reached

across the table for her hand. "I didn't dump you, Noelle."

She'd meant to tease him but realized her remark was insensitive—not to mention plain wrong. "I know. I apologize. Chalk it up to a bad choice of words."

Thom squeezed her hand. "Do you think that's what happened with our mothers?" he asked. "A bad choice of words?"

"How do you mean?"

"Think about it. Just now, you reverted to your old thought pattern—your assumption that you'd been betrayed. It wasn't until after you spoke that you remembered what had really happened."

He was right. The words had slipped out easily, thoughtlessly.

"Our mothers are probably behaving in the same way. After all these years, they're caught in this pattern of disparaging each other, and they can't break the habit."

Noelle wasn't sure she agreed with him. For one thing, she knew her mother had desperately tried to end the feud. Every attempt had been rebuffed. "I don't think it's a good idea to discuss our mothers."

"Why not?"

"Because we argue. You want to defend your mother and I want to defend mine, and the two of us end up fighting. Besides, weren't we talking about the women in your life after I left Rose?"

He chuckled. "You make it sound like there were hordes of them."

"There weren't?" She pretended to be shocked.

He shook his head. "Not really. Two I considered

marrying and a few others I saw for a while. What about you?"

"You keep asking. All right, I was serious once. Paul was a computer programmer, and we both worked for the same company, developing new software. It was an exciting time in the business and we got caught up in the thrill of it all." Paul was actually very sweet and very brilliant, but their romance wasn't meant to be. Noelle had been the first to realize it. She'd ended their brief engagement, and they'd parted on good terms, remaining friends to this day. "After the launch of Curtains, our new operating system, well…it was curtains for our marriage plans, too," she said, smiling at her own feeble pun.

"Just one guy?" Thom asked.

"Don't sound so disappointed." Noelle had told him far more than necessary. He hadn't said a word about either of the women he'd loved.

"Listen, what I said earlier regarding our mothers— I wonder if—"

"I don't want to discuss our mothers, Thom."

"We can't avoid it forever."

"Maybe not," she agreed, "but does it have to be the first thing we talk about?"

"It's not," he argued.

"Look at us," she said. "I haven't been with you fifteen minutes and already we're both on the defensive. This isn't going to work." She was ready to give up and go home, but Thom stopped her.

"Okay, we'll leave our mothers out of the conversation."

Now it seemed neither one had anything to say.

"I kept waiting to hear that you were married," she said after a silence. "But I refused to ask. That's silly I suppose." It was like waiting for the dentist's drill; when it happened there'd be pain and she hadn't been in a hurry to experience it.

"I assumed you'd get married first," he said.

Noelle grinned, shaking her head. "There's something else we need to talk about," she murmured. "What are we going to do now?" She began with the least palatable option—which was also the easiest. "I mean, we could shake hands and say it's great to have this cleared up, then just go back to our respective lives." She waited, watching for a response from him.

His face revealed none of his thoughts. "We could do that," he said. "Or…" He looked at her.

"Or we could renew our friendship."

Thom leaned back in his chair. "I like that option."

So did Noelle. "But, as you said, there's still the situation with our mothers." Now she was the one bringing it up, although she'd hoped to avoid any mention of their mothers' feud. It was futile, she realized. They *couldn't* avoid it, no matter how hard they tried.

"If your mother hadn't borrowed my great-grandmother's tea service," Thom began, "she—"

"My mother?" Noelle cried. "I agree she made a mistake, but she was the first to admit it. Your mother refused to forgive her, and that says a lot about the kind of person she is."

Thom's eyes were flinty with anger. "Don't paint *your* mother as the one who was wronged because—"

Noelle was unwilling to listen to any more. "Listen,

Thom, this isn't going to solve anything. I think it'd be best if we dropped the subject entirely."

"That isn't the only thing you want to drop, is it?"

It was a question she didn't want to answer. A question that implied it would be best for all concerned if they simply walked away from each other right now. Their circumstances hadn't changed, not really; the business with their mothers would always be an obstacle between them. They could ignore it, but it would never disappear.

She stood and gathered her purse, pulled on her coat. This time Thom didn't try to stop her.

"So, you're walking away at the first sign of difficulty," he said.

"No. As a teenager my heart was open to you and your family, but I'm older now."

"What's that got to do with anything?" he demanded.

"This time, my eyes are open, too."

He looked as if he wanted to continue their argument. But she didn't have the heart for it. Obviously Thom didn't, either, because he let her go without another word.

"Help me carry everything in, Greg," Mary Sutton said as she stepped into the house. Her arms were loaded with plastic bags bursting at the seams.

Mary had never understood or appreciated football, and she didn't mind saying so. Her husband's gaze reluctantly left the television screen, where a bunch of men in tight pants and large helmets chased after an oddly shaped ball. As far as she was concerned, it was ridiculous the way they grunted and called out a few numbers now and then and groped their privates right on national television.

"Greg, are you going to help me or not?"

Her husband slowly stood up, his eyes still on the TV. "Honey, it's third down and inches."

He might as well be speaking Greek, but she wasn't going to argue with him. From the sudden reaction of the crowd, something had happened. Greg muttered, shaking his head in a disparaging manner. Mary pretended not to hear and walked back out to the car.

A moment later, he met her in the garage. "We're losing."

"Sorry, darling." She hoped she sounded sympathetic, but she didn't try very hard. Men and their football.

"What on earth did you buy?" he complained, lifting the last of the blue plastic bags from the car's trunk.

"Oh, various things," she said dismissively. "This Christmas basket project hasn't been a positive experience," she went on, following her husband into the house.

"Why not?"

Distressed and angry, she blurted out, "You won't believe this. Sarah McDowell was there!"

"At Walmart?" Even Greg sounded surprised. "Don't tell me we've lost our shopping privileges there, too?"

"Very funny." The incident at the Value-X would haunt her forever.

"So you got along better?"

"I wouldn't say that, but I did discover the problem. We had the same list."

"For the Christmas baskets?"

"Yes." Mary set her load on top of the kitchen counter.

The football game ended, and Greg reached for the remote control to turn off the television set. He opened the first sack and seemed pleasantly surprised to find a stash of candy bars. "For me?" he asked. Without waiting for her to respond, he peeled the wrapper halfway down a Baby Ruth bar and took a bite.

"You can have them all." She threw herself onto the sofa.

Her husband walked into the family room and sat down. "You'd better tell me exactly what happened."

"What makes you think anything did?"

Greg chortled. "I haven't been married to you all these years without knowing when something's bothering you."

"Oh, Greg," she moaned. "I behaved like such an idiot." She longed to cover her face with her hands.

"What went wrong this time?"

She shook her head, unwilling to reveal how low she'd sunk. One thing she'd discovered years ago was still true: Sarah McDowell brought out the very worst in her. It never failed. Mary became another person whenever Sarah was around—a person she didn't like.

"Do you want to talk about it?"

"No. I want to crawl into bed and hide my head in shame." The most embarrassing part of all was that the pastor's wife had seen the whole thing.

"Tomorrow morning, I need to go back to the club."

"For what?"

"I need the second half of the list."

"What's on the list?"

"I won't know until I see it, now will I?" She didn't

mean to be short-tempered, but this afternoon hadn't been one of her best.

"I don't know if I want you driving. There's an ice storm forecast."

"Greg, I have to get that list. I told Sarah I'd take care of this. It's my responsibility."

"Then I'll drive you."

"You will?" Mary felt better already.

"Of course. Can't have you out on icy roads." Her husband finished off the candy bar and returned to the kitchen, where he rummaged through the bags on the counter. "You never did say why you bought all this candy."

Mary looked over at the ten plastic bags that lined her kitchen counter and shuddered. Half of them were filled with candy bars. "You don't want to know."

Greg didn't respond, but she caught him sneaking more Baby Ruth bars into his pockets and the sleeves of his sweater. He wasn't fooling her, but some things were best ignored.

On the other hand, certain things had to be faced. "Greg," she said thoughtfully. "I'm worried about Thom."

"Why?"

"Did you see him with Noelle last night? The two of them were dancing."

"Yes, dear, I saw them."

"Doesn't that concern you?" she asked.

"No." He added a couple of candy bars to his pants pockets, as though she wasn't going to see them protruding.

"Well, it should. Noelle is a sweet girl, but she's her mother's daughter. She's not to be trusted."

"Thom is an adult. He's fully capable of making his own decisions. My advice is to stay out of it."

Mary couldn't believe her husband would say such a thing to her. "You don't mean that! After what happened the last time—"

"You heard me. Stay out of it."

"But Thom is—"

Greg just shook his head. She wanted to say more but swallowed the words. Fathers weren't nearly as caring and concerned about matters of the heart; they lacked sensitivity. Greg hadn't spent time with Thomas the way she had that fateful summer ten years earlier. The McDowell girl had crushed him.

Her husband started toward the garage.

"Greg," she said.

"Yes, dear?"

"Put the candy bars back. I'm adding them to the charity baskets."

He muttered something under his breath, then said, "Yes, dear."

When Thom returned from the mall, he was suffering a full-blown case of the blues. His apartment had never seemed emptier. The small Christmas tree he'd purchased already decorated looked pitiful in the middle of his coffee table. Some Christmas this was turning out to be.

The light on his answering machine blinked, demanding his attention, and for half a heartbeat he thought it might be Noelle. But even as he pressed the Play button, he realized she wouldn't phone.

"Hey, Thom, this is Jonathan Clark," the message said. "Give me a call when you've got a moment."

Thom reached for the phone and punched in the number the investment broker had left. He knew Jonathan but didn't consider him a close friend. He was a business associate and Kristen McDowell's fiancé. This was the first time Jonathan had sought him out socially; Thom hoped it had something to do with Noelle.

After a brief conversation, they agreed to meet at a local pub. Jonathan didn't say why, but it didn't matter. The way Thom felt, he was grateful for any excuse to get out of the house. The walls were closing in around him. Some jovial guy-talk and loud music was exactly what he needed. Although Jonathan was about to marry into the other camp, Thom knew he'd be objective.

Jon was sitting at the bar nursing a dark ale when Thom joined him. The music in the background was Elvis Presley's "Blue Christmas"—appropriate under the circumstances. They exchanged pleasantries and then Jonathan got right to the point.

"I wanted to make sure there weren't any hard feelings about last night."

"You mean finagling it so I ended up dancing with Noelle? No problem."

"I didn't really want to do it, but Kristen seemed to think it was important."

Thom pulled out his wallet and paid for his beer when the bartender delivered it. "Like I said, it wasn't a big deal."

"So you and Kristen's sister were once an item?"

"Once."

"But no more?"

Thom took a deep swallow of the cold beer. "There's trouble between our families."

"Kristen told me about it."

"You're lucky, you know." Jonathan faced none of the challenges he did.

"Very," Jonathan agreed.

There was a pause, not an uncomfortable one. Jon seemed willing to discuss the situation further, but he wouldn't force it. He'd left it up to Thom.

"Noelle and I talked after the dance," he finally ventured.

Jonathan swiveled around on his stool in order to get a better look at Thom. "How'd it go?"

"Last night? Good." His blood warmed at the memory of their kisses. It'd taken every ounce of self-control he'd possessed to let her go. That was one of the reasons he'd suggested they meet at the mall today; it was neutral ground.

"Did you two work everything out?"

"We tried." He waited, half hoping Jonathan would question him about it. Jonathan didn't. Thom sighed, feeling a little discouraged. Now that he'd started, he wanted to talk. "I think we're both leery of getting involved a second time," he continued. "Her home's in Texas now and I live here."

"Right, got ya."

"But it's more than logistics." He tipped back the mug and took another swallow of beer. "We have... this situation. She wants to defend her mother. I want to defend mine."

"Only natural." Jonathan glanced at his watch.

Thom shut up. He had the feeling he was boring the other man. Perhaps he had someplace he needed to be.

Jonathan's next remark surprised him. "Kristen and I were making out our guest list and I put down your name. You'll come, won't you?"

"Sure," Thom answered almost flippantly, and then it occurred to him that if he accepted the invitation, he'd see Noelle again. He found himself eager for the opportunity. "Speaking of the wedding—" well, not really, but he didn't know how else to introduce the topic "—did Kristen ever mention her sister being involved with a guy named Paul?"

Jonathan considered it for a moment, then shook his head. "Not that I can remember. Why?"

"Just curious." And jealous. And worried. Noelle had said it was over between her and this Paul character, but Thom had to wonder. She seemed far too willing to walk away from their conversation this afternoon. Maybe the relationship with Paul wasn't as dead as she'd led him to believe.

"Paul," Jonathan repeated slowly. "Did she give you a surname?"

Thom shook his head.

The door to the pub opened, and Kristen McDowell walked inside. Jonathan glowed like a neon light, he was so pleased to see her. "Over here, sweetheart," he called, waving his hand.

Kristen walked to the bar and slipped her arm around her fiancé's waist. "Hello, Thom," she said as naturally as if they saw each other every day. "How's it going?"

"All right. I understand congratulations are in order."

Kristen smiled up at Jonathan and nodded.

Thom felt like an intruder. Reaching for his overcoat, he was getting ready to go when Kristen stopped him.

"There's no need to rush off."

He was about to pretend he had people to see, places to go, but then decided not to lie. "You sure?"

"Of course I'm sure."

Thom was eager to learn what he could about Noelle, so he lingered and ordered another beer. Jon did, too; Kristen had a glass of red wine.

Thom paid for the second round. The three of them sat on bar stools with Kristen in the middle, talking about Christmas plans for a few minutes. "She had me call you," Jonathan confessed suddenly.

Kristen elbowed her fiancé in the ribs. "You weren't supposed to tell him."

The second beer had loosened Thom's tongue. "She damn near knocked me off my feet when I first saw her."

"Kristen?" Jonathan asked, sounding worried.

"No, Noelle."

"Really?" This appeared to please Noelle's younger sister. "So you're still stuck on her, after all these years."

"Damned if I know," Thom muttered. He did know but he wasn't willing to admit it. "We decided it's not going to work."

"Why not?" Kristen sounded outraged.

"We met and talked this afternoon," Thom informed them both.

Jonathan frowned. "I thought you met last night after the dance."

"We did."

"So you've talked twice in the past twenty-four hours."

"Yeah, and like I said, we both realized there are too many complications."

Kristen raised her hand for the bartender. "We need another round."

"I think we've already done enough damage," Jonathan protested.

"Coffee here," she said, pointing at her fiancé. "Same as before over here." She made a sweeping gesture that included Thom.

The bartender did as requested. As soon as the wine and beer arrived, Kristen turned to face Thom. "I thought you loved my sister."

"I did once." He was still working on his second beer.

"But not now?"

Thom didn't want to answer her. Hell, the last time he'd admitted to loving Noelle he was just a kid. But he'd stood up to his parents and been willing to relinquish everything for Noelle. To say he'd loved her was an understatement. He'd been crazy about her.

"Well?" Kristen pressed. "Don't you have an answer?"

"I do," Thom said, picking up his beer. "I just don't happen to like it."

"What's that mean?" Jonathan asked Kristen.

"I think it means he still has feelings for Noelle." Then, as though she'd suddenly remembered, she said, "Hey! Her birthday's on Christmas Day, you know."

Like he needed a reminder. Not a Christmas passed that Thom forgot.

"She doesn't feel the same way about me," he murmured.

"Yeah, right," Kristen said, exaggerating the words. It took only two beers for him to bare his soul—and it was all for nothing because Noelle didn't love him anymore. It took only two beers to make him maudlin, he thought sourly.

"Yeah, right," Kristen said again.

"It's true," Thom argued. "Did you ask her?"

"Did you?" Kristen asked.

December 22
Afternoon

I blew it. I had the perfect chance to have a rational conversation with Thom. We had a chance to settle this once and for all without the angst and emotion. It didn't happen. Instead I let the opportunity slip through my fingers. Naturally I have a wealth of excuses, the first one being that I didn't sleep more than a couple of hours all night. This situation between Thom and me was on my mind and I couldn't seem to let it go. My feelings swung from happiness to dread and from joy to fear, and then the whole cycle repeated itself. I kept thinking about what I wanted to say when we saw each other again. Then I started worrying what would happen if he kissed me.

How is it that I can develop complicated software programs used all over the world, but when it comes to Thom Sutton I'm hopeless?

Mom's home from shopping, and when Carley asked if she'd gotten everything she needs for the Christmas baskets, it looked as if Mom was about to burst into tears. She said she had a headache, and went to bed. Apparently I wasn't the only one suffering from too little sleep. I have a feeling that something happened with Mrs. Sutton again, which is bad news all the way around.

Kristen wasn't home when I tried to phone, although she hadn't said she was going out. I'd hoped to discuss this with her, get her perspective. She's heard just about everything else that's gone on between Thom and me since I arrived. I could use a sympathetic ear and some sisterly advice.

Everything fell into place so naturally between her and Jonathan, but it sure hasn't been that way with me. I actually considered talking to Carley, which is a sign of how desperate I'm beginning to feel.

I'm not going to see Thom again. We left the mall and nothing more was said. It's over, even though I don't want it to be. It was within my power to change things, and I didn't have the courage to do it. I could've run after him and begged him not to let our relationship end this way, not after we'd come so far. But I didn't, and I'm afraid this is something I'm going to regret for a long time to come.

Six

"You don't need to worry about the dishes," Sarah McDowell protested.

Noelle continued to load the dishwasher. "Mom, quit treating me like a guest in my own home." The menial task gave her something to do. Furthermore, she hoped it would help take her mind off her disastrous meeting with Thom at the mall. She'd reviewed their conversation a dozen times and wished so badly it had taken a different course. Their second attempt at a relationship had staggered to a halt before it had really begun, she thought with regret as she rinsed off the dinner plates and methodically set them inside the dishwasher.

"Thank you, dear. This is a real treat," her mother said, walking into the family room to join her dad.

Sarah had returned from her shopping trip in a subdued mood. Noelle didn't ply her with questions, mainly because she wasn't in a talkative mood herself. Even Carley Sue seemed to be avoiding the rest of the family. Except for dinner, her sister had spent most of the day in her room, first on her computer, and then wrapping Christmas presents.

As Noelle finished wiping the counters, her youngest sister entered the kitchen. Carley glanced into the family room, where her parents sat watching television. Their favorite courtroom drama was on, and they seemed to be absorbed in it.

"Wanna play a game of Yahtzee?" Noelle asked. It was one of Carley's favorites.

Her sister shook her head, then motioned for Noelle to come into her room. Carley nodded toward their parents, then pressed her finger to her lips.

"What's going on?" Noelle asked, drying her hands on a kitchen towel.

"Shh," Carley said, tiptoeing back toward her room.

"What?" Noelle asked impatiently.

Carley opened her bedroom door, grabbed Noelle's hand and pulled her into the bedroom. To her shock, Thom stood in the middle of the room, wearing his overcoat.

"Thom!"

"Shh," both Thom and Carley hissed at her.

"What are you *doing* here?" she whispered.

"When did you trade bedrooms with your sister?" he asked.

"A long time ago." She couldn't believe he was in her family's home. Years ago, he'd come to the house and tapped on her bedroom window, and she'd leaned out on the sill and they'd kissed. Amazingly, her parents hadn't heard—and the neighbors hadn't reported him. "Why are you here?"

"I came to see you."

Okay, that much was obvious. But she still didn't understand why he'd come.

"It was a bit of a surprise to bump into your little sister."

"I didn't mind," Carley said. "But he scared me like crazy when he knocked on the window."

"Sorry," Thom muttered.

"You said he broke your heart," Carley said, directing her remarks at Noelle. "We threw popcorn at him, remember? At least, we thought it was him, but then it wasn't."

Noelle didn't need any further reminders of that unfortunate incident. "I broke his heart, too. It was all a misunderstanding."

"Oh." Carley clasped her hands behind her back and leaned against the door, waiting. She was certainly in no hurry to leave and seemed immoderately interested in what Thom had to say.

Thom glanced at her sister, who refused to take the hint, and then said, "We need to talk."

"Now? Here?"

He nodded and touched her face in the gentlest way. "Listen, I'm sorry about this afternoon. We didn't even talk about what's most important—and that's you and me."

"I'm sorry, too." Unable to resist, Noelle slipped her arms around his waist and they clung to each other.

"This is *so-o-o* romantic," Carley whispered. "Why don't you two sit down and make yourselves comfortable. Can I get you anything to drink?"

Her little sister was as much of a hostess as their

mother, Noelle thought with amusement. "No, but thanks."

Thom shrugged. "I should leave, but—"

"No, don't," Noelle pleaded with him. It might make more sense to meet Thom later, but she didn't want him out of her sight for another second.

Thom sat on the edge of the bed and Noelle sat beside him. He took both her hands in his. "I've been doing a lot of thinking about us."

"I have, too," she said hurriedly.

"I don't want it to end."

"Oh, Thom, I don't, either! Not the way it did this afternoon—and for all the wrong reasons." Noelle was acutely aware of her sister, listening in on their conversation, but she didn't care.

"Noelle, I know what I want, and that's you back in my life."

"Oh, Thom." She bit her lower lip, suddenly on the verge of tears.

Carley sighed again. "This is better than any movie I've ever seen."

Noelle ignored her. "What are we going to do about our families?" They couldn't pretend their relationship wouldn't cause problems.

"I've been thinking about that, but I'm just not sure." Thom stroked the side of her face, and his hand lingered there.

"Oh, this *is* difficult," Carley agreed.

Her little sister was absorbing every word. Had Carley left the room, Noelle was sure Thom would be kissing her by now. Then they'd be lost in the kissing and oblivious to anything else.

"Is there a solution for us? One that doesn't involve alienating our families. Or our mothers, at any rate." Thom didn't look optimistic.

"What about the tea service?" Noelle said, mulling over an idea. "You said there's no replacing it, but maybe if we found a similar one, your mother would be willing to accept it."

"I don't know," he said. "This wasn't just any tea service. It was a family heirloom that belonged to my great-grandmother. We'll never find one exactly like it."

"I know, but finding one even remotely similar would be a start toward rebuilding the relationship, don't you think?"

He didn't seem convinced. "Perhaps."

"Could you find out the style and type?"

Thom shook his head doubtfully. "I could try."

"Please, Thom. And see if there are any photos."

They hugged again and Noelle closed her eyes, savoring the feel of his strong arms around her, inhaling his clean, outdoorsy scent.

Everything had changed for her. The thought of returning to Texas and her life there held little appeal. For years, she'd stayed away from her hometown because it represented a past that had brought her grief, and now—now she knew this was where her future lay.

There was a knock on Carley's door.

Noelle and Thom flew apart and a look of panic came into Carley's eyes.

"The closet," Noelle whispered, quickly ushering Thom inside. No sooner had she shut the door than her little sister admitted their mother into the room.

Noelle figured they must look about as guilty as

any two people could. Carley stared up at the bedroom ceiling and Noelle was tempted to hum a catchy Yuletide tune.

"I thought I'd turn in for the night," her mother said. She obviously hadn't noticed anything out of the ordinary.

"Good idea," Carley told her mother.

"You don't want to wear yourself out," Noelle added, letting her arms swing at her sides. "With Christmas and all…"

Her mother gave them a soft smile. "It does my heart good to see the two of you together. You were like a second mother to Carley when she was a baby."

"Mom!" her little sister wailed.

"I always thought you'd have a house full of your own children one day," she said nostalgically. "Don't you remember how you used to play with all your dolls?"

Noelle wanted to groan, knowing that Thom was listening in on the conversation.

"You'd make a wonderful mother."

"Thank you, Mom," she said. "'Night now. See you in the morning."

"'Night." She stepped out the door.

Noelle sighed with relief and so did Carley. She was about to open the closet when her mother stuck her head back inside the room. "Noelle, do you have plans for the morning?"

"No, why?" she asked, her voice higher than normal.

"I might need some help."

"I'll be glad to do what I can."

"Thank you, sweetheart." And with that she was gone. For good this time.

After a moment, Thom opened the closet door and peered out. "Is it safe?"

"I think so."

"Do you want me to keep watch?" Carley asked. "You know, so you guys can have some privacy." She smiled at Thom. "He's been wanting to kiss you ever since you got here." She lowered her voice. "I think he's kinda cute."

"So do I," Noelle confessed. "And yes, some privacy would be greatly appreciated."

Carley winked at Thom. "I think I'll go out and see what Dad's doing."

The instant the door closed, Thom took her in his arms and lowered his mouth to hers. Noelle groaned softly, welcoming him. Together, they created warm, moist kisses, increasing in intensity and desire. Other than the brief episode in the park, it'd been years since they'd kissed like this. Yet his touch felt so familiar....

"It's always been you," he whispered.

She heard the desperation in his voice. "I know—it's always been you," she echoed.

He kissed her again with a hunger and a need that reflected her own.

"Oh, Thom, what are we going to do?"

"We're going to start with your suggestion and find a silver tea service," he said firmly. "Then we're going to give it to my mother and tell her it's time to mend fences."

"What if we *can't* find one?" She frowned. "Or what if we do and they still won't forgive each other?"

"You worry too much." He kissed the tip of her nose. "And you ask too many questions."

Sarah was sitting up in bed reading a brand-new and highly touted mystery when her husband entered their room.

"You've been quiet this evening," Jake commented as he unbuttoned his shirt.

"Have I?" She gazed at the novel, but her attention kept wandering. She'd read this paragraph at least six times and she couldn't remember what it said. Every word seemed to remind her of a friend she'd lost twenty years ago.

"You haven't been yourself since you got back from shopping."

Sarah decided to ignore his words. "I stopped in and said good-night to the girls before I went to bed. Isn't it nice that Noelle and Carley get along so well?"

"You're changing the subject," Jake said. "And not very subtly."

Sarah set aside the book. In her present frame of mind, she was doing the author and herself a disservice. She reached for the light, but instead of flicking it off, she fell back against her pillows.

"I ran into Mary this afternoon," she told her husband.

"Again?"

"Again," she confirmed. "This meeting didn't go much better than the one at Value-X."

"That bad?"

"Almost. I can't even begin to tell you how horribly the two of us behaved."

Jake chuckled, shaking his head. "Does this have anything to do with the two hundred or so candy bars I found in the back of the big freezer?"

"You saw?"

He nodded. "What is it with you two?"

"Oh, honey, I wish I knew. I *hate* this. I've always hated this animosity. It would've been over years ago if Mary had listened to reason."

Her husband didn't respond.

"Everything was perfectly fine until we were forced to work on this Christmas project. Until then, she ignored me and I ignored her."

"Ignored her, did you?" he asked mildly.

Sarah pretended not to hear his question. "I think Melody Darrington might have planned this." The scheme took shape in her mind. "Melody *must* have."

"Isn't she the club secretary?"

"You know Melody," Sarah snapped. "She's the cute blonde who sold me the tickets to the dance."

"I wasn't there when you picked up the tickets," Jake reminded her as he climbed into bed.

"But you know who I mean."

"If you say so."

"You do. Now listen, because I think I'm on to something here. Melody's the one who told me we couldn't rent the hall for Kristen's wedding unless I performed a community service for the club."

"Yes, I remember, and that's how you got involved in the Christmas basket thing."

"Melody's also the one who assigned me to that project," she went on. "There had to be dozens of other projects I could've done. Plus, she insisted I had to fulfill those hours this year. That makes no sense what-soever."

"Why would Melody do anything like that?"

"How would I know?"

Her husband looked skeptical. "I think you might be jumping to conclusions here."

"Melody gave us half of the same list, too." Out-rage simmered just below the surface as Sarah sorted through the facts. She tossed aside the covers and leaped out of bed. Hands on hips, she glared at her husband. Of course. It all added up. Melody definitely had a role in this, and Sarah didn't like it.

"Hey, I didn't do anything," Jake protested.

"I'm not saying you did." Still not satisfied, she started pacing the area at the foot of the bed. "This is the lowest, dirtiest trick anyone's ever played on me."

"Now, Sarah, you don't have any real proof."

"Of course I do! Why did Melody make a copy of that list, anyway? All she had to do was divide it."

"Sounds like an honest mistake to me. Didn't you tell me the office was hectic that morning? Melody was dealing with you, the phones and everything else when she gave you and Mary the lists."

"Yes, but that's no excuse for what happened."

"You're angrier with yourself than Melody."

Sarah knew the truth when she heard it. The outrage vanished as quickly as it had come, and she climbed back into bed, next to her husband.

For a long time neither spoke. Finally Jake turned on their bedside radio and they listened to "Silent Night" sung by a children's choir. Their pure, sweet voices al-most brought tears to Sarah's eyes.

"In two days, it'll be Christmas," she said in a soft voice.

"And Noelle's birthday." Her husband smiled. "Remember our first year? We could barely afford a Christmas tree, let alone gifts. Yet you managed to give me the most incredible present of all, our Noelle."

"Remember the next Christmas, when I'd just found out I was pregnant with Kristen?" she said fondly. "Our gift to each other was a secondhand washer." In the early years of their marriage, they'd struggled to make ends meet. Yet in many ways, those had been the very best.

Jake smiled. "We were poor as church mice."

"But happy."

"Very happy," he agreed, sliding his arm around her shoulders. "I thought it was clever of you to knit Christmas stockings for the girls the year Noelle turned four. Or was it five?"

"I didn't knit them," Sarah said sadly. "Mary did."

"Mary?"

"Don't you remember? She knit all the kids' stockings, and I baked the cookies and we exchanged?"

"Ah, yes. You two had quite a barter system worked out."

"If we hadn't traded babysitting, none of us would've been able to afford an evening out." Once a month, they'd taken the girls over to their dearest friends' home for the night; Mary and Greg had done the same. It'd been a lifesaver in those early years. She and Jake had never been able to afford anything elaborate, but a night out, just the two of them, had been heaven. Mary and Greg had cherished their nights, as well.

"I miss her," Sarah admitted. "Even after all these years, I miss my friend."

"I know." Jake gently squeezed her shoulder.

"I'd give anything never to have borrowed the silver tea service."

"You were trying to help someone out."

"That's how it started, but I should've been honest with Mary. I should've told her the tea service wasn't for my open house, but for Cheryl's."

"Why didn't you?"

She'd had years to think about the answer to that question. "Because Mary didn't like Cheryl. I assumed she was jealous. Now... I don't know."

Sarah remembered the circumstances well. She'd recently begun selling real estate and Cheryl Carlson had given her suggestions and advice. Cheryl had wanted something to enhance the look of the dining room for her open house, and Sarah had volunteered to bring in the tea service. When she'd asked Mary, her friend had hesitated, but then agreed. Sarah had let Mary assume it was for her own open house.

"You were so upset when you found out the tea service had been stolen."

To this day her stomach knotted at the memory of having to face Mary and confess what had happened. Soon afterward, Cheryl had left the agency and hired on with another firm, and Sarah had lost touch with her.

"I'd always hoped that one day Mary would find it in her heart to forgive me."

"I did, too."

"I'm so sorry, sweetheart," Sarah whispered, resting her head against her husband's shoulder.

"Why are you apologizing to me?"

"Because you and Greg used to be good friends, too."

"Oh."

"Remember how you used to golf together."

"Yes."

"I wonder if Greg still plays."

"I see him out at the club every now and then," Jake told her.

"Does he speak to you?"

"Yes."

Sarah was comforted knowing that. "I'm glad."

"So am I," her husband said, then kissed her good-night.

On December twenty-third, Thom's office was running on a skeleton crew. His secretary was in for half a day and he immediately handed her the assignment of locating every antiques store in a hundred-mile radius.

He'd called his father before eight that morning. "Tell me what you know about Mom's old tea service."

"Tell you what I know?" he repeated. "It was stolen, remember?"

"I realize that," Thom said impatiently.

"What makes you ask?"

"I thought I'd buy her a replacement for Christmas."

"Don't you think you're leaving your shopping a little late?"

"Could be." Thom didn't feel comfortable sharing what this was really about, but he was going to do whatever he could to replace that damn tea service.

"I think we might have a picture of it somewhere."

Thom perked up.

"For years your mother looked for a replacement, you know. We hadn't actually taken a picture of the tea set, but it was in the background of another photograph."

Thom remembered now. His parents had the photo enlarged in order to get as much detail as possible.

"Do you still have the photograph? Or better yet, the enlargement?"

"I think it might be around here somewhere. I assume you need this ASAP."

"You got it."

"Well, I promised to drive your mother out to the Women's Century Club this morning and then to the grocery store. You're welcome to stop by the house and look."

"Where do you figure it might be?"

His father considered that for a moment. "Maybe the bottom drawer of my desk. There are a few old photographs there. That's my best suggestion."

"Anyplace else I should look?"

"Your mother's briefcase. Every once in a while she visits an antiques store, but for the most part she's given up hope. She's still got her name in with several of the bigger places. If anything even vaguely similar comes in, the stores promised to give her a call."

"Has she gotten many calls?"

"Only two in all these years," his father told him. "Both of them excited her so much she could barely sleep until she'd checked them out. They turned out to be completely the wrong style."

Thom didn't know if he'd have any better success, but he had to try.

"Good luck, son."

"Thanks, Dad."

As soon as he hung up, Thom called Noelle's cell phone. She answered right away.

"Morning," he said, warming to the sound of her voice. "I hope you're free to do a bit of investigating."

"I am. I canceled out on Mom—told her I was meeting an old friend."

"Did she ask any questions?"

"No, but I could tell she was disappointed. I do so hope we're successful."

"Me, too. Listen, I've got news." Thom told her about the old photograph and what his father had said earlier. He hoped it would encourage Noelle, but she seemed disheartened when she spoke again.

"If your parents searched all these years, what are the chances of us finding a replacement now?"

"We'll just keep working on it. I'm not giving up, and I'm guessing you feel the same way."

"I do—of course."

"Good. How soon before we can meet?"

"Fifteen minutes."

"I'll wait for you at my parents' place."

On his way out the door, Thom grabbed the list Martha, his secretary, had compiled and when he read it over, he knew why he paid this woman top dollar. Not only had she given him the name and address of every store in the entire state, she'd also listed their websites and any other internet information.

"Merry Christmas," he said, then gave her the rest of the day off with pay.

Noelle was already parked outside his parents' house

when Thom arrived. She got out of her car and joined him as he pulled into the driveway.

"Hi," she said softly.

Thom leaned over and kissed her. "Hi." The key to the house was under a decorative rock. He unlocked the door and turned off the burglar alarm. Holding Noelle's hand, he led her into his parents' home.

Noelle stopped in the entryway and glanced around. It'd been many, many years since she'd walked into this house. It wasn't really familiar—everything had been redecorated and repainted since she was a little girl—but the place had a comfortable relaxed feel. Big furniture dominated the living room, hand-knit stockings hung on the fireplace and the mantel was decorated with holly. The scent of the fresh Christmas tree filled the air.

"Your mother has a wonderful eye for color and design," she commented, taking in the bright red bows on the tree and all the red ornaments.

Still holding her hand, Thom led her into his father's den. The oak rolltop desk sat in the corner, and Thom immediately started searching through the bottom drawer. He found the stack of photographs his father had mentioned and sorted through them with Noelle looking over his shoulder. She leaned against him, and he wondered if she realized how good it felt to have her pressed so close to him. Or how tempting it was to turn and kiss her...

"That's it," she cried triumphantly when he flipped past a black-and-white picture. She grabbed it before he had a chance to take a second look. Examining the print, she murmured, "It really was exquisite, wasn't it?" She passed it back to him.

"It *is* beautiful," he said, emphasizing the present tense. Thom wasn't sure why he insisted on being this optimistic about finding a replacement. He suspected that wanting it so badly had a lot to do with it.

Reaching into his coat pocket, he pulled out the list Martha had compiled for him.

"Now that we have a picture," Noelle said, "I'll go home and scan it into Carley's computer. Then I'll send it out to these addresses and see what comes back."

"Great. But before you do, I'll get a copy of this photograph and start contacting local dealers. They might be able to steer me in a different direction."

"Oh, Thom, it'd mean so much to me if we could bring our mothers back together."

They kissed, and it would've been the easiest thing in the world to become immersed in the wonder of having found each other again. Her mouth was warm, soft to the touch. She enticed him, fulfilled him and tempted him beyond any woman he'd ever known or loved. He didn't know much about her present life. They'd spoken very little of their accomplishments, their friends, their jobs. It wasn't necessary. Thom *knew* her. The girl he'd loved in high school had matured into a capable, beautiful and very desirable adult.

"It's hard to think about anything else when you kiss me," she whispered.

"It is for me, too."

Before leaving the Sutton home, Thom put everything back as it was, and remembered to reset the burglar alarm.

After making a photocopy at his office, Thom gave her the original, thinking that would scan best.

"I'll go back to the house now and plead with Carley to let me on the computer," she told him.

"Okay, and I'll see what a little old-fashioned foot-work turns up."

Noelle started to get into her car, then paused. "What'll happen if we don't find a replacement before I return to Texas?"

Thom didn't want to think about that yet. "I don't know," he had to admit.

"Want to meet in the park at midnight?" she asked.

Thom chuckled. "I'm a little old to be sneaking around to meet my girlfriend."

"That didn't stop you from climbing in my bedroom window last night."

True, but his need to see her had overwhelmed his caution, not to mention his good sense.

"I love you, Noelle." There, he'd said it. He'd placed his heart in her hands, to accept or reject.

Tears glistened in her eyes. "I love you, too—I never stopped loving you."

"Even when you hated me?"

She laughed shakily. "Even then."

NOELLE McDOWELL'S
JOURNAL

December 23
11:00 a.m.

I feel as if I'm on an emotional roller coaster. One moment I'm feeling as low as I can get, and the next I'm soaring into the clouds. Just now, I'm in the cloud phase. Thom found the picture of the tea set! We're determined to locate one as close to the original as possible. As I said to Thom, I'm hoping for a Christmas miracle. (I never knew I was such a romantic.) Normally I scoff at things like miracles, but that's what both Thom and I need. We've already had one miracle—we have each other back.

Before we parted this morning, Thom said he loved me. I love him, too. I've always loved Thom, and that's what made his deception—or what I believed was his deception—so terribly painful.

Now all we've got to do is keep our mothers out of the picture until we can replace the tea service. I know it's a challenging task, but we're up to it.

As of right now, we each have our assignments. Car-

ley's using the computer for ten more minutes and then it's all mine. My job is to scan in the picture he found at his parents' house and send it to as many online antiques dealers as I can. Thom is off checking local dealers and has some errands to run. We're going to meet up again later.

I had to cancel a lunch date with Kristen and Jonathan, but my sister understood. She's excited about Thom and me getting back together. Apparently she's had more of a hand in this than I realized. I really owe her.

Finding a tea service to replace the one that was stolen is turning out to be even harder than I expected— but we have to try. I believe in miracles. I was a doubter less than a week ago, but now I'm convinced.

Seven

"How many turkeys did you say we had to buy?"

"Six," Mary said, checking the list to make sure she was correct. December twenty-third, and the grocery store was a nightmare. The aisles were crowded, and many of the shelves needed restocking. The last thing Mary wanted to do was fight the Christmas rush, but that couldn't be helped. Next year, she'd leave the filling of these Christmas baskets to someone else.

"Get six bags of potatoes while you're at it," she told her husband as they rolled past a stack of ten-pound bags.

"Getting a little bossy, aren't you?" Greg muttered.

"Sorry, it's just that there are a hundred other things I'd rather be doing right now."

"Then you should've given the task to Sarah Mc-Dowell. Didn't you tell me she offered?"

Mary didn't want to hear the other woman's name. "I don't trust her to see that it's done properly."

"Don't you think you're being a little harsh?"

"No." That should be plain enough. The more she

thought about her last encounter with Sarah McDowell, the more she realized how glad she'd be when they'd completed this project. "Being around Sarah has dredged up a whole slew of bad memories," she informed her husband.

Greg dutifully loaded sixty pounds of potatoes into the cart. As soon as he'd finished, Mary headed down the next aisle.

"My Christmas has been ruined," she said through gritted teeth.

"How's that?"

"Greg, don't be obtuse." She reached for several cans of evaporated milk and added them to the food piled high in their cart. "I've had to deal with *her*."

"Yes, but—"

"Never mind," Mary said, cutting him off. She didn't expect Greg to understand. Her husband had never really grasped the sense of loss she'd felt when Sarah destroyed their friendship with her deception. The silver tea service was irreplaceable; so was the friendship its disappearance had shattered.

"Hello, Mary." Jean Cummings, a friend who edited the society page, pulled her cart alongside Mary's. "Merry Christmas, Greg."

Her husband had the look of a deer caught in the headlights. He no more knew who Jean was than he would a stranger, although he'd attended numerous social functions with the woman.

"You remember Jean, don't you?" she said, hoping to prompt his memory.

"Of course," he lied. "Good to see you again."

"It looks like you're feeding a big crowd," Jean said, surveying the contents of Mary's cart.

Mary didn't bother to explain about the Christmas baskets. "Is your family coming for the holidays?" she asked.

"Oh, yes, and yours, too, I imagine?"

"Of course." Mary was eager to get about her business. She didn't have time to dillydally. As soon as she was finished with the shopping, she could go back to planning her own family's Christmas dinner. Greg would need to order the fresh Dungeness crabs they always had on Christmas Eve; he could do that while they were here.

"Tell me," Jean said, leaning close to Mary and talking in a stage whisper. "Am I going to get the scoop on Thom?"

"Thom?" Mary didn't know what she was talking about.

"I saw him just now in Mendleson's."

It was well known that the jeweler specialized in engagement rings.

"Thom's one of the most eligible bachelors in town. I know plenty of hearts will be broken when he finally chooses a bride."

Mary was speechless. She'd had lunch with her son on Friday and although he'd hinted, he certainly hadn't said anything that suggested he was on the verge of proposing. She didn't even know who he was currently seeing.

"I'm sure Thom would prefer to do his own announcing," Greg said coolly, answering for Mary.

"Oh, drat," Jean muttered. "I was hoping you'd let the cat out of the bag."

"My lips are sealed," Mary said, recovering. "Have a wonderful Christmas."

"You, too." Jean pushed her cart past them.

As soon as the society page editor was out of earshot, Mary gripped her husband's forearm. "Has Thom spoken to you lately?"

"This morning," Greg told her. "But he didn't say anything about getting engaged."

"Who could it be?" Mary cried, aghast that she was so completely in the dark. As his mother, she should know these things.

"If he was serious about any woman, we'd know."

Mary wasn't buying it.

"Let's not leap to conclusions just because our son happened to walk into a certain jewelry store. I'm sure there's a perfectly logical reason Thom was in Mendleson's and I'll bet it hasn't got a thing to do with buying an engagement ring."

"This is all Sarah's fault," she murmured.

Her husband looked at her as though she were speaking in a foreign language.

"I mean it, Greg. I've been so preoccupied with the whole mess Sarah's created about these baskets, I haven't had time to pay attention to my son. Why, just on Friday when we had lunch…" Suddenly disheartened, Mary let her words fade.

"What's wrong?" Greg asked.

All the combativeness went out of her. "I can't blame Sarah entirely—I played a role in this, too."

"What role?"

Once again, she was amazed by her husband's obliviousness. "This business with Thom. Now that I think about it, I'm convinced he wanted to talk over his engagement with me, only I was so rattled by the Value-X incident I didn't give him a chance. Oh, Greg, how could I have been so self-absorbed?"

"What makes you think he was going to tell you he was getting engaged? Why don't we call and ask him when we get home?" Greg suggested.

"And let him think we're interfering in his life? We can't do that!"

"Why not?"

"We'd ruin his surprise, if indeed there is one."

Greg merely sighed as they wheeled the cart to the checkout counter.

Ten minutes later, once everything was safely inside the trunk, Mary turned to him. "I just don't know what I'll do if *she's* the one he's interested in. I couldn't stand it if he married into *that* family."

"I don't think we need to worry about it," he told her as they started back to the house. "There's no evidence whatsoever."

"He *danced* with Noelle McDowell!"

"He danced with lots of girls."

The engine made a coughing sound as they approached the first intersection. "What's that?" Mary asked.

"It's time for an oil change," her husband said. "I'll have the car looked at after the holidays."

She nodded. She trusted the upkeep of their vehicles to her husband and immediately put the thought out of her mind. Car troubles were minor in the greater scheme of things.

* * *

By the end of the day, when clouds thickened the sky and the cold swept in, fierce and chilling, Thom finally had to admit that replacing the silver tea service wasn't going to be easy.

He'd tried everything he could think of, called friends and associates who might know where he could find an antiques dealer who specialized in silver—anyone who might lead him to his prize. Far more than a gift lay in the balance. It was possible that his and Noelle's entire future hinged on this.

At seven, after an exhaustive all-day search, he went home. The first thing he did was check his answering machine, hoping to hear from Noelle. Sure enough, the message light was flashing. Without waiting to remove his coat, he pushed the button and grabbed paper and a pen.

A female voice, high and excited, spilled out. "It's Carley Sue. Remember me? I'm Noelle's sister. Anyway, Noelle asked me to call you. She'd call you herself, but I asked if I could do it, 'cause it was my bedroom window you knocked on. And my computer Noelle used."

Thom laughed out loud, almost missing the second half of the message.

"Anyway, Noelle wanted to know if you could meet her at the park tomorrow morning. She said you should be there early. She said six o'clock 'cause you have to drive all the way to Portland. She said you'd know why, but she wouldn't tell me. When you see Noelle, please tell her it's not nice to keep secrets from her sister, will you?" She giggled. "Never mind, I could get it out of her if I really wanted to. Bye."

Thom smiled, feeling a surge of energy. Obviously Noelle had had better luck than he did.

A second message followed the first.

"Thom, it's me. I wasn't sure Carley got the entire message to you. When we meet at the park, come with a full tank of gas. If this conflicts with your Christmas Eve plans, call me on my cell phone." There was a short pause. "I don't want you to get your hopes up. I found a tea service that's not *exactly* like your grandmother's, but I'm looking for a Christmas miracle. We'll need to compare it to the picture. The dealer's only keeping his store open until noon, which is why we need to leave here so early. I'm sorry I can't see you tonight. I wish I could, but I've got family obligations. I know you understand."

He did understand—all too well. A third message started; he was certainly popular today. It was his mother and she sounded worried.

"It's Mom… I ran into a friend from the newspaper this morning and she mentioned seeing you at Mendleson's Jewelers. Were you…buying an engagement ring? Thom, it isn't that McDowell girl, is it? Call me, will you? I need reassurance that you're not about to make a big mistake."

This was what happened when you lived in a small town. Everyone knew your business. So, his mother had heard, and even with the wrong facts, she'd put together the right answer. Yes, he'd been at Mendleson's. And yes, it *was* "that McDowell girl."

Thom decided he had to talk about all of this with someone who understood the situation and knew all the people involved. Someone discreet, who had his best interests at heart. Someone with no agenda, hidden or otherwise.

The one person he could trust was his older sister. Suzanne was three years his senior, married and living ten miles outside of town; she and her husband, Rob, owned a hazelnut orchard. Thom didn't see Suzanne often, but he was godfather to his five-year-old nephew, Cameron.

A brief phone call assured him that his sister was available and eager to see him. Off he went, grabbing a chunk of cheese and an apple to eat on the way. Maybe his sister would have some wisdom to share with him…. How quickly life can change, he mused, and never more so than at Christmas.

Suzanne had a mug of hot cider waiting when he arrived. Rob was out, dealing with some late deliveries. His family owned the orchard and leased it to him. Rob worked long hours making a success of their business, and so did Suzanne. Both his sister and brother-in-law were honest, hardworking people, and he trusted their advice.

"This is a surprise," Suzanne said, pulling out a chair at the large oak table in the center of her country kitchen.

"Cameron's in bed already?" Thom asked, disappointed to miss seeing his nephew.

"He thinks if he goes to bed early Santa will come sooner." She gave a shrug. "Never mind that this is only the twenty-third. I guess he's hoping he can make time speed up," she said with a smile. "By the way, he had a ridiculous tale about you and some woman at the movies the other day. Throwing popcorn was a big theme in this story."

"I don't know what he told you, but more than likely it's true. We bumped into Noelle McDowell and her little sister at the theater."

"Noelle. Oh, no." Suzanne was instantly sympathetic. "That must've been uncomfortable."

"Yes and no." He hesitated, wondering to what extent his sister's attitude was a reflection of their parents'. "It was difficult at first, because we didn't exactly part on the best of terms."

"At first?"

His sister had picked up on that fast enough. "We've talked since and resolved our difficulties."

"Resolved them, did you?" Suzanne raised her eyebrows.

"I love Noelle." There, he'd said it.

"Who's Noelle?" Rob asked as he walked in through the kitchen door, shedding hat, scarf and gloves.

"I'll explain later," Suzanne promised, ladling a cup of cider from the pot on the stove. "Here, honey."

"Our families don't get along," Thom explained.

"Do Mom and Dad know?" his sister asked.

"Not yet, but Mom got wind of me going to Mendleson's. She must have her suspicions, since she left a message on my machine practically begging me to tell her I'm not seeing Noelle."

"Did you buy a ring?"

"That's not the point."

"Okay," his sister said slowly. "What *do* you plan to tell Mom and Dad?"

"I don't know."

Suzanne sipped her cider, then put down the mug to

focus on him. "You're going to wait until Christmas is over before you say anything, right?"

Thom didn't know if he could. His mother was already besieging him with questions and she'd keep at him until she got answers—preferably the answers she wanted. He needed an ally and he hoped he could count on Suzanne.

"Let me play devil's advocate here a moment," his sister suggested.

"Please."

"Put yourself in Mom's place. Noelle's family has hurt our family. And now you're asking Mom to welcome Noelle into our lives and our hearts."

"Noelle is already in my heart."

"I know," Suzanne told him, "but there's more than one person involved in this. How does her family feel about you, for instance?"

That was a question Thom didn't want to consider. This wouldn't be easy for Noelle, either. Kristen and Carley were obviously supportive, but Sarah McDowell—well, she was another matter.

"We were ready to defy everyone as teenagers," he said, reminding his sister of the difficult stand he'd taken at eighteen.

"You were a kid."

"I was in love with her then, and I'm still in love with her."

"Yes," Suzanne said, "but you're more responsible now."

"I can't live my life to suit everyone else," he said, frustrated by her response.

"He's got a point," Rob said. "I don't understand the

family dynamics here, but I have a fairly good idea what you're talking about. I say if Thom feels this strongly about Noelle after all these years, he should go for it. He should live his own life."

Thom felt a rush of gratitude for his brother-in-law's enouragement.

"That's what you wanted to hear, isn't it?" Suzanne said, smiling. "For what it's worth, I agree with my husband."

"Thanks," Thom said. "That means a lot, you guys." He shook his head. "Noelle and I are well aware of the problems we face as a couple. We'd hoped to come to our parents with a solution."

"What kind of solution?"

"I've been pounding the pavement all day, checking out antiques stores and jewelry stores for a replacement tea service. Noelle's been doing an internet search."

His sister frowned. "I don't want to discourage you, but you're not going to find one."

She certainly had a way of cutting to the chase. "Thank you for that note of optimism. Anyway, how can you be so sure? Noelle thinks she might have a lead."

"Hey, that's good," Rob said. "It's worth trying to find…whatever this thing is that you're looking for."

"An antique silver tea service—I'll fill you in later, Rob." She turned to her brother. "I don't want to be pessimistic. It's just that Mom and Dad looked for years. They've given up now, but for a long time they left no stone unturned."

"If we find one, we'll consider it a Christmas miracle."

"Definitely," Suzanne agreed. "And I'd consider it a lucky omen, too."

"But you don't think we'll succeed."

"No," his sister told him. "I don't think so, but who knows?"

"If I ask Noelle to be part of my life, will you accept her?"

"Of course." Suzanne didn't hesitate. "But I'm not the one whose opinion matters. However, Rob's right, you've got to live your own life, and we'll support you in whatever choice you make."

He visited with his sister a while longer and assured her that no matter what he decided, he'd meet the family for the annual Christmas Eve dinner, followed by church services.

The next morning Noelle was waiting in the park at the appointed time and place when he got there. His heart reacted instantly to the sight of her. She looked like an angel in her long white wool coat and cashmere scarf. A Christmas angel. He smiled at the thought—even if he *was* getting sentimental in his old age.

"Merry Christmas," he said.

"Merry Christmas, Thom." Her eyes brightened as he approached.

Thom folded her in his arms and their kisses were deep and urgent. His mouth lingered on hers, gradually easing into gentler kisses. Finally he whispered, "Ready to go?"

"I hope this isn't a wild-goose chase," Noelle told him as she leaned her head against his shoulder.

"I do, too." But if it was, at least he'd be spending the day with her.

If they couldn't carry out their quest, they'd simply have to find some other way to persuade both mothers to accept the truth—that Thomas Sutton and Noelle McDowell were in love.

It was Christmas Eve, nine in the morning, and Sarah McDowell was eager to finish with the Christmas baskets. She'd skillfully wrapped each gift to transport to the Salvation Army.

"You're coming with me, aren't you?" she asked her husband.

Jake glanced up from the morning paper, frowning. "I can't."

"Why not?" Sarah didn't know if she could face Mary alone—not again. She'd assumed Jake would drive with her.

"I've got errands of my own. It's Christmas Eve."

"What about you, Carley?" she said, looking hopefully toward her daughter.

"Can't, Mom, sorry."

But not nearly sorry enough, Sarah thought. Her family was abandoning her in this hour of need. "Where's Noelle?" she asked. Surely she could count on Noelle.

"Out," Carley informed her.

"She's left already?"

Carley nodded.

Sarah thought she saw Jake wink at Carley. Apparently those two were involved in some sort of conspiracy against her.

At least Jake helped her load up the car, shifting his golf clubs to the backseat, but he disappeared soon afterward. Grumbling under her breath, Sarah drove out to the Women's Century Club.

Mary's car was already in the lot when she arrived. So, Mary Sutton was breaking a lifelong habit of tardiness in her eagerness to finish this charity project. For that, Sarah couldn't blame her. She, too, had reached her limit.

The cold air cut through her winter coat the instant she climbed out of the car. The radio station had mentioned the possibility of an ice storm later in the day. Sarah only hoped it wouldn't materialize.

"Merry Christmas," Melody called out as Sarah struggled through the front door, carrying the largest and most awkward of the boxes.

Sarah muttered a reply. Her Christmas Eve was *not* getting off to a good start.

"Mary's waiting for you," Melody told her. "I understand there was a mix-up with the lists. I'm so sorry. It was crazy that morning, wasn't it?"

Sarah wasn't fooled by the other woman's cheerful attitude. Melody Darrington had done her utmost to manipulate the two of them into working on this project together, and Sarah, for one, didn't take kindly to the interference. It was clear that Mary hadn't realized anything was amiss, but then Mary Sutton wasn't the most perceptive person in the world. Still, Sarah wasn't going to make a federal case of it, on the off chance that it *had* all been an innocent mistake as Melody was implying.

Sarah made her way into the meeting room, where Mary had the six baskets set up on a long table, as well as six large boxes, already filled with the makings for Christmas dinner.

"Is that everything you've got?" Mary asked, peering into Sarah's carton. Her tone insinuated that Sarah had contributed less than required.

"Of course not," she snapped. "I have two more boxes in the car."

Neither woman leaped up to help her carry them inside, although Melody did make a halfhearted offer when Sarah headed out the front door.

"No thanks—you've already done enough," she said pointedly.

"You're sure you don't need the help?" Melody asked.

Shaking her head, Sarah brought in the second of the boxes and set it on the table.

"I thought you'd bring one of the girls with you," Mary said in that stiff way of hers.

"They're busy." She started back for the last of the cartons.

"Noelle isn't with Thom, is she?"

The question caught her off guard. No one had said where Noelle had gone, but it couldn't be to meet Thom Sutton. Could it? No, she wouldn't do that. Not her daughter.

"Absolutely not," Sarah insisted. Noelle had already learned her lesson when it came to the Suttons.

"Good," Mary said.

"Noelle's with friends," Sarah returned and then, because she had to know, she asked a question of her own. "What makes you ask?"

"Oh—no reason."

Sarah didn't believe that for a moment. "You tell your son Noelle's under no illusions about him. She won't be so easily fooled a second time."

"Now just one minute—"

"We both know what he did."

"You're wrong, Sarah—but then you often are."

Melody stepped into the meeting room and stopped abruptly. With a shocked look, she regarded both women. "Come on, you two! It's Christmas."

"And your point is?" Sarah asked.

"My point is that the least you can do is work together on this. These baskets need to get to the Salvation Army right away. They're late already, and my husband just phoned and said there's definitely an ice storm coming, so you shouldn't delay."

"I'll get them there in time," Mary promised. "If we could get the baskets filled…"

"Fine," Sarah said. "I'll bring in the last box."

"We wouldn't be this late if you'd—"

Sarah ignored her and hurried out the door, only to hear Melody mutter something about an ice storm developing right in this room.

She knew that the minute she left, Melody and Mary would talk about her. However, she didn't care. Right after Kristen's wedding, she was letting her membership in the Women's Century Club lapse.

Once the third box was safely inside, Sarah placed the gifts in the correct baskets. Then both women sorted through the family names by checking the tag on each present. Sarah had spent a lot of time wrapping her gifts, wanting to please the recipients…and, to be honest, impress Mary and Melody with her talents. Given the opportunity, she could have decorated the clubhouse to match Mary's efforts. No, to exceed them.

"You did get that Firefighter Barbie doll, didn't you?" Mary asked.

"Of course I did," she answered scornfully.

They attached ribbons to each basket, then prepared everything—gifts and groceries—for transport.

"Would you like help loading up your car?" Sarah asked. Since Mary was driving and this was a joint project, she felt constrained to offer.

Mary seemed surprised, then shook her head. "I can manage. But…thanks."

Sarah had wanted to make a quick getaway, but Melody stopped her at the door, appointment book in hand.

"I have a few questions about Kristen's wedding."

"What do you need to know?"

Melody flipped open the book. "Will you require the use of our kitchen?"

"I'm not sure because we haven't picked the caterer yet, but we'll do that right after the first of the year."

"I have a list, if you'd like to look at it."

"I would." Sarah wanted to make her daughter's day as special as she could. But as she answered Melody's questions, her mind drifted to Noelle. Mary had brought up a frightening possibility. Noelle had been absent from the house quite a bit since the dance on Saturday night. She was at the mall on Sunday, and then on Monday—oh, yes, she'd worked on Carley's computer most of the day. Reassured now, Sarah relaxed. Mary's fears about her son and Noelle were unfounded.

She glanced around the lot; Mary's car was gone. She'd apparently left for the Salvation Army already. She must have moved her vehicle to the side entrance in order to load up the baskets and boxes more easily and Sarah hadn't seen her drive off. That was just fine. Maybe this was the last she needed to see of Mary Sutton.

Now she could enjoy Christmas.

"Merry Christmas, Melody," she said. "I'm sorry for the way I snapped at you earlier."

Melody accepted her apology. "I realize this was hard on both of you but what's important are the Christmas baskets."

"I couldn't agree with you more."

Sarah's spirits lifted considerably as she walked to her car or rather, Jake's. He'd insisted she take his SUV, and she was glad of it. If possible, it seemed even colder out; she drew her coat more closely around her and bent her head as she trudged toward the car.

As she turned out of the parking lot, she saw that the roads were icing over. The warning of an ice storm had become a reality, and even earlier than expected. This weather made her nervous, and Sarah drove carefully, hoping she wouldn't run into any problem.

She hadn't gone a mile when she noticed a car pulled off to the side of the road. She slowed down and was surprised to see Mary Sutton in the driver's seat. Mary was on her cell phone; she looked out the passenger window as Sarah slowed down. Mary's eyes met hers, and then she waved her on, declining help before Sarah could even offer it.

A Note From
Noelle McDowell

Christmas Eve

Dear Carley Sue,
Good morning. I'll be gone by the time you read this.
I'm meeting Thom in the park and we're driving to an
antiques store outside Portland to check out a tea ser-
vice. Kristen knows I'm with Thom, but not why.

I'm asking you to keep my whereabouts a secret for
now. No, wait—you can mention it to Dad if you want.
Mom's the only one who really can't know. I don't think
she'll ask, because she's got a lot to do this morning
delivering the Christmas baskets.

This whole mix-up with those baskets has really got
her in a tizzy. I find it all rather humorous and I sus-
pect Dad does, too.

I'm trusting you with this information, little sister.
I figured you (and your romantic heart) would want
to know.

Love,
Noelle

Eight

The car had made a grinding noise as soon as Mary started it—the same sound as the day before. Greg had said he'd look into it after the holidays, but she'd assumed it was safe to drive. Apparently not.

The car had slowed to a crawl, sputtered and then died. That was just great. The Salvation Army was waiting for these Christmas baskets, which, according to Melody, were already late. If Mary didn't hurry up and deliver them to the organization's office before closing time, six needy families would miss out on Christmas. She couldn't let that happen.

Reaching for her cell phone, she punched in her home number and hoped Greg was home. She needed rescuing, and soon. Greg would know what to do. The phone had just begun to ring when Sarah McDowell drove past.

Mary bit her lip hard. Pride demanded that she wave her on. She didn't need that woman's help. Still, she felt Sarah should've stopped; it was no less than any decent human being would do.

Well, she should know better than to expect compas-

sion or concern from Sarah McDowell. Good Christian
that she professed to be, Sarah had shown not the slight-
est interest in Mary's safety.

Mary clenched her teeth in fury. So, fine, Sarah
didn't care whether *she* froze the death, but what about
the Christmas baskets? What about the families, the
children, whose Christmas depended on them? The truth
was, Sarah simply didn't care what happened to Mary
or the Christmas baskets.

The phone was still ringing—where on earth was
Greg? Suddenly an operator's tinny voice came on with
a recorded message. "I'm sorry, but we are unable to
connect your call at this time."

"*You're* sorry?" Mary cried. She punched in Thom's
number and then Suzanne's and got the same response.
She tossed the phone back in her purse and waited. The
Women's Century Club was on the outskirts of Rose.
On Christmas Eve, with an ice storm bearing down,
the prospect of a Good Samaritan was highly unlikely.

"Great," she muttered. She might be stuck here for
God knows how long. Surely *someone* would realize
she wasn't where she was supposed to be. Still, it might
take hours before anyone came looking for her. And
even more hours before she was found.

With the engine off, the heater wasn't working, and
Mary was astonished by how quickly the cold seeped
into the car's interior. She tried her cell phone again
and got the same message. There was obviously trouble
with the transmitters; maybe it would clear up soon. She
struggled to remain optimistic, but another depressing
thought overshadowed the first. How long could she
last in this cold? She could imagine herself still sitting

in the car days from now, frozen stiff, abandoned and forgotten on Christmas Eve.

Trying to ward off panic, she decided to stand on the side of the road to see if that would help her cell phone reception. That way, she'd also be ready to wave for assistance if someone drove by.

She retrieved her phone, climbed out of the car and immediately became aware of how much colder it was outside. Hands shaking, she tried the phone. Same recorded response. She tucked her hands inside her pockets and waited for what seemed like an eternity. Then she tried her cell phone again.

Nothing. Just that damned recording.

Resigned to waiting for a passerby, she huddled in her coat.

Five minutes passed. The icy wind made it feel more like five hours. The air was so frigid that after a few moments it hurt to breathe. Her teeth began to chatter, and her feet lost feeling, but that was what she got for wearing slip-on loafers instead of winter boots.

A car appeared in the distance and Mary was so happy she wanted to cry. Greg was definitely going to hear about this! Once she got safely home, of course.

Stepping into the middle of the road, she raised her hand and then groaned aloud. It wasn't some stranger coming to her rescue, but Sarah McDowell. Desperate though she was, Mary would rather have seen just about anyone else.

Sarah pulled up alongside her and rolled down the window. "What's wrong?"

"Wh-what does it l-look like? M-my car broke down." She wished she could control the chattering of her teeth.

"Is someone coming for you?"

"N-not yet… I c-can't get through on my cell phone."

"I'm here now. Would you like me to deliver the Christmas baskets?"

Mary hesitated. If the gifts were to get to the families in time, she didn't really have much choice. "M-maybe you should."

Sarah edged her vehicle closer to Mary's and with some difficulty they transferred the six heavy baskets and the boxes of groceries from one car to the next.

"Thanks," Mary said grudgingly.

Sarah nodded curtly. "Go ahead and call Greg again," she suggested.

"Okay." Mary punched out the number and waited, hoping against hope that the call would connect. Once again, she got the "I'm sorry" recording.

"Won't go through."

"Would you like to use my phone?" Sarah asked.

"I doubt your phone will work if mine doesn't." It was so irritating—Sarah always seemed to believe that whatever she had was better.

"It won't hurt to try."

"True," Mary admitted. She accepted Sarah's phone and tried again. It gave her no satisfaction to be right.

"Go ahead and deliver the baskets," Mary said, putting on a brave front.

"I'm not going to leave you here."

Mary hardened her resolve. "Someone will come by soon enough."

"Don't be ridiculous!" Sarah practically shouted.

"Oh, all right, you can drive me back to the club. And then deliver the baskets."

Sarah glared at her. "Aren't you being a little stubborn? I could just as easily drive you home."

Mary didn't answer. She intended to make it clear that she preferred to wait for Greg to rescue her rather than ride to town with Sarah.

"Fine, if that's what you want," Sarah said coldly.

"I'm grateful you came back," Mary told her—and she was. "I don't know how long I could've stood out here."

This time Sarah didn't respond.

"What's most important is getting these baskets to the families."

"At least we can agree on that," Sarah told her.

Mary climbed into the passenger side of Sarah's SUV and nearly sighed aloud when Sarah started the engine. A blast of hot air hit her feet and she moaned in pleasure.

Sarah was right, she decided. She *was* being unnecessarily stubborn. "If you don't mind," she said tentatively, "I would appreciate a ride home."

Sarah glanced at her as she started down the winding country road. "That wasn't so hard, now was it?"

"What?" she asked, pretending not to understand.

Just then, Sarah hit a patch of ice and the vehicle slid scarily into the other lane. With almost no traction, Sarah did what she could to keep the car on the road. "Hold on!" she cried. She struggled to maintain control but the tires refused to grip the asphalt.

"Oh, no," Mary breathed. "We're going into the ditch!" At that instant the car slid sideways, then swerved and went front-first into the irrigation ditch.

Mary fell forward, bracing her hands against the console. The car sat there, nose down. A frozen turkey rolled out of its box and lodged in the space between the two bucket seats, tail pointed at the ceiling. Sarah's eyes were wide as she held the steering wheel in a death grip.

Neither spoke for several moments. Then in a slightly breathless voice, Sarah asked, "Are you hurt?"

"No, are you?"

"I'm okay, but I think I broke three nails clutching the steering wheel."

Mary couldn't keep from smiling. Sarah had always been vain about her fingernails.

"Do you think we should try to climb out of the car?" Sarah murmured.

"I don't know."

"One of us should."

"I will," Mary offered. After all, Sarah would've been home by now if she hadn't come back to help.

"No, I think I should," Sarah said. "You must be freezing."

"I've warmed up—some. Listen, I'll go get Melody."

"It's at least a mile to the club."

"I know how far it is," Mary snapped. Sarah argued about everything.

"Why can't you just accept my help?"

"I'm in your car, aren't I?" She resisted the urge to remind Sarah that she hadn't actually been much help. Now they were both stuck, a hundred feet from where she'd been stranded. The charity baskets were no closer to their destination, either.

"Maybe another car will come by."

"Don't count on it," Mary told her.

"Why not?"

"Think about it. We're in the middle of an ice storm.

It's Christmas Eve. Anyone with half a brain is home in front of a warm fireplace."

"Oh. Yes."

"I'll walk to the club."

"No," Sarah insisted.

"Why not?"

Sarah didn't say anything for a moment. "I don't want to stay here alone," she finally admitted.

Mary pondered that confession and realized she wouldn't want to wait in the car by herself, either. "Okay," she said. "We'll both go."

"Tell me what you found out about the tea service," Thom said as they headed toward the freeway on-ramp.

"The internet was great. Your secretary's list was a big help, too. I scanned in the photograph you gave me and got an immediate hit with the man we're going to see this morning."

"Hey, you did well."

"I have a good feeling about this." Noelle's voice rose with excitement.

Thom didn't entirely share her enthusiasm. "I don't think we should put too much stock in this," he said cautiously.

"Why not?"

"Don't forget, my mom and dad searched for years. It's unrealistic to think we can locate a replacement after just one day."

"But your parents didn't have the internet."

She was right, but not all antiques stores were online. Under the circumstances, it would be far too easy to build up their expectations only to face disappointment. "You said yourself this could be a wild-goose chase."

"I know." Noelle sounded discouraged now.

Thom reached out and gently clasped her fingers. "Don't worry—we're going to keep trying for as long as it takes." The road was icy, so he returned his hand to the steering wheel. "Looks like we're in for a spell of bad weather."

"I heard there's an ice storm on the way."

Thom nodded. The roads were growing treacherous, and he wondered if they should have risked the drive. However, they were on their way and at this point, he wanted to see it through as much as Noelle did.

What was normally a two-and-a-half-hour trip into Portland took almost four. Fortunately, the roads seemed to improve as they neared the city.

"I'm beginning to wonder if we should've come," Noelle said, echoing his thoughts as they passed an abandoned car angled off to the side of the road.

"We'll be fine." They were in Lake Oswego on the outskirts of Portland already—almost there.

"It's just that this is so important."

"I know."

"Maybe we should discuss what we're going to do if we don't find the tea service," Noelle said as they sought out the Lake Oswego business address.

"We'll deal with that when we have to, all right?"

She nodded.

The antiques store was situated in a strip mall between a Thai restaurant and a beauty parlor. Thom parked the car. "You ready?" he asked, turning to her.

Noelle smiled encouragingly.

They held hands as they walked to the store. A bell above the door chimed merrily when they entered, and they found themselves in a long, narrow room crammed with glassware, china and polished wood furniture. Every conceivable space and surface had been put to use. A slightly moldy odor filled the air, competing with the piney scent of a small Christmas tree. Thom had to turn sideways to get past a quantity of comic books stacked on a chest of drawers next to the entrance. He led Noelle around the obstacles to the counter, where the cash register sat.

"Hello," Noelle called out. "Anyone here?"

"Be with you in a minute," a voice called back from a hidden location deep inside the store.

While Noelle examined the brooches, pins and old jewelry beneath the glass counter, Thom glanced around. A collection of women's hats filled a shelf to the right. He couldn't imagine his mother wearing anything with feathers, but if she'd lived in a different era…

He studied a pile of old games next, but they all seemed to be missing pieces. This looked less and less promising.

"Sorry to keep you waiting." A thin older man with a full crop of white hair ambled into the room. He was slightly stooped and brushed dust from his hands as he walked.

"Hello, my name is Noelle McDowell," she said. "We spoke yesterday."

"Ah, yes."

"Thom Sutton." Thom stepped forward and offered his hand.

"Peter Bright." His handshake was firm, belying his

rather frail appearance. "I didn't know if you'd make it or not, with the storm and all."

"We're grateful you're open this close to Christmas," Noelle told him.

"I don't plan on staying open for long. But I wanted to escape the house for a few hours before Estelle found an excuse to put me to work in the kitchen." He chuckled. "Would you like to take a look at the tea service?"

"Please."

"I have it back here." He started slowly toward the rear of the store; Thom and Noelle followed him.

Noelle reached for Thom's hand again. Although he'd warned her against building up their expectations, he couldn't help feeling a wave of anticipation.

"Now, let me see…" Peter mumbled as he began shifting boxes around. "You know, a lot of people tell me they're coming in and then never show up." He smiled. "Like I said, I didn't really expect you to drive all the way from Rose in the middle of an ice storm." He removed an ancient Remington typewriter and set it aside, then lifted the lid of an army-green metal chest.

"I've had this tea service for maybe twenty years," Peter explained as he extracted a Navy sea bag.

"Do you remember how you came to get it?"

"Oh, sure. An English lady sold it to me. I displayed it for a while. People looked but no one bought."

"Why keep it in the chest now?" Noelle asked.

"I didn't like having to polish it," Peter said. "Folks have trouble seeing past the tarnish." He straightened and met Thom's gaze. "Same with people. Ever notice that?"

"I have," Thom said. Even on short acquaintance, he liked Peter Bright.

Nodding vigorously, Peter extracted a purple pouch from the duffel bag and peeled back the cloth to display a creamer. He set it on the green chest for their examination.

Noelle pulled the photograph from her purse and handed it to Thom, who studied the style. The picture wasn't particularly clear, so he found it impossible to tell if this was the same creamer, but there was definitely a similarity.

The sugar bowl was next. Peter set it out, waiting for Thom and Noelle's reaction. The photograph showed a slightly better view of that.

"This isn't the one," Noelle said. "But it's close, I think."

"Since you drove all this way, it won't hurt to look at all the pieces."

Thom agreed, but he already knew it had been a futile trip. He tried to hide his disappointment. Against all the odds, he'd held high hopes for this. Like Noelle, he'd been waiting for a Christmas miracle but apparently it wasn't going to happen.

Bending low, Peter thrust his arm inside the canvas bag and extracted two more objects. He carefully unwrapped the silver teapot and then the coffeepot and offered them a moment to scrutinize his wares.

The elaborate tray was last. Carefully arranging each piece on top of it, Peter stepped back to give them a full view of the service. "It's a magnificent find, don't you think?"

"It's lovely," Noelle said.

"But it's not the one we're looking for."

He accepted their news with good grace. "That's a shame."

"You see, this service—" she held out the picture "—was stolen years ago, and Thom and I are hoping to replace it with one that's exactly the same. Or as much like it as possible."

Peter reached for the photograph and studied it a moment. "I guess I should've looked closer and saved you folks the drive."

"No problem," Thom said. "Thanks for getting back to us."

"Yes, thank you for your trouble," Noelle said as they left the store. "It's a beautiful service."

"I'll give you a good price on it if you change your mind," the old man said, following them to the front door. "I'll be here another hour or so if you want to come back."

"Thank you," Thom said, but he didn't think there was much chance they'd be back. It wasn't the tea service they needed.

"How about lunch before we head home," he suggested. The Thai restaurant appeared to be open.

"Sure," Noelle agreed.

Thom shared her discouragement, but he was determined to maintain her optimism—and his own. "Hey, we've only started to look. It's too early to give up."

"I know. You're right, it was foolish of me to think we'd find it so quickly. It's just that…oh, I don't know, I guess I thought it *would* be easy because everything else fell into place for us."

They were the only customers in the restaurant. A charming waitress greeted them and escorted them to a table near the window.

Thom waited until they were seated before he spoke. "I guess this means we go to Plan B."

"What about pad thai and—" Noelle glanced up at him over the menu. "What exactly is Plan B?"

Thom reached inside his coat pocket and set the jeweler's box in the middle of the table.

"Thom?" Noelle put her menu down.

This wasn't the way he'd intended to propose, but— as the cliché had it—there was no time like the present. "I love you, Noelle, and I'm not going to let this feud stand between us. Our parents will have to understand that we're entitled to our own happiness."

Tears glistened in her eyes. "Oh, Thom."

"I'm asking you to be my wife."

She stretched her arm across the table and they joined hands. "And I'm telling you it would be the greatest honor of my life to accept. I have a request, though."

"Anything."

"I want to buy that tea service. Not you. Me."

Thom frowned. "Why?"

"I want to give it to your mother. From me to her. I can't replace the original, but maybe I can build a bridge between our families with this one."

Thom's fingers tightened around hers. "It's worth a try."

"I think so, too," she whispered.

"I'm going to try my phone again," Sarah said. Technology had betrayed them, but surely it would come to their rescue. Eventually. Walking a mile in the bitter cold was something she'd rather avoid.

"Go ahead," Mary urged. She didn't seem any more eager than Sarah to make the long trek.

Sarah got her phone and speed dialed her home number. Hope sprang up when the call instantly connected, but was dashed just as quickly when she heard the recording once again.

"Any luck?" Mary asked, her eyes bright and teary in the cold.

She shook her head.

"Damn," Mary muttered. "I guess that means there's no option but to hoof it."

"Appears that way."

"I think we should have a little fortification first, though," Sarah said. Her husband's golf bags were in the backseat, and she knew he often carried a flask.

"Fortification?"

"A little Scotch might save our lives."

Mary's look was skeptical. "I'm all for Scotch, but where are we going to find any out here?"

"Jake." She opened the back door and grabbed the golf bag. Sure enough, there was a flask.

"I don't remember you liking Scotch," Mary said.

"I don't, but at this point I can't be choosy."

"Right."

Sarah removed the top and tipped the flask, taking a sizable gulp. Wiping her mouth with the back of her hand, she swallowed, then shook her head briskly. "Oh my, that's strong." The liquor burned all the way down to her stomach, but as soon as it hit bottom, a welcoming warmth spread through her limbs.

"My turn," Mary said.

Sarah handed her the flask and watched as Mary rubbed the top, then tilted it back and took a deep swallow. She, too, closed her eyes and shook her head. Soon, however, she was smiling. "That wasn't so bad."

"It might ward off hypothermia."

"You're right. You'd better have another."

"You think?"

Mary nodded and after a moment, Sarah agreed. Luckily Jake had refilled the flask. The second swallow didn't taste nearly as nasty as the first. It didn't burn this time, either. Instead it enhanced the warm glow spreading through her system.

"How do you feel?"

"Better," Sarah said, giving Mary the flask.

Mary didn't need encouragement. She took her turn with the flask, then growled like a grizzly bear.

Sarah didn't know why she found that so amusing, but she did. She laughed uproariously. In fact, she laughed until she started to cough.

"What?" Mary asked, grinning broadly.

"Oh, dear." She coughed again. "I didn't know you did animal impressions."

"I do when I drink Scotch."

Then, as if they'd both become aware that they were having an actual conversation, they pulled back into themselves. Sarah noticed that Mary's expression suddenly grew dignified, as though she'd realized she was laughing and joking with her enemy.

"We should get moving, don't you think?" Mary said in a dispassionate voice.

"You're right." Sarah put the flask back in the golf bag and wrapped her scarf more tightly around her neck and face. Fortified in all respects, she was ready to face the storm. "It's a good thing we're walking together. Anything could happen on a day like this."

They'd gone about the length of a football field when Mary said, "I'm cold again."

"I am, too."

"You should've brought along the Scotch."

"We'll have to go back for it."

"I think we should," Mary agreed solemnly. "We could freeze to death before we reach the club."

"Yes. The Scotch might make the difference between survival and death."

Back at the car, they climbed in and shared the flask again. Soon, for no apparent reason, they were giggling.

"I think we're drunk," Mary said.

"Oh, hardly. I can hold my liquor better than this."

Mary burst into peals of laughter. "No, you can't. Don't you remember the night of our Halloween party?"

"That was—what?—twenty-two years ago!"

"I know, but I haven't forgotten how silly those margaritas made you."

"You were the one who kept filling my glass."

"You were the one who kept telling me how good they were."

Sarah nearly doubled over with hysterics. "Next thing I knew, I was standing on the coffee table singing 'Guantanamera' at the top of my lungs."

"You sounded fabulous, too. And then when you started to dance—"

"I *what?*" All Sarah recalled was the blinding headache she'd suffered the next morning. When she woke and could barely lift her head from the pillow without stabbing pain, she'd phoned her dearest, best friend in the world. Mary had dropped everything and rushed over. She'd mixed Sarah a tomato-juice concoction that had saved her life, or so she'd felt at the time.

Both women were silent. "I miss those days," Sarah whispered.

"I do, too," Mary said.

Sarah sniffled. It was the cold that made her eyes water. Digging through her purse, she couldn't find a single tissue. Mary gave her one.

"I've missed you," Sarah said and loudly blew her nose.

"I've missed you, too."

The cold must have intensified, because her eyes began to water even more. Using her coat sleeve, she wiped her nose.

"Here," she said to Mary, handing her the flask. "I want you to have this. Take the rest."

"The Scotch?"

Sarah nodded. "If we're not found until it's too late— I want you to have the liquor. It might keep you alive long enough for the rescue people to revive you."

Mary looked as though she was close to bursting into tears. "You'd die for—me?" She hiccuped on the last word.

Sarah nodded again.

"That's the most beautiful thing anyone's ever said to me."

"But before I die, I need to ask you something."

"Anything," Mary told her. "Anything at all."

Sarah sniffled and swallowed a sob. Leaning her forehead against the steering wheel, she whispered, "Forgive me."

Mary placed her hand on Sarah's shoulder. "I do

forgive you, but first you have to forgive *me* for acting so badly. You were right—I *was* jealous of Cheryl. I thought you liked her better than me."

"Never. She's one of those people who move in and out of a person's life, but you—you're my...my soul sister. I've missed you so much."

"We're idiots." Mary returned the flask. "I can't accept this Scotch. If we freeze, we freeze together."

Sarah was feeling downright toasty at the moment. The world was spinning, but that was probably because she was drunker than a skunk. The thought made her giggle.

"What's so funny?" Mary wanted to know.

"We're drunk," she muttered. "Drunk as skunks. Drunk as skunks," she recited in a singsong voice.

"Isn't it wonderful?"

They laughed again.

"Jake always insists I eat something when I've had too much to drink."

"We have lots of food," Mary said, sitting up straight.

"Yes, but most of it's half-frozen by now."

Mary's eyes gleamed bright. "Not everything. I'm sure the families would want us to take what we need, don't you think?"

"I'm sure you're right," Sarah said as Mary climbed over the front seat and into the back, her coat flipping over her head.

Sarah laughed so hard she nearly peed her pants.

Women's Century Club
Rose, Oregon

December 24

Dear Mary and Sarah,

Just a note to let you know how much the Women's Century Club appreciates the effort that went into preparing these Christmas baskets. You two did a splendid job. I could see from the number of gifts filling the baskets that you went far beyond the items listed on the sheet I gave you. Both of you have been generous to a fault.

Sarah, I realize it was difficult to come into this project at the last minute, but you are to be commended for your cooperation.

Mary, you did a wonderful job making all the arrangements, and I'm confident the baskets will reach the Salvation Army in plenty of time to be distributed for the holidays.

If you're both willing to take up the task again next year, I'd be happy to recommend you for the job.

Sincerely,
Melody Darrington

Nine

Jake McDowell glanced at the kitchen clock and frowned. "What time did your mother say she'd be home?"

"I don't know." His youngest daughter was certainly a fount of information. Carley lay flat on her stomach in front of the Christmas tree, her arms outstretched as she examined a small package.

"She should be back by now, don't you think?" Jake asked, looking at the clock again.

"I suppose."

"When will Noelle be home?"

Unconcerned, Carley shrugged.

Jake decided he wasn't going to get any answers here and tried Sarah's cell for perhaps the fiftieth time. Whenever he punched in the number, he received the same irritating message. "I'm sorry. We are unable to connect your call…."

Not knowing what else to do, he phoned his golfing partner. Greg Sutton answered on the first ring.

"I thought you were Mary," he said, sounding as worried as Jake was.

"You haven't heard from Mary?"

"Not a word. Is Sarah back?"

"No," Jake said. "That's why I was calling you."

"What do you think happened?"

"No idea. I could understand if one of them was missing, but not both."

Greg didn't say anything for a moment. "Did you phone the Women's Century Club?"

"I did. Melody said they were there and left two hours ago. She told me the ice storm's pretty bad in her area. She's going to stay put until her husband can come and get her this afternoon."

"What did she say about Mary and Sarah?"

"Not much. Just that they got the baskets all sorted and loaded into Mary's vehicle. Melody did make some comment about Sarah and Mary being pretty hostile toward each other. According to her, they left at different times."

"That doesn't explain why they're both missing."

"What if one of them had an accident and the other stopped to help?" Greg suggested.

Jake hadn't considered that. "But wouldn't they have been back by now?"

"Unless they got stuck."

"Together?"

"I wouldn't know."

Jake laughed grimly. "If that's the case, God help us all."

"What do you think we should do?"

"We can't leave them out there."

"You're right," Greg said. "But I have to tell you the

idea is somewhat appealing. If they *are* stuck with each other for a while, they just might settle this mess."

"They could murder each other, too." Jake knew his wife far too well. When it came to Mary Sutton, she could be downright unreasonable. "I say we go after them—together."

Jake had no objection to that. Greg owned a large four-wheel-drive truck that handled better on the ice than most vehicles. "You want to pick me up?"

"I'm on my way," Greg said.

Sarah reached for another Christmas cookie. "What did you call these again?" she asked, studying the package. Unfortunately, the letters wouldn't quite come into focus.

"Pfeffernusse."

"Try to say *that* three times when you're too drunk to stand up."

Mary giggled and helped herself to one of the glazed ginger cookies. "They're German. One family on the list had a German-sounding name and I thought they might be familiar with these cookies."

Sarah was touched. Tears filled her eyes. "You're so thoughtful."

"Not really," Mary said with a sob. "I… I was trying to outdo you." She was weeping in earnest now. "How could I have been so silly?"

"I did the same thing." Sarah wrapped her arm around Mary's shoulders. "I was the one who got us thrown out of Value-X."

Mary sniffled and dried her eyes. "I'm never going to let anything come between us again."

"I won't, either," Sarah vowed. "I think this has been the best Christmas of my life."

"Christmas!" Mary jerked upright. "Oh, Sarah, we've got to get these baskets to the Salvation Army!"

"But how? We can't carry all this stuff."

"True, but we can't just sit here, either." She looked into the distance, in the direction of the Women's Century Club. "We're going to have to walk, after all."

Her friend was right. They had to take matters into their own hands and work together. "We can do it."

"We can. We'll walk to the club and send someone to get the baskets. Then we'll call Triple A. See? We have a plan. A good plan. There isn't anything we can't do if we stick together."

Sarah felt the tears sting her eyes again. "Is there any Scotch left?"

"No," Mary said, sounding sad. "We're going to have to make it on our own."

Clambering out of the car, Sarah was astonished by how icy the road had become in the hour or so they'd dawdled over their comforting Scotch. Luckily, she was wearing her boots, whereas Mary wore loafers.

Her friend gave a small cry and then, arms flailing, struggled to regain her balance. "My goodness, it's slippery out here."

"How are we going to do this?" Sarah asked. "You can't walk on this ice."

"Sure I can," Mary assured her, straightening with resolve. But she soon lost her balance again and grabbed hold of the car door, just managing to save herself.

"It's like you said—we'll do it together," Sarah declared. "We have to, because I'm not leaving you behind."

With Mary's arm around Sarah's waist and Sarah's arm about Mary's shoulder, they started walking down the center of the road. The treacherous ice slowed them down, and their progress was halting, especially since both of them were drunk and weepy with emotion.

"I wonder how long it'll take Greg to realize I'm not home," Mary said. Her husband was in trouble as it was, leaving her a defective vehicle to drive.

"Probably a lot longer than Jake. I told him I wouldn't be more than an hour."

"I'm sure there's some football game on TV that Greg's busy staring at. He won't notice I'm not there until Suzanne and Thom arrive for dinner." Mary went strangely quiet.

"Are you okay?" Sarah asked, tightening her hold on her friend.

"Yes, but… Thom. I was thinking about Thom. He's in love with Noelle, you know."

"Noelle's been in love with Thom since she was sixteen. It broke her heart when he dumped her."

"Thom didn't dump her. She dumped him."

Sarah bristled. "She did not!"

"You mean to say something else happened?"

"It must have, because I know for a fact that Noelle's always loved Thom."

"And Thom feels the same about her."

"We have to do something," Sarah said. "We've got to find a way to get them back together."

"I think they might've been secretly seeing each other," Mary confessed.

Sarah shook her head, which made her feel slightly dizzy. "Noelle would've told me. We're this close." She attempted to cross two fingers, but couldn't manage it. Must be because of her gloves, she decided. Yes, that was it.

"We're drunk," Mary said. "Really and truly drunk. The cookies didn't help one bit."

"I don't care. We're best friends again and this time it's for life."

"For life," Mary vowed.

"We're on a mission."

"A mission," Mary repeated. She paused "What's our mission again?"

Sarah had to stop and think about it. "First, we need to deliver the Christmas baskets."

Mary slapped her hand against her forehead. "Right! How could I forget?"

"Then…"

"There's more?" Mary looked confused.

"Yes, lots more. Then we need to convince Noelle and Thom that they were meant to be together."

"Poor Thom," Mary said. "Oh no." She covered her mouth with her hand.

"What?"

"I left a message on his answering machine. I may not remember much right now, but I remember that. I told him I didn't think he should marry Noelle…."

"Why would you do that?"

"Well, because—oh dear, Sarah, I might have ruined everything."

"We'll deal with it as soon as we're home," Sarah said firmly.

A car sounded from behind them. "Someone's coming," Mary cried, her voice rising with excitement.

"We've got to hitch a ride." Sarah whirled around and held out her thumb as prominently as she could.

"That's not going to work," Mary insisted, thrusting out her leg. "Don't you remember that old Clark Gable movie?"

"Clark Gable got a ride by showing off his ankle?"

"No… Claudette Colbert did."

The truck turned the corner; Sarah wasn't willing to trust in either her thumb or Mary's leg, so she raised both hands above her head and waved frantically.

"It's Greg," Mary cried in relief.

"And Jake's with him." Thank God. Sarah had never been happier to see her husband.

To their shock and anger, the two men drove directly past them.

"Hey!" Mary shouted after her husband. "I am in no mood for games."

The truck stopped, and the driver and passenger doors opened at the same time. Greg climbed down and headed over to Mary, while Jake hurried toward Sarah.

"We're friends for life," Mary told her husband, throwing her arm around Sarah again.

"You're drunk," Greg said. "Just what have you been drinking?"

"I know exactly what I'm doing," she answered with offended dignity.

"Do *you*?" Jake asked Sarah.

"Of course I do."

"We're on a mission," Mary told the two men.

Jake frowned. "What happened to the car?"

"I'll tell you all about it later," Sarah promised, enunciating very carefully.

"What mission?" Jake asked.

Sarah exchanged an exasperated look with Mary. "Why do we have to explain everything?"

"Men," Mary said in a low voice. "Can't live with 'em, can't live without 'em."

Her friend was so wise.

The drive back to Rose took even longer than the trip into Portland. The roads seemed to get icier and more slippery with every mile. Keeping her eyes on the road, Noelle knew how tense Thom must be.

"Would you rather wait until after Christmas?" she asked as they neared her family's home. It might be better if they got through the holidays before making their announcement and throwing their families into chaos. Noelle hated the thought of dissension on Christmas Day.

"Wait? You mean to announce our engagement?" Thom clarified. "I don't think we should. You're going to marry me, and I want to tell the whole world. I refuse to keep this a secret simply because our mothers don't happen to get along. They'll just have to adjust."

"But—"

"I've waited all these years for you. I'm not waiting any longer. All right?"

"All right." Noelle was overwhelmed by contradictory emotions. Love for Thom—and love for her family. Excitement and nervousness. Happiness and guilt.

"Do you know what I like most about Christmas?" Thom asked, breaking into her thoughts.

"Tell me, and then I'll tell you what I like."

"Mom has a tradition she started when Suzanne entered high school. On Christmas Eve, she serves fresh Dungeness crab. We all love it. She has them cooked at the market because she can't bear to do it herself, then Dad brings them home. Mom's got the butter melted and the bibs ready and we sit around the table and start cracking."

"Oh, that sounds delicious."

"It is. Does your family have a Christmas Eve tradition?"

"Bingo."

"Bingo?"

"Christmas Bingo. We play after the Christmas Eve service at church. The prizes aren't worth more than five dollars, but Mom's so good at getting neat stuff. I haven't been home for Christmas in years, but Mom always makes up for it by mailing me three or four little Bingo gifts."

"My favorite carol is 'What Child Is This,'" he said next.

"Mine's 'Silent Night.'"

"What was your favorite gift as a kid?"

"Hmm, that's a toss-up," she said. "There was a Christmas Barbie I adored. Another year I got a set of classic Disney videos that I watched over and over."

Thom smiled. "As a little boy, I loved my Matchbox

car garage. I got it for Christmas when I was ten. Mom's kept it all these years. She has Dad drag it out every year and tells me she's saving it to give to my son one day."

She sighed, at peace with herself and this man she loved. "I want to have your babies, Thom," she said in a soft voice.

His eyes left the street to meet hers. The sky had darkened and he looked quickly back at the road. "You make it hard to concentrate on driving."

"Tell me some of the other things you love about Christmas. It makes me feel good to hear them."

"It's your turn," he said.

"The orange in the bottom of my stocking. Every year there's one in the toe. It's supposed to commemorate the Christmases my great-grandparents had—an orange was a pretty special thing back then."

"I like Christmas cookies. Especially meringue star ones."

"Mexican tea cakes for me," she said. "I'll ask your mother for the recipe for star cookies and bake you a batch every Christmas."

"That sounds like a very wifely thing to do."

"I want to be a good wife to my husband." Noelle suddenly realized that she was genuinely grateful they hadn't married so young. Yes, the years had brought pain, but they'd brought wisdom and perspective, too. The love she and Thom felt for each other would deepen with time. They were so much more capable now of valuing what they had together.

"What's it like to be born on Christmas Day?" Thom asked.

"It's not so bad," Noelle said. "First, I share a birthday with Jesus—that's the good part. The not-so-good is having the two biggest celebrations of the year fall on the same day. When I was a kid, Mom used to throw me a party in June to celebrate my half-year birthday."

"I remember that."

"Do you remember teasing me by saying it really wasn't my birthday so you didn't need to bring a gift?"

Thom chuckled. "What I remember is getting my ears boxed for saying it."

Twenty minutes later, they were almost at her family's house. They'd decided to confront her parents first. Their laughter, which had filled the car seconds earlier, immediately faded.

"You ready?" Thom asked as he stopped in front of the house.

Noelle nodded and swallowed hard. "No matter what happens, I want you to remember I love you."

His hand squeezed hers.

Glancing at her family's home, Noelle noticed a truck parked outside. "Looks like we have company." She didn't know whether to feel relief or disappointment.

"Oh, no." Thom's voice was barely above a whisper.

"What is it?"

"That's my parents' truck."

Dread slipped over her. "They must've found out that we spent the day together. That's my fault—I left a note for Carley telling her I was with you." Noelle could imagine what was taking place inside. Her mother would be shouting at Thom's, and their fathers would be trying to keep the two women apart.

"Should we wait?" Noelle asked, just as she had earlier.

"For another time?" His jaw tensed. "No, we face them here and now, for better or worse. Agreed?"

Noelle nodded. "Okay...just promise me you won't let them change your mind."

He snorted inelegantly. "I'd like to see them try."

Thom parked behind the truck and turned off the engine. Together, holding hands, they approached the house. Never had Noelle been more nervous. If this encounter went wrong, she might alienate her mother, and that was something she didn't want to do. In high school, she'd self-righteously cast her family aside in the name of love. But if the years in Dallas had taught her independence, they'd also taught her the importance of home and family. Her self-imposed exile was over now, and she'd learned from it. Listening to Thom talk about his Christmas traditions, she'd realized that he'd find it equally hard to turn his back on his parents.

He was about to ring the doorbell when she stopped him. "Remember how I said I was looking for a Christmas miracle?"

Thom nodded. "You mean finding a tea service similar to my grandmother's?"

"Yes. But if I could be granted only one miracle this Christmas, it wouldn't be that. I'd want our families to rekindle the love and friendship they once had."

"That would be my wish, too." Thom gathered her

in his arms and kissed her with a passion that readily found a matching fire in her. The kiss was a reminder of their love, and it sealed their bargain. No matter what happened once they entered the house, they would face it together.

"Actually, this is a blessing in disguise," Thom said. "We can confront both families at the same time and be done with it." He reached for the doorbell again, and again Noelle stopped him.

"This is my home. We don't need to ring the bell." Stepping forward, she opened the door.

Noelle wasn't sure what she expected, but certainly not the scene that greeted her. Her parents and two sisters, plus Thom's entire family, sat around the dining room table. Her mother and Mrs. Sutton, both wearing aprons, stood in the background, while her father and Thom's dished up whole Dungeness crabs, with Jonathan pouring wine.

"Thom!" his mother shouted joyfully. "It's about time you got here."

"What took you so long?" Sarah asked Noelle.

Stunned, Thom and Noelle looked at each other for an explanation.

"There's room here," Carley called out, motioning to the empty chairs beside her.

Noelle couldn't do anything other than stare.

"What…happened?" Thom asked.

"It's a long story. Sit down. We'll explain everything later."

"But…"

Thom put his arm around Noelle's shoulder. "Before

we sit down, I want everyone to know that I've asked Noelle to be my wife and she's accepted."

"Nothing you say or do will make us change our minds," Noelle said quickly, before anyone else could react.

"Why would we want to change your minds?" her father asked. "We're absolutely delighted."

"You can fight and argue, threaten and yell, and it won't make any difference," Thom added. "We're getting married!"

"Glad to hear it," his father said.

A round of cheers followed his announcement.

Thom's mother and Noelle's mother embraced in joy.

"One thing this family refuses to tolerate anymore is fighting," his mother declared.

"Absolutely," her own mother agreed.

Both Thom and Noelle stared back at them, shocked into speechlessness.

"There's no reason to stand there like a couple of strangers," her mother said. "Sit down. You wouldn't believe the day we had."

Sarah and Mary put their arms around each other's shoulders. "At least the Christmas baskets got delivered on time," Mary said with a satisfied nod.

"And no one mentioned that the two of us smelled like Scotch when we got there," her mother pointed out.

They both giggled.

"What happened?" Noelle asked.

Her father waved aside her question. "You don't want to know," he groaned.

"I'll tell you later," her mother promised.

Thom leaned close to her and whispered, "Either we just walked into the middle of an *X-Files* episode or we got our Christmas miracle."

Noelle slipped an arm around his waist. "I think you must be right."

Sarah McDowell
9 Orchard Lane
Rose, Oregon

December 26

Dear Melody,
Mary and I found your note when we delivered the baskets on Christmas Eve. We did have a wonderful time, and Mary has agreed to head up the committee next year. I promised I'd be her cochair.

Now, about using the club for Kristen's wedding reception… Well, it seems there's going to be another wedding in the family, and fairly soon. Mary and I will be in touch with you about that right after New Year's.

Sincerely,
Sarah McDowell

* * * * *

LET IT SNOW

For Virelle Kidder and Suzanne Carter
My Florida soul sisters

One

"Ladies and gentlemen, this is your captain speaking."

Shelly Griffin's fingers compressed around the armrest until her neatly manicured nails threatened to cut into the fabric. Flying had never thrilled her, and she avoided it whenever possible. It had taken her the better part of a month to convince herself that this trip would be perfectly safe. She told herself that of course the Boeing 727 that had taken off without incident from San Francisco almost ninety minutes ago would land unscathed just a little while from now in Seattle. Still, if it wasn't Christmas, if she wasn't so homesick, and if she'd had more than four days off, she would have done anything except fly to get home for the holidays.

"Seattle is reporting heavy snow and limited visibility," the captain continued. "We've been rerouted to Portland International until the Seattle runways can be cleared."

A low groan filled the plane.

She forced herself to relax. Snow. She could handle snow, right? She wasn't overjoyed at the prospect of having to land twice, but she was so close to home now that she would willingly suffer anything to see a welcoming smile light up her father's eyes.

In an effort to divert her thoughts from impending tragedy, she studied the passengers around her. A grandmotherly type slept sedately in the seat beside her. The man sitting across the aisle was such a classic businessman that he was intriguing. Almost from the moment they'd left San Francisco, he'd been working out of his briefcase. He hadn't so much as cracked a smile during the entire flight. The captain's announcement had produced little more than a disgruntled flicker in his staid expression.

She had seen enough men like him in her job as a reporter in the federal court to catalog him quickly. Polished. Professional. Impeccable. Handsome, too, she supposed, if she was interested—which she wasn't. She preferred her men a little less intense. She managed to suppress a tight laugh. Men? What men? In the ten months she'd been living in the City by the Bay, she hadn't exactly developed a following. A few interesting prospects now and again, but nothing serious.

As the plane made its descent, Shelly gripped the armrest with renewed tension. Her gaze skimmed the emergency exits as she repeated affirmations on the safety of flying. She mumbled them under her breath as the plane angled sharply to the right, aligning its giant bulk with the narrow runway ahead.

Keeping her eyes centered on the seat in front of her, she held her breath until she felt the wheels gently bounce against the runway in a flawless landing. She braced herself as the brakes quickly slowed the aircraft to a crawl.

The oxygen rushed from her lungs in a heartfelt sigh of relief. Somehow the landings were so much worse than the takeoffs. As the tension eased from her rigid body, she looked around to discover the businessman slanting his idle gaze over her. His dark eyes contained a look of surprise. He seemed amazed that anyone could be afraid of flying. The blood mounted briefly in her pale features, and she decided she definitely didn't like his cold attitude, no matter how handsome he was.

The elderly woman sitting next to her placed a hand on Shelly's forearm. "Are you all right, dear?"

"Of course." Relief throbbed in her voice. Now that they were on the ground, she could feign the composure that seemed to come so easily to the other passengers.

"I hope we aren't delayed long. My daughter's taking off work to meet me."

"My dad's forty minutes from the airport," Shelly offered, hoping that he'd called the airline to check if her flight was on time. She hated the thought of him anxiously waiting for her.

The other woman craned her neck to peek out the small side window. "It doesn't seem to be snowing much here. Just a few flakes. They look a bit like floating goose feathers, don't you think?"

Shelly grinned at the image. "Let's hope it stays that way."

She remained seated while several of the other passengers got up and took advantage of the captain's offer to leave the plane during the delay. The businessman was among those who quickly vacated their seats. But since the captain had said he didn't expect them to be in Portland long, Shelly didn't want to take a chance of missing the flight when it was ready to take off again.

After checking her watch every ten minutes for forty minutes, she was starting to think that they would never leave Oregon. The blizzard had hit the area, and whirling snow buffeted the quiet plane with growing intensity. Her anxieties mounted with equal force. Suddenly her dire musings were interrupted.

"This is the captain speaking." His faint Southern drawl filled the plane. "Unfortunately, Seattle reports that visibility hasn't improved. They're asking that we remain here in Portland for another half hour, possibly longer."

Frustration and disappointment erupted from the remaining passengers, and they all began speaking at once.

"This is the captain again," the pilot added, his tone one of wry humor. "I'd like to remind those of you who are upset by our situation that it's far better to be on the ground wishing you were in the sky than to be in the sky *praying* you were on the ground."

Shelly added a silent amen to that. As it was, she was beginning to feel claustrophobic, trapped inside the plane. She grabbed her purse and reached for her cell, then discovered when she tried to turn it on that she must have forgotten to charge it, because the battery was dead. Unsnapping her seat belt, she stood and headed down the narrow aisle toward the front of the plane.

"Do I have time to make a phone call? My cell is dead," she explained.

"Sure," the flight attendant answered with a cordial smile. "Don't be long, though. The conditions in Seattle could change quickly."

"I won't," Shelly promised, and made her way into the terminal. Thank heavens airports still had payphones, she thought as she found two lonely phones sandwiched between a newsstand and a bagel shop.

She claimed the only unoccupied one, then frowned when she saw the "Out of Order" sign taped over the credit card slot. It wasn't until she was sorting through her purse for change that she noted that the unsympathetic businessman from her flight was sitting at the other phone. Apparently even someone as focused as he seemed to be could forget to charge his phone, too.

"This is Slade Garner again," he announced with the faintest trace of impatience creeping into his voice. "My plane's still in Portland."

Shelly scowled at her wallet. She didn't have change for the phone.

"Yes, yes, I understand the snow's a problem on your end as well," he continued smoothly. "I doubt that I'll make it in this afternoon. Perhaps we should arrange the meeting for first thing tomorrow morning. Nine o'clock?" Another pause. "Of course I realize it's the day before Christmas."

Rummaging in her purse, Shelly managed to dredge up a token for the cable car, a breath mint and a lost button.

Pressing her lips tightly together, she mused about how coldhearted Slade Garner was to insist on a meeting so close to Christmas. Instantly she felt guilty because her thoughts were so judgmental. Of course he would want to keep his appointment. He obviously hadn't taken this flight for fun. Her second regret was that she realized she had intentionally eavesdropped on his conversation, looking for excuses to justify her dislike of him. Such behavior was hardly in keeping with the Christmas spirit.

Pasting on a pleasant smile, she stepped forward when he replaced the receiver, thinking to claim the working phone, but someone practically knocked her over and got there first.

"Excuse me," she said politely as Slade turned in her direction. He refused to meet her gaze, and for a second she didn't think he'd heard her.

"Yes?" He finally looked her way, his expression bored, frustrated.

"Have you got change, by any chance?"

He uninterestedly checked the contents of his pocket, then looked down at the few coins in his palm. "Sorry." Dispassionately he tucked them back in his pocket and turned away.

She was ready to approach someone else when he turned back to her. His dark brows drew together in a frown, something about her apparently registering in his mind despite his preoccupied thoughts. "You were on the Seattle flight, weren't you?"

"Yes."

"Here." He handed her what change he had.

The corners of her mouth curved up in surprise. "Thanks." He was already walking briskly away, and she was convinced he hadn't even heard her. She didn't know what difference it made that they'd shared the same plane, but without analyzing his generosity any further, she dropped the first coin in the slot, then shifted her weight from one foot to the other while the phone rang, hoping her father—one of the last holdouts against owning a cell—wasn't already at the airport waiting for her. She was pleased when he answered.

"Dad, I'm so glad I caught you."

"Merry Christmas, Shortcake."

Her father had bestowed this affectionate title on her when she was thirteen and her friends had sprouted up around her. To her dismay she had remained at a deplorable five feet until she was seventeen. Then, within six months, she had grown five inches. Her height and other attributes of puberty had been hormonal afterthoughts.

"I'm in Portland."

"I know. When I phoned the airline they told me you'd been forced to land there. How are you doing?"

"Fine." She wasn't about to reveal her fear of flying or how much she was dreading getting back on that plane. "I'm sorry about the delay."

"It's not your fault."

"But I hate wasting precious time sitting here when I could be with you."

"Don't worry about it. We'll have plenty of time together."

"Have you decorated the tree yet?" Since her mother's death three years before, she and her father had made a ritual of placing the homemade ornaments on the tree together.

"I haven't even bought one. I thought we'd do that first thing in the morning."

She closed her eyes, savoring the warm feeling of

love and security that the sound of her father's voice always gave her. "I've got a fantastic surprise for you."

"What's that?" he prompted.

"It wouldn't be a surprise if I told you, would it?"

Her father chuckled, and she could visualize him rubbing his finger over his upper lip the way he did when something amused him. They chatted for another minute, and then she realized she should check on the status of her flight.

"I've missed you, Dad."

"I've missed you, too."

"Take care."

"I will." She was about to hang up, but then... "Dad," she added hastily, her thoughts churning as she focused on a huge advertisement for a rental car agency. "Listen, don't go to the airport until I phone."

"But—"

"I'll be hungry by then, so I'll grab some lunch and be waiting outside for you. That way you won't have to park."

"I don't mind parking, Shortcake."

"I know, but I'd rather do it my way."

"If you insist."

"I do." Her brothers claimed that their father was partial to his only daughter. It was a long-standing family joke that she was the only one capable of swaying him once he'd made a decision. "I insist."

They said their goodbyes, and she disconnected, feeling light-hearted and relieved. Instead of heading back down the concourse toward the plane, she ventured in the opposite direction, taking the escalators to the lower level, where the rental car agencies were located.

To her surprise, she saw Slade Garner talking with a young man at the first agency. Shelly walked past him to the second counter.

"How much would it cost to rent a car here and drop it off in Seattle?" she asked brightly.

The woman on duty hardly looked up from her computer screen. "Sorry, we don't have any cars available."

"None?" Shelly found that hard to believe.

"Lots of people had the same idea you did," the agent explained. "A plane hasn't landed in Seattle in hours. No one wants to sit around the airport waiting. Especially at Christmas."

"Thanks anyway." Shelly hurried down to the third agency and repeated her question.

"Yes, we do," the agent said with a wide grin. "We have exactly one car available." She named a sum that caused Shelly to swallow heavily. But already the idea had gained traction in her mind. Every minute the plane remained on the ground robbed her of precious time with her father. And from what he'd told her, the snow was coming down fast and furiously. It could be hours before the plane was able to take off, if it took off today at all. She freely admitted that another landing at another airport in the middle of the worst snowstorm of the year wasn't her idea of a good time. As it was, her Christmas bonus was burning a hole in her purse. And this was a good cause. Surely there was some unwritten rule that stated every favorite daughter should spend Christmas with her father.

"I'll take the car."

She looked up and saw Slade Garner standing a mere six inches away. A wide, confident smile spread across his handsome features, and his aura of self-assurance bordered on arrogance.

"I'm already taking it," she said firmly.

"I have to get to Seattle."

"So do I," she informed him primly. And then, in case he decided to remind her that she was indebted to him, she added, "But give me an address and I'll make sure to reimburse you while I'm there."

"I've got an important meeting."

"As a matter of fact, so do I." Turning back to the counter, she picked up a pen and prepared to fill in the rental form.

"How much?" he asked.

"I beg your pardon?"

"How much do you want for the car?" He slipped his hand into the pocket of his coat, apparently prepared to pay her price.

Squaring her shoulders, she exchanged looks with the rental agent, then turned back to Slade and said, "Get your own car."

"There's only one car available. This one."

"And I've got it," she told him with a deceptively calm smile. The more she saw of this man, the more aggravating he became.

His jaw tightened. "I don't think you understand," he said, and breathed out with sharp impatience. "My meeting's extremely important."

"So is mine. I'm—"

"You could share the car," the agent suggested, causing both Shelly and Slade to turn their eyes his way, shocked by his impromptu peacemaking.

Shelly hesitated.

Slade's brows arched and he met her eyes. "I'll pay the full fee for the car," he offered.

"You mention money one more time and the deal's off," she shot back hotly.

"Don't be unreasonable."

"I'm not being unreasonable. You are."

He rubbed a hand along the back of his neck and forcefully expelled his breath. "Do we or do we not have a deal?"

"I'm not going to Seattle."

He gave her a sharp look of reproach. "I just heard you say Seattle."

"I'm headed for Maple Valley. That's in south King County."

"Fine. I'll drop you off and return the car to the rental office myself."

That would save her one hassle. Still, she hesitated. Two minutes together and they were already arguing. How would they possibly manage three hours cooped up in the close confines of a car?

"Listen," he argued, his voice tinged with exasperation. "If I make it to Seattle this afternoon, I might be able to get this meeting over with early. That way I can be back home in San Francisco for Christmas."

Without knowing it, he'd found the weakest links in her chain of defense. Christmas and home were important to her.

"All right," she mumbled. "But I'll pay my share of the cost."

"Whatever you want."

For the first time since she'd seen him, Slade Garner smiled.

Two

"What about your luggage?" Slade asked as they strolled down the concourse toward the plane.

"I only have one bag. It's above my seat." Her honey-brown hair curled around her neck, and she absently lifted a strand and looped it over her ear. A farm girl's wardrobe didn't fit in with the formal business attire she needed in San Francisco so she had left most of her clothes with her father. And it hadn't been hard to fit four days' worth of clothes into her carry-on. The brevity of her vacation was turning out to be a blessing in disguise.

Her spirits rose as they neared the plane. She was heading home for Christmas, and she wasn't flying!

"Good. I only have a garment bag with me."

She hesitated. "I do have a tote bag filled with presents."

His gaze collided briefly with hers. "That shouldn't be any problem."

When he saw the monstrosity, he might change his mind, she mused with an inner smile. In addition to a variety of odd-sized gifts, she was bringing her father several long loaves of sourdough bread. The huge package was awkward, and she had required a flight attendant's assistance to fit it in the compartment above her seat. Normally she would have put everything in a second suitcase and checked it, but loaves of bread were so long—sticking out of her bag like doughy antennas—that none of her suitcases had been big enough.

The plane was nearly empty when they boarded, confirming her suspicion that the delay was going to be far longer than originally anticipated. Checking her watch, she discovered that it was nearly noon. The other passengers had probably gone to get something to eat.

Standing on tiptoes, she opened the luggage compartment.

"Do you need help?" Slade asked. A dark gray garment bag was folded neatly over his forearm.

"Here." She handed him her one small bag. She heard him mumble something about appreciating a woman who packed light and smiled to herself.

Straining to stretch as far as she could to get a good grip on her bag of gifts, she heard Slade grumble.

"Look at what some idiot put up there."

"Pardon?"

"That bag. Good grief, people should know better than to try to force a tuba case up there."

"That's mine, and it isn't a tuba case." Extracting the bag containing the bread, so the bigger bag would be easier to extricate, she handed it down to him.

Slade looked at it as if something were about to leap out and bite him. "Good heavens, what is this?"

What was it? What was wrong with his eyes? Bread had to be the most recognizable item in the world.

"A suitcase for a snake," she replied sarcastically.

The beginnings of a grin touched his usually impassive features as he gently moved in front of her. "Let me get that thing down before you drop it on your head."

She stepped aside so he could put the bread and their carry-ons on her empty seat.

"Suitcase for a snake, huh?" Unexpectedly he smiled again.

The effect on her was dazzling. She had the feeling that this man didn't often take the time to enjoy life. Only minutes before she'd classified him as cheerless and intense. But when he smiled, the carefully guarded facade cracked and she felt she was being given a rare glimpse of the intriguing man inside. And he fascinated her.

By the time they'd arranged things with the airline, the courtesy van from the rental agency had arrived to deliver them to their vehicle.

"I put everything in my name," Slade said on a serious note as he unlocked their car.

The snow continued to fall, creating a picturesque view and making her happier than ever that she wasn't getting back on that plane. "That's fine." He'd taken the small carry-on from her, leaving her to cope with the huge bag filled with Christmas goodies.

"It means I'll be doing all the driving."

After another glance at the snowstorm, she was grateful.

"Well?" He looked as though he expected an argument.

"Do you have a driver's license?"

Again a grin cracked the tight line of his mouth, touching his eyes. "Yes."

"Then there shouldn't be any problem."

He paused, looking down at her, and smiled again. "Are you always so witty?"

Shelly chuckled, experiencing a rush of pleasure at her ability to make him smile. "Only when I try to be. Come on, loosen up. It's Christmas."

"I've got a meeting to attend. Just because it happens to fall close to a holiday doesn't make a bit of difference."

"Yeah, but just think, once you're through, you can hurry home and spend the holidays with your family."

"Right."

The jagged edge of his clipped reply was revealing. She wondered if he had a family.

As they deposited their luggage in the trunk of the rented Taurus, she had the opportunity to study him. The proud, withdrawn look revealed little of his thoughts; there was an air of independence about him. Even after their minimal conversation, she realized that he possessed a keen and agile mind. He was a man of contrasts—pensive yet decisive, his highly organized façade covering his sense of humor.

The young man at the rental desk had given Slade a map of the city and highlighted the route to the nearest freeway entrance ramp, apologizing for the fact that the car's built-in GPS was broken. Since that explained why the car was available at all, neither she nor Slade had objected.

Now Slade pulled the map from his pocket and handed it to her. "Are you ready?"

"Forward, James," she teased, climbing into the passenger seat and rubbing her bare hands together to generate some warmth. When she'd left San Francisco that morning, she hadn't dressed for snow.

With a turn of the key, Slade started the engine and adjusted the heater. "You'll be warm in a minute."

Shelly nodded, burying her hands in her jacket pockets. "You know, if it gets much colder, we might get snow before we reach Seattle."

"Very funny," he muttered dryly, snapping his seat belt into place. Hands gripping the wheel, he hesitated. "Do you want to call your husband before we hit the road and I need you to navigate?"

"I'm visiting my dad," she corrected him. "I'm not married. And no. If I told him what we're doing, he'd only worry."

Slade shifted gears, and they pulled onto the road.

"Do you want to contact…your wife?"

"I'm not married, either."

"Oh." She prayed that her tone wouldn't reveal her satisfaction at the information. It wasn't often that she found herself so fascinated by a man. The crazy part was that she wasn't entirely sure she liked him, but he certainly attracted her.

"I'm engaged," he added.

"Oh." She swallowed convulsively. So much for that. "When's the wedding?"

The windshield wipers hummed ominously. "In approximately two years."

Shelly nearly choked in an effort to hide her shock.

"Margaret and I have professional and financial goals we hope to accomplish before we marry." He drove with his back suddenly stiff, his expression turning chilly. "Margaret feels we should save fifty thousand dollars before we think about marriage, and I agree. We both feel that having a firm financial foundation is the basis for a lasting marriage."

"I can't imagine waiting two years to marry the man I loved."

"But then you're entirely different from Margaret."

As far as Shelly was concerned, that was the nicest thing anyone had said to her all day. "We do agree on one thing, though. I feel a marriage should last forever." But for her, love had to be more spontaneous and far less calculated. "My parents had a marvelous marriage," she said, filling the silence. "I only hope that when I marry, my own will be as happy." She went on to explain that her parents had met one Christmas and been married less than two months later on Valentine's Day. Their marriage, she told him with a sad smile, had been blessed with love and happiness for nearly twenty-seven years before her mother's unexpected death. It took great restraint for her not to mention that her parents had barely had twenty dollars between them when they'd taken their vows. At the time her father had been studying veterinary medicine, with only two years of vet school behind him. They'd managed without a huge bank balance.

From the tight lines around his mouth, she could tell that Slade found the whole story trite.

"Is your sweet tale of romance supposed to touch my heart?"

Stung, she straightened and looked out the side window at the snow-covered trees that lined the side of Interstate 5. "No. I was just trying to find out if you had one."

"Karate mouth strikes again," he mumbled.

"Karate mouth?" She was too stunned by his unexpected display of wit to do anything more than repeat his statement.

"You have the quickest comeback of anyone I know." But he said it with a small smile, and admiration flashed unchecked in his gaze before he turned his attention back to the freeway.

Shelly was interested in learning more about Margaret, so she steered the conversation away from herself. "I imagine you're anxious to get back to spend Christmas with Margaret." She regretted her earlier judgmental attitude toward Slade. He had good reason for wanting his meeting over with.

"Margaret's visiting an aunt in Arizona over the holidays. She left a couple of days ago."

"So you won't be together." The more she heard about his fiancée, the more curious she was about a woman who actively wanted to wait two years for marriage. "Did she give you your Christmas gift before she left?" The type of gift one gave was always telling, she felt.

He hesitated. "Margaret and I agreed to forgo giving gifts this year."

"No presents? That's terrible."

"I told you. We have financial goals," he growled irritably. "Wasting money on trivialities simply deters us from our two-year plan. Christmas gifts aren't going to advance our desires."

At the moment Shelly sincerely doubted that good ol' Margaret and Slade *had* "desires."

"I bet she's just saying she doesn't want a gift," Shelly said. "She's probably secretly hoping you'll break down and buy her something. It doesn't have to be something big. Any woman appreciates roses."

Slade gave an expressive shrug. "I thought flowers would be a nice touch myself, but she claims they make her sneeze. Besides, roses at Christmas are ridiculously expensive. A total waste of money, when you think about it."

"Total," Shelly echoed under her breath. She was beginning to get a clearer and far less flattering picture of Slade Garner and his insanely-practical fiancée.

"Did you say something?" A hint of challenge echoed in his cool tone.

"Not really." Leaning forward, she fiddled with the radio, trying to find some decent music. "What's Margaret do, by the way?"

"She's a systems analyst."

Shelly arched both eyebrows in mute comment. That was exactly the type of occupation she would have expected from a nuts-and-bolts person like Margaret. "What about children?"

"What about them?"

She realized that she was prying, but she couldn't help herself. "Are you planning a family?"

"Of course. We're hoping that Margaret can schedule a leave of absence in eight years."

"Eight years?" She looked at him assessingly. "You'll be nearly thirty!" The exclamation burst from her lips before she could hold it back.

"Thirty-one, actually. Do you disapprove of that, too?"

She swallowed uncomfortably and paid an inordinate amount of attention to the radio, frustrated because she couldn't find a single radio station. "I apologize. I didn't mean to sound so judgmental. It's just that—"

"It's just that you've never been goal oriented."

"But I have," she argued. "I've always wanted to be a court reporter. It's a fascinating job."

"I imagine that you're good at anything you put your mind to."

The unexpected compliment caught her completely off guard. "What a nice thing to say."

"If you put your mind to it, you might figure out why you can't get the radio working."

Her gaze flickered automatically from Slade to the dial. Before she could comment, he reached over and pushed a button. "It's a bit difficult to hear anything when the radio isn't turned on."

"Right." She'd been too preoccupied with asking about Margaret to notice. Color flooded into her cheeks at her own stupidity. Slade flustered her as no man had in a long time. She had the feeling that, in a battle of words, he would parry her barbs as expertly as a professional swordsman.

She found a station playing Christmas carols, and music filled the car. Warm and snug, she leaned back against the headrest and hummed along, gazing at the falling flakes.

"With the snow and all, it really feels like Christmas," she murmured, fearing more questions would destroy the tranquil mood.

"It's caused nothing but problems."

"I suppose, but it's so lovely."

"Of course *you* think it's lovely. You're sitting in a warm chauffeur-driven car, listening to 'Silent Night.'"

"Grumble, grumble, grumble," she tossed back lightly. "Bah, humbug!"

"Bah, humbug," he echoed, and then, to her astonishment, he laughed.

The sound of it was rich and full, and she couldn't stop herself from laughing with him. When the next song was a Bing Crosby Christmas favorite, she sang along. Soon Slade's deep baritone joined her clear soprano in sweet harmony. The lyrics spoke of dreaming, and her mind conjured up her own longings. Despite his rough edges, she found herself comfortable with this man, when she'd expected to find a dozen reasons to dislike him. Instead, she'd discovered that she was attracted to someone who was engaged to another woman. A man whose responses showed he was intensely loyal. That was the usual way her life ran. She was attracted to a man she couldn't have, experiencing feelings that would lead nowhere. She wasn't even entirely sure that her insights about him were on base. As uncharitable as it sounded, she might be overestimating his appeal simply because she considered him too good for someone like Margaret.

Disgusted with herself, she closed her eyes and rested her head against the window. The only sounds were the soft melodies playing on the radio and the discordant swish of the windshield wipers. Occasionally a gust of wind would cause the car to veer slightly. She decided to ignore her troublesome feelings and lost herself in thoughts of Christmas.

The next thing she knew, she was being shaken by a gentle hand on her shoulder. "Shelly."

With a start she bolted upright. "What's wrong?"

Slade had pulled over to the shoulder of the freeway. The snow was so thick that she couldn't see two feet in front of her.

"I don't think we can go any further," he announced.

Three

"We can't stay *here*," Shelly insisted, looking at their precarious position beside the road. Snow was whirling in every direction. The ferocity of the storm shocked her as it whipped and howled around them. While she'd slept, the storm had worsened drastically. She found it little short of amazing that Slade had been able to steer the car at all.

"Do you have any other suggestions?" he asked, and breathed out sharply.

He was angry, but his irritation wasn't directed at her. Wearily she lifted the hair from her neck. "No, I guess I don't."

Silence seeped around them as Slade turned off the engine. Gone was the soothing sound of Christmas music, the hum of the engine and the rhythmic swish of the wipers. Together they sat waiting for nature's fury to lessen so they could get going again. Staring out at the surrounding area between bursts of wind and snow, she guessed that they weren't far from Castle Rock and Mount St. Helens.

After ten minutes of uneasiness, she decided to be the first to break the gloom. "Are you hungry?" She stared at the passive, unyielding face beside her as she spoke.

"No."

"I am."

"Have some of that bread." He cocked his head toward the back seat, where she'd stuck the huge loaves of sourdough.

"I couldn't eat Dad's bread. He'd never forgive me."

"He'd never forgive you if you starved to death, either."

Glancing down at her pudgy thighs, Shelly sadly shook her head. "There's no chance of that."

"What makes you say that? You're not fat. In fact, I'd say you were just about perfect."

"Me? Perfect?" A burst of embarrassed laughter slid from her throat. Reaching for her purse, she removed her wallet.

"What are you doing?"

"I'm going to pay you for saying that."

Slade chuckled. "What makes you think you're overweight?"

"You mean aside from the fat all over my body?"

"I'm serious."

She shrugged. "I don't know. I just feel chubby. Since leaving home, I don't get enough exercise. I couldn't very well bring Sampson with me when I moved to San Francisco."

"Sampson?"

"My horse. I used to ride him every day."

"If you've gained any weight, it's in all the right places."

His gaze fell to her lips, and her senses churned in quivering awareness. He stared into her dark eyes and blinked, as if not believing what he saw. For her part, she studied him with open curiosity. His eyes were smoky dark, his face blunt and sensual. His brow was creased, as though he was giving the moment grave consideration. Thick eyebrows arched heavily over his eyes.

Abruptly he pulled his gaze away and leaned forward to start the engine. The accumulated snow on the windshield was brushed aside with a flip of the wiper switch. "Isn't that a McDonald's up ahead?"

Shelly squinted to catch a glimpse of the world-famous golden arches through a momentary break in the storm. "Hey, I think it is."

"The exit can't be far, then."

"Do you think we can make it?"

"I think we'd better," he mumbled.

She understood. The car had become their private cocoon, unexpectedly intimate and far too tempting. Under normal circumstances they wouldn't have given each other more than a passing glance. What was happening now was magical, and far more exhilarating than the real life that seemed very far away right now.

With the wipers beating furiously against the window, Slade inched the car toward the exit, which proved to be less than a half mile away.

Slowly they crawled down the side road that paralleled the freeway. With some difficulty he was able to find a place to park in the restaurant lot. Shelly sighed with relief. This was the worst storm she could remember. Wrapping her coat securely around her, she reached for her purse.

"You ready?" she blurted out, opening her door.

"Anytime."

Hurriedly he joined her, tightly grasping her elbow as they stepped together toward the entrance. Pausing just inside the door to stamp the snow from their shoes, they glanced up to note that several other travelers were stranded there, as well.

They ordered hamburgers and coffee, and sat down by the window.

"How long do you think we'll be here?" she asked, not really expecting an answer. She needed reassurance more than anything. This Christmas holiday hadn't started out on the right foot. But of one thing she was confident: their plane hadn't left Portland yet.

"Your guess is as good as mine."

"I'll say two hours, then," she murmured, taking a bite of her burger.

"Why two hours?"

"I don't know. It sounds reasonable. If I thought it would be longer than that I might start to panic. But, if worse comes to worst, I can think of less desirable places to spend Christmas. At least we won't starve."

He muttered something unintelligible under his breath and continued eating. When he finished, he excused himself and returned to the car for his briefcase.

She bought two more cups of coffee and propped her feet on the seat opposite her. Taking the latest issue of *Mad* from her purse, she was absorbed in the magazine by the time he returned. Her gaze dared him to comment on her reading material. Her love of *Mad* was a long-standing joke between her and her father. He even read each issue himself so he could tease her about the contents. Since moving, she'd fallen behind by several issues and wanted to be prepared when she saw her dad again. She didn't expect Slade to understand her tastes.

He gave her little more than a glance before reclaiming his seat and briskly opening the *Wall Street Journal.*

Their reading choices said a lot about them, she realized. Rarely had two people been less alike. A lump grew in her throat. She liked Slade. He was the type of man she would willingly give up *Mad* for.

An hour later she contentedly set the magazine aside and reached in her purse for the romance novel she kept tucked away. It wasn't often that she was so at ease with a man. She didn't feel the overwhelming urge to keep a conversation going or fill the silence with chatter. They were comfortable together.

Without a word she went to the counter and bought a large order of fries and placed it in the middle of the table. Now and then, her eyes never leaving the printed page, she blindly reached for a fry. Once her groping hand bumped another, and her startled gaze collided with Slade's.

"Sorry," he muttered.

"Don't be. They're for us both."

"They get to be addictive, don't they?"

"Sort of like reading the *Wall Street Journal?*"

"I wondered if you'd comment on that."

She laughed. "I was expecting you to mention *my* choice."

"*Mad* is exactly what I'd expect from you." He said it in such a way that she couldn't possibly be offended.

"At least we agree on one thing."

He raised his thick brows in question.

"The fries."

"Right." Lifting one, he held it out for her.

She leaned toward him and captured the fry in her mouth. The gesture was oddly intimate, and her smile faded as her gaze met his. It was happening again. That heart-pounding, room-fading-away, shallow-breathing syndrome. Obviously this…feeling…had something to do with the weather. Maybe she could blame it on the season of love and goodwill toward all mankind. Apparently she was overly endowed with benevolence this Christmas. Given the sensations she was already experiencing, heaven only knew what would happen if she spied some mistletoe.

Slade raked his hand through his well-groomed hair, mussing it. Quickly he diverted his gaze out the window. "It looks like it might be letting up a little."

"Yes, it does," she agreed without so much as checking the weather. The French fries seemed to demand her full attention.

"I suppose we should think about heading out."

"I suppose." A glance at her watch confirmed that it was well into the afternoon. "I'm sorry about your appointment."

He looked at her blankly for a moment. "Oh, that. I knew when we left that there was little likelihood I'd be able to make it in time today. Luckily I've already made arrangements to meet tomorrow morning."

"It's been an enjoyable break."

"Very," he agreed.

"Do you think we'll have any more problems?"

"We could, but there are enough businesses along

the way that we don't need to worry about getting stranded."

"In other words, we could hit every fast-food spot between here and Seattle."

He responded with a soft chuckle. "Right."

"Well, in that case, bring on the French fries."

By the time they were back on the freeway, Shelly saw that the storm had indeed lessened, though it was far from over. And when the radio issued a weather update that called for more snow, Slade groaned.

"You could always spend Christmas with me and Dad," she offered, broaching the subject carefully. "We'd like to have you. Honest."

He tossed her a disbelieving glare. "You don't mean that."

"Of course I do."

"But I'm a stranger."

"I've shared French fries with you. It's been a long time since I've been that intimate with a man. In fact, it would be best if you didn't mention it to my dad. He might be inclined to reach for his shotgun."

It took a minute for Slade to understand the implication. "A shotgun wedding?"

"I *am* getting on in years. Dad would like to see me married off and producing grandchildren. My brothers have been lax in that department." For the moment she'd forgotten about Margaret. When she remembered, she felt her exhilaration rush out of her with all the force of a deflating balloon. "Don't worry," she was quick to add. "All you need to do is tell Dad about your fiancée and he'll let you off the hook." Somehow she managed to keep her voice cheerful.

"It's a good thing I didn't take a bite of your hamburger."

"Are you kidding? That would have put me directly into your last will and testament."

"I was afraid of that," he said, laughing good-naturedly.

Once again she noticed how rich and deep the sound of his laughter was. It had the most overwhelming effect on her. She discovered that, when he laughed, nothing could keep her spirits down.

Their progress was hampered by the still-swirling snow, and finally their forward movement became little more than a crawl. She didn't mind. They chatted, joked and sang along with the radio. She discovered that she enjoyed his wit. Although a bit dry, under that gruff, serious exterior lay an interesting man with a warm but subtle sense of humor. Given any other set of circumstances, she would have loved to get to know Slade Garner better.

"What'd you buy your dad for Christmas?"

The question came so unexpectedly that it took her a moment to realize that he was speaking to her.

"Are you concerned that I have soup in my bag?"

He scowled, momentarily puzzled. "Ah, to go with the bread. No, I was just curious."

"First I got him a box of his favorite chocolate-covered cherries."

"I should have known it'd be food."

"That's not all," she countered a bit testily. "We exchange the normal father-daughter gifts. You know. Things like stirrup irons, bridles and horse blankets. That's what Dad got me last Christmas."

He cleared his throat. "Just the usual items every father buys his daughter. What about this year?"

"Since Sampson and I aren't even living in the same state, I imagine he'll resort to the old standbys, like towels and sheets for my apartment." She was half hoping that, at the mention of her place in San Francisco, Slade would turn the conversation in that direction and ask her something about herself. He didn't, and she was hard-pressed to hide her disappointment.

"What about you?" she asked into the silence.

"Me?" His gaze flickered momentarily from the road.

"What did you buy your family?"

He gave her an uncomfortable look. "Well, actually, I didn't. It seemed simpler this year just to send them money."

"I see." She knew that was perfectly acceptable in some cases, but it sounded so cold and uncaring for a son to resort to a gift of money. Undoubtedly, once he and Margaret were married, they would shop together for something appropriate.

"I wish now that I hadn't. I think my parents would have enjoyed fresh sourdough bread and chocolate-covered cherries." He hesitated for an instant. "I'm not as confident about the stirrups and horse blankets, however."

As they neared Tacoma, Shelly was surprised at how heavy the traffic had gotten. The closer they came to Maple Valley, the more anxious she became.

"My exit isn't far," she told him, growing impatient. "Good grief, you would expect people to stay off the roads in weather like this."

"Exactly," he agreed without hesitation.

It wasn't until she heard the soft timbre of his chuckle that she realized he was teasing her. "You know what I mean."

He didn't answer as he edged the car ahead. Already the night was pitch-dark. Snow continued to fall with astonishing vigor. She wondered when it would stop. She was concerned about Slade driving alone from Maple Valley to Seattle.

"Maybe I should phone my dad," she suggested, momentarily forgetting that her cell was dead.

"Why?"

"That way he could come and pick me up, and you wouldn't—"

"I agreed to deliver you to Maple Creek, and I intend to do exactly that."

"Maple Valley," she corrected.

"Wherever. A deal is a deal. Right?"

A rush of pleasure assaulted her vulnerable heart. Slade wasn't any more eager to put an end to their adventure than she was.

"It's the next exit," she informed him, giving him the directions to the ten-acre spread on the outskirts of town. Taking out a pen and paper, she drew a detailed map for him so he wouldn't get lost on the return trip to the freeway. Under the cover of night, there was little to distinguish one road from another, and he could easily become confused.

Sitting straighter, she excitedly pointed to her left. "Turn here."

Apparently in preparation for his departure for the

airport, her father had plowed the snow from the long driveway.

The headlights cut into the night, revealing the long, sprawling ranch house that had been Shelly's childhood home. A tall figure appeared at the window, and almost immediately the front door opened.

Slade had barely put the car into Park when Shelly threw open the door.

"Shortcake!"

"Dad." Disregarding the snow and wind, she flew into his arms.

"You little… Why didn't you tell me you were coming by car?"

"We rented it." Remembering Slade, she looped an arm around her father's waist. "Dad, I'd like you to meet Slade Garner."

Her father stepped forward. "Don Griffin," he said, and extended his hand. "So you're Shelly's surprise. Welcome to our home. I'd say it was about time my daughter brought a young man home for her father to meet."

Four

Slade extended his hand to Shelly's father and grinned. "I believe you've got me confused with sourdough bread."

"Sourdough bread?"

"Dad, Slade and I met this morning on the plane." Shelly's cheeks brightened in a self-conscious pink flush.

"When it looked like the flight wasn't going to make it to Seattle, we rented the car," Slade explained further.

A curious glint darkened Don Griffin's deep blue eyes as he glanced briefly from his daughter to Slade and ran a hand through is thick thatch of dark hair. "It's a good thing you did. The last time I phoned the airline, I learned your plane still hadn't left Portland."

"Slade has an important meeting first thing tomorrow." Her eyes were telling him that she was ready to make the break. She could say goodbye and wish him every happiness. Their time together had been too short for any regrets. Hadn't it?

"There's no need for us to stand out here in the cold

discussing your itinerary," her father inserted and motioned toward the warm lights of the house.

Slade hesitated. "I should be getting into Seattle."

"Come in for some coffee first," her father invited.

"Shelly?" Slade sought her approval. The unasked question in his eyes pinned her gaze.

"I wish you would." *Fool!* her mind cried out. It would be better to sever the relationship quickly, sharply and without delay, before he had the opportunity to touch her tender heart. But her heart refused to listen to her mind.

"For that matter," her father continued, seemingly oblivious to the undercurrents between Slade and Shelly, "stay for dinner."

"I couldn't. Really." Slade made a show of glancing at his wristwatch.

"We insist," Shelly said quickly. "After hauling this bread from here to kingdom come, the least I can offer you is a share of it."

To her astonishment Slade grinned, his dark eyes crinkling at the edges. The smile was both spontaneous and personal—a reminder of the joke between them. "All right," he agreed.

"That settles it, then." Don grinned and moved to the rear of the car while Slade extracted Shelly's suitcase and the huge tote bag. "What's all this?"

"Presents," she said.

"For me?"

"Well, who else would I be bringing gifts for?"

"A man. It's time you started thinking about a husband."

"Dad!" If her cheeks had been bright pink previously, now the color deepened into fire-engine red. In order to minimize further embarrassment, she returned to the car and rescued the bread. Her father carried the gifts inside, while Slade brought up the rear with her carry-on.

The house contained all the warmth and welcome that she always associated with home. She paused in just inside the open doorway, her gaze skimming over the crackling fireplace and the large array of family photos that decorated the mantel. Ol' Dan, their thirteen-year-old Labrador, slept on the braided rug and did little more than raise his head when Don and Slade entered the house. But on seeing Shelly, the elderly dog got slowly to his feet and with difficulty ambled to her side, tail wagging. She set the bread aside and fell to her knees.

"How's my loyal mangy mutt?" she asked, affectionately ruffling his ears and hugging him. "You keeping Dad company these days?"

"Yeah, but he's doing a poor job of it," her father complained loudly. "Ol' Dan still can't play a decent game of chess."

"Do *you* play?" Slade asked her father as his gaze scanned the living room for a board.

"Forty years or more. What about you?"

"Now and again."

"Could I interest you in a match?"

Slade was already unbuttoning his overcoat. "I'd enjoy that, sir."

"Call me Don, everyone does."

"Right, Don."

Within a minute the chessboard was out and set up on the coffee table, while the two men sat opposite each other on matching ottomans.

Suspecting that the contest could last a while, she checked the prime rib roasting in the oven and added large potatoes, wrapping each in aluminum foil. The refrigerator contained a fresh green salad and her favorite cherry pie from the local bakery. There were also some carrots in the vegetable drawer; she snatched a couple and put them in her pocket.

After grabbing her denim jacket with its thick wool padding from the peg on the back porch and slipping into her cowboy boots, she made her way out to the barn.

The scent of hay and horses greeted her, and she paused, taking in the rich, earthy odors. "Howdy, Sampson," she said, greeting her favorite horse first.

The sleek black horse whinnied a welcome as she approached the stall, then accepted the proffered carrot without pause.

"Have you missed me, boy?"

Pokey, an Appaloosa mare, stuck her head out of her stall, seeking a treat, too. Laughing, Shelly pulled another carrot from her pocket. Midnight, her father's horse and Sampson's sire, stamped his foot, and she made her way down to his stall.

After stroking his sleek neck, she took out the brushes and returned to Sampson. "I suppose Dad's letting you get fat and lazy now that I'm not around to work you." She glided a brush down his muscled flank. "All right, I'll admit it. Living in San Francisco has made *me* fat and lazy, too. I haven't gained any weight, but I feel flabby. I suppose I could take up jogging, but it's foggy and rainy and—"

"Shelly?"

Slade was standing just inside the barn door, looking a bit uneasy. "Do you always carry on conversations with your horse?"

"Sure. I've talked out many a frustration with Sampson. Isn't that right, boy?"

Slade gave a startled blink when the horse answered with a loud snort and a toss of his head, as if agreeing with her.

"Come in and meet my favorite male," she invited, opening the stall door.

Hands buried deep in his pockets, Slade shook his head. "No, thanks."

"You don't like horses?"

"Not exactly."

Having lived all her life around animals, she had trouble understanding his reticence. "Why not?"

"The last time I was this close to a horse was when I was ten and at summer camp."

"Sampson won't bite you."

"It's not his mouth I'm worried about."

"He's harmless."

"So is flying."

Surprised, Shelly dropped her hand from Sampson's hindquarters.

Slade strolled over to the stall, a grin lifting the edges of his mouth. "From the look on your face when we landed, one would assume that your will alone was holding up the plane."

"It was!"

He chuckled and tentatively reached out to rub Sampson's ebony forehead.

She went back to grooming the horse. "Is your chess match over already?"

"I should have warned your father. I was on the university chess team."

Now it was her turn to look amused. She paused in midstroke. "Did you wound Dad's ego?"

"I might have, but he's regrouping now. I came out here because I wanted to have a look at the famous Sampson before I headed for Seattle."

"Sampson's honored to make your acquaintance." *I am, too,* her heart echoed.

Slade took a step in retreat. "I guess I'll get back to the house. No doubt your dad's got the board set for a rematch."

"Be gentle with him," she called out, trying to hide a saucy grin. Her father wasn't an amateur when it came to the game. He'd been a member of the local chess club for years, and she wondered just what his strategy was tonight. Donald Griffin seldom lost at any game.

An hour later she stamped the snow from her boots and entered the kitchen through the back door. She shed the thick coat and hung it back on its peg, then went to check the roast and the baked potatoes. Both were done to perfection, and she turned off the oven.

Seeing that her father and Slade were absorbed in their game, she stepped up behind her father and slipped her arms around his neck, resting her chin on the top of his head.

"Dinner's ready," she murmured, not wanting to break his concentration.

"In a minute," he grumbled.

Slade moved his bishop, leaving his hand on the piece

for a couple of seconds. Seemingly pleased, he released the piece and relaxed. As though sensing her gaze on him, he lifted his incredibly dark eyes, which locked with hers. They stared at each other for long, uninterrupted moments. She felt her heart lurch as she basked in the warmth of his look. She wanted to hold on to this moment, forget San Francisco, Margaret, the snowstorm. It felt paramount that she capture this magic with both hands and hold on to it forever.

"It's your move." Don's words cut into the stillness.

"Pardon?" Abruptly Slade dropped his eyes to the chessboard.

"It's your move," her father repeated.

"Of course." Slade studied the board and moved a pawn.

Don scowled. "I hadn't counted on your doing that."

"Hey, you two, didn't you hear me? Dinner's ready." She was shocked at how normal and unaffected her voice sounded.

Slade got to his feet. "Shall we consider it a draw, then?"

"I guess we better, but I demand a rematch someday."

Shelly's throat constricted. There wouldn't be another day for her and Slade. They were two strangers who had briefly touched each other's lives. Ships passing in the night and all the other clichés she had never expected would happen to her. But somehow she had the feeling that she would never be the same again. Surely she wouldn't be so swift to judge another man. Slade had taught her that, and she would always be grateful.

The three of them chatted easily during dinner, and Shelly learned things about Slade that she hadn't thought to ask. He was a salesman, specializing in intricate software programs, and was meeting with a Seattle-based company, hoping to agree on the first steps of a possible distribution agreement. It was little wonder that he'd considered his meeting so important. It was. And although he hadn't mentioned it specifically, she was acutely aware that if his meeting was successful, he would be that much closer to achieving his financial and professional goals—and that much closer to marrying coldly practical Margaret.

Shelly was clearing the dishes from the table when Slade set his napkin aside and rose. "I don't remember when I've enjoyed a meal more, especially the sourdough bread."

"A man gets the feel of a kitchen sooner or later," Don said with a crusty chuckle. "It took me a whole year to learn how to turn on the oven."

"That's the truth," she added, sharing a smile with her father. "He thought it was easier to use the microwave. The problem was, he couldn't quite get the hang of that, either. Everything came out the texture of beef jerky."

"We survived," her father grumbled, affectionately looping an arm around Shelly's waist. The first eighteen months after her mother's death had been the most difficult for the family, but life went on, and almost against their wills they'd adjusted.

Slade paused in the living room to stare out the window. "I can't remember it ever snowing this much in the Pacific Northwest."

"Rarely," Don agreed. "It's been three winters since we've had any snow at all. I'll admit this is a pleasant surprise."

"How long will it be before the snowplows are out?"

"Snow*plow*, you mean?" Don said with a gruff laugh. "King County is lucky if they have more than a handful. There isn't that much call for them." He walked to the picture window and held back the draperies with one hand. "You know, it might not be a bad idea if you stayed the night and left first thing in the morning."

Slade hesitated. "I don't know. If I miss this meeting, it'll mean having to wait over the Christmas holiday to reschedule."

"You'll have a better chance of making it safely to Seattle in the morning. The roads tonight are going to be treacherous."

Slade slowly expelled his breath. "I have the distinct feeling you may be right. Without any streetlights, Lord knows where I'd end up."

"I believe you'd be wise to delay your drive. Besides, that will give us time for another game."

Slade's gaze shifted to Shelly and softened. "Right," he concurred.

The two men were up until well past midnight, engrossed in one chess match after another. After watching a few games, Shelly decided to say good-night and go to bed.

Half an hour later Shelly lay in her bed in her darkened room, dreading the approach of morning. In some ways it would have been easier if Slade had left immediately after dropping her off. And in other ways it was far better that he'd stayed.

She fell asleep with the bright red numbers of the clock insidiously counting down the minutes to six o'clock when Slade would be leaving. There was nothing she could do to hold back time.

Before even being aware that she'd fallen asleep, she was startled into wakefulness by the discordant drone of the alarm.

Tossing aside the covers, she automatically reached for the thick housecoat she kept at her father's. Pausing only long enough to run a comb through her hair and brush her teeth, she rushed into the living room.

Slade was already dressed and holding a cup of coffee. "I guess it's time to say goodbye."

Five

Shelly ran a hand over her weary eyes and blinked. "You're right," she murmured, forcing a smile. "The time has come."

"Shelly—"

"Listen—"

"You first," Slade said, and gestured toward her with his open hand.

Dropping her gaze, she shrugged one shoulder. "It's nothing, really. I just wanted to wish you and Margaret every happiness."

His gaze softened, and she wondered if he knew what it had cost her to murmur those few words. She did wish him happiness, but she was convinced that he wouldn't find it with a cold fish like Margaret. Forcefully she directed her gaze across the room. For all her good intentions, she was doing it again—judging someone else. And she hadn't even met Margaret.

When she turned back his eyes delved into hers. "Thank you."

"You wanted to say something?" she prompted softly.

He hesitated. "Be happy, Shelly."

A knot formed in her throat as she nodded. He was telling her goodbye, *really* goodbye. He wouldn't see her again, because it would be too dangerous for them both. Their lives were already plotted, their courses set. And whatever it was that they'd shared so briefly, it wasn't meant to be anything more than a passing fancy.

The front door opened and her father entered, brushing the snow from his pant legs. A burst of frigid air accompanied him, and she shivered.

"As far as I can see you shouldn't have a problem," Don said to Slade. "We've got maybe seven to ten inches of snow, but there're plenty of tire tracks on the road. Just follow those."

Unable to listen anymore, she headed into the kitchen and poured herself a cup of hot black coffee. Clasping the mug with both hands, she braced her hip against the counter and closed her eyes. Whatever Slade and her father were saying to each other didn't matter to her. She was safer in the kitchen, where she wouldn't be forced to watch him leave. The only sound that registered in her mind was the clicking of the front door opening and closing.

Slade had left. He was gone from the house. Gone from her life. Gone forever. She refused to mope. He'd touched her heart, and she should be glad. For a long time she'd begun to wonder if there was something physically wrong with her because she couldn't respond to a man. Slade hadn't so much as kissed her, but she'd experienced a closeness to him that she hadn't felt with all the men she'd dated in San Francisco. Without even realizing it, he had granted her the priceless gift of expectancy. If he was capable of stirring her restless heart, then so would another.

Humming softly, she set a skillet on the burner and laid thick slices of bacon across it. This was the day before Christmas, and it promised to be a full one. She couldn't be sad or filled with regrets when she was surrounded by everything she held dear.

The door opened again, and her father called cheerfully, "Well, he's off."

"Good." She hoped her tone didn't give away her feelings.

"He's an interesting man. I wouldn't mind having someone like him for a son-in-law." He entered the kitchen and reached for the coffeepot.

"He's engaged."

He sighed, and there was a hint of censure in his voice when he spoke. "That figures. The good ones always seem to be spoken for."

"It doesn't matter. We're about as different as any two people can be."

"That's not always bad, you know. Couples often complement each other that way. Your mother was the shy one, whereas I was far more outgoing. Our lives would have been havoc if we'd had identical personalities."

Silently Shelly agreed, but to admit as much would reveal more than she wanted to. "I suppose," she murmured softly, and turned over the sizzling slices of bacon.

A few minutes later she was sliding the eggs easily from the hot grease onto plates when there was a loud pounding on the front door.

Her gaze rose instantly and met her father's.

"Slade," they said simultaneously.

Her father rushed to answer the door, and a breathless Slade stumbled into the house. She turned off the stove and hurried out to meet him.

"Are you all right?" Her voice was laced with concern. Heart pounding, she looked him over for any obvious signs of injury.

"I'm fine. I'm just out of breath. That was quite a hike."

"How far'd you get?" Don asked.

"A mile at the most. I was gathering speed to make it to the top of an incline when the wheels skidded on a patch of ice. The car, unfortunately, is in a ditch."

"What about your meeting?" Now that she'd determined that he was unscathed, her first concern was the appointment that he considered so important to his future.

"I don't know."

"Dad and I could take you into town," she offered.

"No. If I couldn't make it, you won't be able to, either."

"But you said this meeting is vital."

"It's not important enough to risk your getting hurt."

"Not to mention my truck has been acting up, so I took it in for servicing," her father said, then smiled. "But there's always the tractor."

"Dad! You'll be lucky if the old engine so much as coughs. You haven't used that antique in years." As far as she knew, it was collecting dust in the back of the barn.

"It's worth a try," her father argued, looking to Slade. "At least we can pull your car out of the ditch."

"I'll contact the county road department and find

out how long it'll be before the plows come this way," Shelly said. She didn't hold much hope for the tractor, but if she could convince the county how important it was to clear the roads near their place, Slade might be able to make his meeting somehow.

Two hours later, Shelly was dressed in dark cords and a thick cable-knit sweater the color of winter wheat as she paced the living room carpet. Every few minutes she paused to glance out the large front window for signs of either her father or Slade. Through some miracle they'd managed to fire up the tractor, but how much they could accomplish with the old machine was pure conjecture. If they were able to rescue Slade's car from the ditch, then there was always the possibility of towing it up the incline so he could try again to make it into the city.

The sound of a car pulling into the driveway captured her attention, and she rushed onto the front porch just as Slade was easing the Taurus to a stop. He climbed out of the vehicle.

"I called the county. The road crew will try to make it out this way before nightfall," she told him, rubbing her palms together to ward off the chill. "I'm sorry, Slade, it's the best they could do."

"Don't worry." His gaze caressed her. "It's not your fault."

"But I can't help feeling that it is," she said, following him into the house. "I was the one who insisted you bring me here."

"Shelly." He cupped her shoulder with a warm hand. "Stop blaming yourself. I'll contact Walt Bauer, the man

I was planning to see. He'll understand. It's possible he didn't make it to the office, either."

Granting him the privacy he needed to make his call, she donned her coat and walked to the end of the driveway to see if she could locate her father. Only a couple of minutes passed before she saw him proudly steering the tractor, his back and head held regally, like a benevolent king surveying all he owned.

Laughing, she waved.

He pulled to a stop alongside her. "What's so funny?"

"I can't believe you, sitting on top of a 1948 Harvester like you own the world."

"Don't be silly, serf," he teased.

"We've got a bit of a problem, you know." She realized she shouldn't feel guilty about Slade, but she did.

"If you mean Slade, we talked about this unexpected delay. It might not be as bad as it looks. To his way of thinking, it's best not to appear overeager with this business anyway. A delay may be just the thing to get the other company thinking."

It would be just like Slade to say something like that, she thought. "Maybe."

"At any rate, it won't do him any good to stew about it now. He's stuck with us until the snowplows clear the roads. No one's going to make it to the freeway unless they have a four-wheel drive. It's impossible out there."

"But, Dad, I feel terrible."

"Don't. If Slade's not concerned, then you shouldn't be. Besides, I've got a job for you two."

Shelly didn't like the sound of that. "What?"

"We aren't going to be able to go out and buy a Christmas tree."

She hadn't thought of that. "We'll survive without one." But Christmas wouldn't be the same.

"There's no need to. Not when we've got a good ten acres of fir and pine. I want the two of you to go out and chop one down like we used to do in the good old days."

It didn't take much to realize her father's game. He was looking for excuses to get her together with Slade.

"What's this, an extra Christmas present?" she teased.

"Nonsense. Being out in the cold would only irritate my rheumatism."

"What rheumatism?"

"The one in my old bones."

She hesitated. "What did Slade have to say about this?"

"He's agreeable."

"He is?"

"Think about it, Shortcake. He's stuck here. He wants to make the best of the situation."

It wasn't until they were back at the house and Slade had changed into borrowed jeans and a flannel shirt, along with a pair of heavy boots, that she truly believed he'd fallen in with her father's scheme.

"You don't have to do this, you know," she told him on the way to the barn.

"Did you think I was going to let you traipse into the woods alone?"

"I could."

"No doubt, but there isn't any reason why you *should*. Not when I'm here."

She brought out the old sled from a storage room in the rear of the barn, wiping away the thin layer of dust with her gloves.

He located a saw, and she eyed him warily.

"What's wrong now?"

"The saw."

"What's the matter with it?" He tested the sharpness by carefully running his thumb over the jagged teeth and raised questioning eyes to her.

"Nothing. If we use that rusty old thing, we shouldn't have any trouble bringing home a good-sized rhododendron."

"I wasn't planning to chop down a California redwood."

"But I want something a bit larger than a poinsettia." She grabbed an axe and headed for the door.

He paused, then followed her out of the barn. "Are you always this difficult to get along with?"

Dragging the sled along behind her in the snow, she turned and said, "There's nothing wrong with me. It's you."

"Right," he growled.

Shelly realized that she was acting like a shrew, but her behavior was a defense mechanism against the attraction she felt for Slade. If he was irritated with her, it would be easier for her to control her own feelings for him.

"If my presence is such an annoyance to you, I can walk into town."

"Don't be silly."

"She crabs at me about cutting down rhododendrons and *I'm* silly?" He appeared to be speaking to the sky.

Plowing through the snow, Shelly refused to look back. She started determinedly up a small incline toward the woods. "I just want you to know I can do this on my own."

He laid his hand on her shoulder, stopping her in her tracks. "Shelly, listen to me, would you?"

She hesitated, her gaze falling on the long line of trees ahead. "What now?"

"I like the prospect of finding a Christmas tree with you, but if you find my company so unpleasant, I'll go back to the house."

"That's not it," she murmured, feeling ridiculous. "I have fun when I'm with you."

"Then why are we arguing?"

Against her will she smiled. "I don't know," she admitted.

"Friends?" He offered her his gloved hand.

She clasped it in her own and nodded wordlessly at him.

"Now that we've got that out of the way, just how big a tree were you thinking of?"

"*Big.*"

"Obviously. But remember, it's got to fit inside the house, so that sixty-foot fir straight ahead is out."

"But the top six feet isn't," she teased.

Chuckling, Slade draped his arm across her shoulder. "Yes, it is."

They were still within sight of the house. "Don't worry. I don't want to cut down something obvious."

"How do you mean?"

"In years to come, I don't want to look out the back window and see a hole in the landscape."

"Don't be ridiculous. You've got a whole forest back here."

"I want to go a bit deeper into the woods."

"Listen, Shortcake, I'm not Lewis and Clark."

Shelly paused. "What did you call me?"

"Shortcake. It fits."

"How's that?"

His gaze roamed over her, his eyes narrowing as he studied her full mouth. It took every ounce of control, but she managed not to moisten her lips. A tingling sensation attacked her stomach, and she lowered her gaze. The hesitation lasted no longer than a heartbeat.

His breath hissed through his teeth before he asked, "How about this tree?" He pointed to a small fir that barely reached his waist.

She couldn't keep from laughing. "It should be illegal to cut down anything that small."

"Do you have a better suggestion?"

"Yes."

"What?"

"That tree over there." She marched ahead, pointing out a seven-foot pine.

"You're being ridiculous. We wouldn't be able to get that one through the front door."

"Of course we'd need to trim it."

"Like in half," he mocked.

She refused to be dissuaded. "Don't be a spoilsport."

"Forget it. This tree would be a nice compromise." He indicated another small tree that was only slightly bigger than the first one he'd chosen.

Without hesitating, she reached down and packed a thick ball of snow. "I'm not willing to compromise my beliefs."

He turned to her, exasperation written all over his

features, and she let him have it with the snowball. The accuracy of her toss astonished her, and she cried out with a mixture of surprise and delight when the snowball slammed against his chest, spraying snow in his face.

His reaction was so speedy that she had no time to run before he was only inches away. "Slade, I'm sorry," she said, taking a giant step backward. "I don't know what came over me. I didn't mean to hit you. Actually, I was aiming at that bush behind you. Honest."

For every step she retreated, he advanced, packing a snowball between his gloved hands.

"Slade, you wouldn't," she implored him, arms wide in surrender.

"Yes, I would."

"No!" she cried, and turned, running for all she was worth. He overtook her almost immediately, grabbing her shoulder and turning her to face him. She stumbled, and they went crashing together to the snow-covered ground.

His heavy body pressed her deeper into the snow. "Are you all right?" he asked urgently, fear and concern evident in the tone of his voice as he tenderly pushed the hair from her face.

"Yes," she murmured, breathless. But her lack of air couldn't be attributed to the fall. Having Slade this close, his warm breath fanning her face, was responsible for that. Even through their thick coats she could feel the pounding rhythm of his heart echoing hers.

"Shelly." He ground out her name like a man driven to the brink of insanity. Slowly he slanted his mouth over hers, claiming her lips in a kiss that rocked the very core of her being. In seconds they were both panting and nearly breathless.

Her arms locked around his neck, and she arched against him, wanting the kiss to go on and on.

"Shelly…" he said again as his hands closed around her wrists, pulling free of her embrace. He sat up with his back to her. All she could see was the uneven rise and fall of his shoulders as he dragged in air.

"Don't worry," she breathed in a voice so weak that it trembled. "I won't tell Margaret."

Six

"That shouldn't have happened," Slade said at last.

"I suppose you want an apology," Shelly responded, standing and brushing the snow from her pants. In spite of her efforts to appear normal, her hands trembled and her pulse continued to hammer away madly. From the beginning she'd known that his kiss would have this effect on her, and she cursed her traitorous heart.

He stared, clearly shocked that she would suggest such a thing. "*I* should be the one to apologize to *you*."

"Why? Because you kissed me?"

"And because I'm engaged."

"I know." Her voice rose several decibels. "What's in a kiss, anyway? It wasn't a big deal. Right?" *Liar,* her heart accused, continuing to beat erratically. It had been the sweetest, most wonderful kiss of her life. One that would haunt her forever.

"It won't happen again," he said without looking at her. He rose and held himself stiffly, staying a good two feet away from her. His facade slipped tightly into place, locking his expression right before her eyes. She was reminded of the man she'd first seen on the plane—that polished, impeccable businessman who looked at the world with undisguised indifference.

"As I said, it wasn't a big deal."

"Right," he answered. Her dismissive attitude toward his kiss didn't appear to please him. He stalked in the direction of the trees and stopped at the one he'd offered as a compromise. Without soliciting her opinion, he began sawing away at its narrow trunk.

Within minutes the tree toppled to the ground, stirring up the snow. She walked over, prepared to help him load the small fir onto the sled, but he wouldn't let her.

"I'll do it," he muttered gruffly.

Offended, she folded her arms and stepped back, feeling awkward. She knew she would feel better if they could discuss the kiss openly and honestly.

"I knew it was going to happen." She'd been wanting him to kiss her all morning, in fact.

"What?" he barked, heading in the direction of the house, tugging the sled and Christmas tree behind him.

"The kiss," she called after him. "And if I was honest, I'd also admit that I wanted it to happen. I was even hoping it would."

"If you don't mind, I'd rather not talk about it."

He was making her angrier every time he opened his mouth. "I said *if* I was being honest, but since neither of us is, then apparently you're right to suggest we drop the issue entirely."

This time he ignored her, taking long strides and forcing her into a clumsy jog behind him. The north wind whipped her scarf across her mouth, and she tucked it more securely around her neck. Then she turned and walked backward, so the bitter wind stopped buffeting her face.

Unexpectedly her boot hit a small rock hidden under the snow, and she momentarily lost her balance. Flinging her arms out in an effort to catch herself, she went tumbling down the hill, somersaulting head over heels until she lay spread-eagled at the base of the slope.

Slade raced after her, falling to his knees at her side, his eyes clouded with emotion. "Do you have to make a game out of everything?"

What was he talking about? She'd nearly killed herself, and he was accusing her of acrobatics in the snow. She struggled to give him a sassy comeback, but the wind had been knocked from her lungs and she discovered that she couldn't speak.

"Are you all right?" He looked genuinely concerned.

"I don't know," she whispered tightly. Getting the appropriate amount of oxygen to her lungs seemed to require all her energy.

"Don't move."

"I couldn't if I wanted to."

"Where does it hurt?"

"'Where doesn't it?' would be a more fitting question." Then, giving the lie to her previous answer, she levered herself up on one elbow and wiggled her legs. "I do this now and then so I can appreciate how good it feels to breathe," she muttered sarcastically.

"I said don't move," Slade barked. "You could've seriously injured something."

"I did," she admitted. "My pride." She got slowly to her feet, then bowed mockingly before him and said,

"Stay tuned for my next trick when I'll single-handedly leap tall buildings and alter the course of the mighty Columbia River."

"You're not funny."

"There goes my career in comedy, then."

"Here." He tucked a hand under her elbow. "Let me help you back to the house."

"This may come as a shock to you, but I'm perfectly capable of walking on my own."

"Nothing you do anymore could shock me."

"That sounds amazingly like a challenge."

His indifference visibly melted away as he stared down at her with warm, vulnerable eyes. "Trust me, it isn't." He claimed her hand, lacing his fingers with hers. "Come on, your father's probably getting worried."

Shelly sincerely doubted it. What Slade was really saying was that things would be safer for them both back at the house. Temptation could more easily be kept at bay with someone else present.

He let go of her hand and placed his palm at the small of her back, and they continued their short sojourn across the snowy landscape.

The house looked amazingly still and dark as they approached. Only a whisper of smoke drifted into the clear sky from the chimney, as though the fire had been allowed to die. She had expected to hear Andy Williams crooning from the stereo and perhaps smell the lingering scent of freshly popped popcorn.

Instead, they were greeted by an empty, almost eerie silence.

While Slade leaned the tree against the side of the house, she ventured inside. A note propped against the sugar bowl in the middle of the kitchen table commanded her attention. She walked into the room and picked it up.

Sick horse at the Adlers' place. Ted W came for me and will bring me home. Call if you need me.
Love,
Dad.

She swallowed tightly, clenching the paper in her hand as the back door shut.

"Dad got called out to a neighbor's. Sick horse," she announced without turning around. "Would you like a cup of coffee? The pot's full, although it doesn't look too fresh. Dad must have put it on before he left. He knew how cold we'd be when we got back." She realized she was babbling and immediately stopped. Without waiting for his response, she reached for two mugs.

"Coffee sounds fine." His voice was heavy with dread. The same dread she felt pressing against her heart. Her father was the buffer they needed, and now he was gone.

She heard Slade drag out a kitchen chair, and she placed the mug in front of him. Her thick lashes fanned downward as she avoided his gaze.

Reluctantly she pulled out the chair opposite his and joined him at the table. "I suppose we should put up the tree."

He paused, then said, "We could."

From all the enthusiasm he displayed, they could have been discussing income taxes. Her heart ached, and she felt embarrassed for having made the suggestion. No doubt Margaret had her tree flocked and decorated without ever involving Slade.

Her hands tightened around the mug, the heat burning the sensitive skin of her palms.

"Well?" he prompted.

"I think I'll wait until Dad's back. We—every year since Mom died, we've done it together. It's a fun time." The walls of the kitchen seemed to be closing in on them. With every breath she drew, she became more aware of the man sitting across from her. They'd tried to pretend, but the kiss had changed everything. The taste of him lingered on her lips, and unconsciously she ran her tongue over them, wanting to recapture that sensation before it disappeared forever.

His eyes followed her movement, and he abruptly stood and marched across the kitchen to place his half-full mug in the sink.

"I'll see to the fire," he offered, hastily leaving the room.

"Thank you."

After emptying her own mug in the sink, she joined him, standing in the archway between the kitchen and living room.

She watched as he placed a small log in the red coals, and in moments flames were sizzling over the dry bark. Soon the fire crackled and hissed, hungry flames attacking the fresh supply of wood. Ol' Dan got slowly off the couch where he'd been sleeping and lay down in front of the fire with a comfortable sigh.

"I wonder what's happening with the road crew," Slade said.

"They could be here anytime."

They turned simultaneously toward the phone and collided. She felt the full impact of the unexpected contact, and her breath caught somewhere between her lungs and her throat, but not from pain.

"Shelly." His arms went around her faster than a shooting star. "Did I hurt you?"

One hand was trapped against his broad chest, while the other hung loosely at her side. "I'm fine," she managed, her voice as unsteady as his. Still, he didn't release her.

Savoring his nearness and warmth, she closed her eyes and pressed her head to his chest, listening to the beat of his heart beneath her ear.

Slade went utterly still, and then his arms tightened around her and he groaned her name.

Could anything that felt this wonderful, this good, be wrong? Shelly knew the answer, and her head buzzed with a warning. Even though her eyes were closed, she could see flashing red lights. Slade had held and kissed her only once, and he had instantly regretted it. He'd even refused to talk about it, closing himself off from her. This couldn't end well.

Yet all the logical arguments melted away like snow in a spring thaw when she was in his arms. His lips moved to her hair, and he breathed in deeply, as though to capture her scent.

"Shelly," he pleaded, his voice husky with emotion. "Tell me to stop."

The words wouldn't form. She knew that she should break away and save them both the agony of guilt. But she couldn't.

"I want you to hold me," she whispered. "Just hold me."

His arms tightened even further, anchoring her against him, and his lips nuzzled her ear, shooting tingles of pleasure down her spine. From her ear he found her cheek, her hair. For an eternity he hesitated.

The phone rang and they broke apart with a suddenness that made her lose her balance. Slade's hand on her shoulder steadied her. Brushing the hair from her face, she drew a steadying breath and picked up the phone.

"Hello." Her voice was barely above a whisper.

"Shelly? Are you all right? You don't sound like yourself."

"Oh, hi, Dad." She glanced up guiltily at Slade. His returning look was heavy with his own unhappiness. He brushed a hand through his hair and walked to the picture window, and she returned her attention to the call. "We got the tree."

"That's good." Her father paused. "Are you sure everything's fine?"

"Of course I'm sure," she answered, somewhat defensively. "How are things at the Adlers'?"

"Not good. I may be here awhile. I'm sorry to be away from you, but Slade's there to keep you company."

"How…long will you be?"

"A couple of hours, three at the most. You and Slade will be all right, won't you?"

But her father didn't sound any more convinced than she felt when she replied, "Oh, sure."

She replaced the receiver. Without the call as a buffer, the air in the room seemed to vibrate with Slade's presence. He turned around and met her gaze. "I've got to get to Seattle. Bauer said he's going to be at the office late anyway, finishing up some things so he can enjoy Christmas without work hanging over his head. I've really got to get there."

What he was really saying was that he had to get away from her. "I know," she told him. "But how?"

"How'd your dad get to that sick horse?"

"The Adlers' neighbor, Ted Wilkens, has a pickup with a plow blade. He came for Dad."

"Would it be possible for him to take me into Seattle?"

Shelly hadn't thought of that. "I'm not sure. I'll call."

"Although…it's Christmas Eve." He sounded hesitant, so different from the man she'd overheard on the phone yesterday, the man who hadn't cared about setting up a meeting for Christmas Eve.

"They're good people," she said, reaching for the phone. Slade paced nearby while she talked to Connie Wilkens.

"Well?" He studied her expectantly as she hung up the phone.

"Ted's out helping someone else, but Connie thinks he'll be back before dark. She suggested that we head their way, and by the time we arrive, Ted should be home."

"You're sure he won't mind?"

"Positive. Ted and Connie are always happy to help out their friends."

"They really are good people—like you and your dad," he murmured softly.

She laced her fingers together in front of her. "We're neighbors, although they're a good four miles from here. And friends." She scooted down in front of Ol' Dan and petted him in long, soothing strokes. "I told Connie that we'd start out soon."

Slade's brow furrowed as her words sank in. "But how? The tractor?"

"I couldn't run that thing if my life depended on it."

"Shelly, we can't trek that distance on foot."

"I wasn't thinking of walking."

"What other way is there?"

A smile graced her soft features until it touched her eyes, which sparkled with mischief. "We can always take the horses."

Seven

"**Y**ou have to be kidding!" Slade gave her a look of pure disbelief.

"No," Shelly insisted, swallowing a laugh. "It's the only possible way I know to get there. We can go up through the woods, where the snow isn't as deep."

Rubbing a hand over his eyes, Slade stalked to the far side of the room, made an abrupt about-face and returned to his former position. "I don't know. You seem to view life as one big adventure after another. I'm not used to…"

"Pokey's as gentle as a lamb," she murmured coaxingly.

"Pokey?"

"Unless you'd rather ride Midnight."

"Good grief, no. Pokey sounds more my speed."

Doing her best to hold back a devilish grin, she led the way into the kitchen.

"What are you doing now?"

"Making us a thermos of hot chocolate."

"Why?"

"I thought we'd stop and have a picnic along the way."

"You're doing it again," he murmured, but she noticed that an indulgent smile lurked just behind his intense dark eyes. He was a man who needed a little fun in his life, and she was determined to provide it. If she was only allowed to touch his life briefly, then she wanted to bring laughter and sunshine with her. Margaret would have him forever. But these few hours were hers, and she was determined to make the most of them.

"It'll be fun," she declared enthusiastically.

"No doubt Custer said the same thing to his men," he grumbled as they put their coats and boots back on, and he followed her out to the barn.

"Cynic," she teased, holding the barn door for him.

Reluctantly he preceded her inside.

"How do you feel about a lazy stroll in the snow, Pokey?" she asked as she reached the Appaloosa's stall and petted the horse's nose. "I know Sampson's ready anytime."

"Don't let her kid you, Pokey," Slade added from behind her. "Good grief, now you've got *me* doing it."

"Doing what?"

"Talking to the animals."

"Animals often share human characteristics," she said. "It's only natural for people to express their feelings to the animals that share their lives."

"In which case we're in trouble. Pokey is going to have a lot to say about how I feel when I climb on her back."

"You'll be fine."

"Sure, but will Pokey?"

"You both will. Now stop worrying."

When Shelly brought out the tack, Slade just stared at her, hands buried deep in his pockets, but then he stepped up and did what he could to help her saddle the two horses. Mostly he circled her awkwardly, looking doubtful.

When she'd finished, she led the horses out of the barn. Holding on to both sets of reins, she motioned for him to mount first. "Do you need any help?" she asked. He looked so different from the staid executive she'd met in Portland that she had trouble remembering that he really was the same person. The man facing her now was clearly out of his element, nothing like the unflappable man on the airplane.

"I don't think so," he said, reaching for the saddle and trying to follow Shelly's directions. Without much difficulty he swung himself onto Pokey's back. The horse barely stirred.

Looking pleased with himself, he smiled down at Shelly. "I suppose you told her to be gentle with me."

"I did," she teased in return. Double-checking the cinch, she asked, "Do you need me to adjust the stirrups or anything?"

"No." He shifted his weight slightly and accepted the reins she handed him. "I'm ready anytime you are."

She mounted with an ease that spoke of years in the saddle. "It's going to be a cold ride until we get under the cover of the trees. Follow me."

"Anywhere."

She was sure she must have misheard him. "What did you say?" she asked, twisting around in the saddle.

"Nothing." But he was grinning, and she found him

so devastatingly appealing that it demanded all her will-power to turn around and lead the way.

They quickly reached the path that took them through the woods. Gusts of swift wind blew the snow from the trees. The swirling flakes were nearly as bad as the storm had been. Even Pokey protested at having to be outside.

"Shelly," Slade said, edging the Appaloosa to Sampson's side. "This may not have been the most brilliant idea. Maybe we should head back."

"Don't be ridiculous."

"I don't want you catching cold on my account."

"I'm as snug as a bug in a rug," she said, using one of her father's favorite expressions.

"Liar," he purred softly.

"I want you to have something to remember me by." She realized she must sound like some lovesick romantic. He would be gone soon, and she had to accept that she probably would never see him again.

"Like what? Frostbite?"

She laughed. The musical sound was carried by the wind and seemed to echo in the trees around them. "How can you complain? This is wonderful. Riding along like this makes me want to sing."

He grumbled something unintelligible under his breath.

"What are you complaining about now?"

"Who says I'm complaining?"

She grinned, her head bobbing slightly with the gentle sway of Sampson's gait. "I'm beginning to know you."

"All right, if you insist on knowing, I happen to be

humming. My enthusiasm for this venture doesn't compel me to burst into song. But I'm doing the best I can."

Holding an unexpectedly contented feeling to her heart, she tried not to think about what would happen when they reached the Wilkens place. She was prepared to smile at him and bid him farewell, freely sending him out of her life. But that would have been easier before he'd held her in his arms and she'd experienced the gentle persuasion of his kiss. So very much easier.

Together, their horses side by side, they ambled along, not speaking but singing Christmas songs one after the other until they were breathless and giddy. Their voices blended magically in two-part harmony. More than once they shared a lingering gaze. But Shelly felt her high spirits evaporating as they neared the landmark that marked the half-way point of their journey.

"My backside is ready for a break," Slade announced unexpectedly.

"You aren't nearly as anxious to scoff at my picnic idea now, are you?" she returned.

"Not when I'm discovering on what part of their anatomy cowboys get calluses." A grin curved his sensuous mouth.

They paused in a small clearing, looping the horses' reins around the trunk of a nearby fir tree.

While she took the hot chocolate and some homemade cookies from her saddlebags, he exercised his stiff legs, walking around as though he were on stilts.

"We'll have to share the cup," she announced, holding out the plastic top of the thermos. She stood between the two horses, munching on a large oatmeal cookie.

Slade lifted the cup to his lips and hesitated as their

eyes met. He paused, slowly lowering the cup without breaking eye contact.

Her breath came in shallow gasps. "Is something wrong?" she asked with difficulty.

"You're lovely."

"Sure." She forced a laugh. "My nose looks like a maraschino cherry and—"

"Don't joke, Shelly. I mean it." His voice was gruff, almost harsh.

"Then thank you."

He removed his glove and placed his warm hand on her cold face, cupping her cheek. The moment was almost unbearably tender, and she swallowed the surging emotion that clogged her throat. It would be the easiest thing in the world to walk into his arms, lose herself in his kiss and love him the way he deserved to be loved.

As if reading her thoughts, Sampson shifted, bumping her back and delivering her into Slade's arms. He dropped the hot chocolate and hauled her against him like a man in desperate need.

"I told myself this wouldn't happen again," he whispered against her hair. "Every time I hold you, it becomes harder to let you go."

Her heart gave a small leap of pleasure at his words. She didn't want him to let her go. Not ever. Everything felt right between them. Too right and too good.

How long he held her, Shelly didn't know. Far longer than was necessary and not nearly long enough. Each second seemed to stretch, sustaining her tender heart for the moment when she would have to bid him farewell.

Not until they broke apart did she notice that it was

snowing again. Huge crystalline flakes filled the sky with their icy purity.

"What should we do?" he asked, looking doubtful.

Her first instinct was to suggest that they return to the house, but she hesitated. The thought of their inevitable goodbye became more difficult to bear every minute.

"We're going back," he said, answering his own question.

"Why?"

"I'm not leaving you and your father to deal with the horses. It's bad enough that I dragged you this far." Placing his foot in the stirrup, he reached for the saddle and remounted. "Come on, before this snow gets any worse."

"But we can make it to the Wilkens place."

"Not now." He raised his eyes skyward and scowled. "It's already getting dark."

Grumbling, she repacked her saddlebags, tugged Sampson's reins free of the tree trunk and lifted her body onto his back with the agile grace of a ballerina.

The house was in sight when Slade finally spoke again. "Once we get back, I need to contact Margaret. She'll be waiting. I told her I'd call Christmas Eve."

Shelly's heart constricted at the mention of the other woman's name. Until now, unless she'd asked about Margaret, Slade hadn't volunteered any information about his fiancée. Now he had freely thrust her between them.

"She's a good woman," he said when Shelly stayed silent.

She didn't know who he was trying to convince. "I didn't think you'd love a woman who wasn't."

"I've known Margaret a lot of years."

"Of course you have." And he'd only known *her* a few days. She understood what he was saying. It was almost as if he were apologizing because Margaret had prior claim to his loyalties and his heart. He didn't need to. She'd accepted that from the beginning.

When they left the cover of the woods, she spoke, managing to keep her voice level and unemotional. "You'll never get a cell signal way out here, not in this weather. You go in and use the phone," she said, surprised that her voice could remain so even. "I'll take care of the horses so you can make your call in private, and I'll call the Wilkenses when I'm done."

"I won't talk long."

"Don't cut the conversation short on my account."

He wiped his forearm across his brow. The movement brought her attention to the confusion in his eyes. "I won't."

By then they were at the barn, where she dismounted slowly, lowering both booted feet to the ground. He did the same, but she avoided his gaze as she opened the barn door and led the horses through. The wind followed her inside the dimly lit building. The cold nipped at her heels.

With a heavy heart she lifted the saddle from Pokey's back before she noticed Slade's dark form blocking the doorway. Her hands tightened around the smooth leather. "Is there a problem?"

"No."

After cross-tying Pokey in the aisle, Shelly turned back to Slade, only to find that he'd left.

Taking extra time with the horses, she put off entering the house as long as possible. Removing the gloves from her hands one finger at a time, she walked in the back door to discover Slade sitting in the living room staring blindly into the roaring fire. She walked quickly to the phone and called the Wilkenses. Connie was glad to hear from her and admitted that after a full day driving neighbors around in the snow, Ted was exhausted.

"I don't know about you," she called out cheerfully after hanging up the phone, "but I'm starved." The tip of her tongue burned with questions that pride refused to let her ask. She was dying to know what Slade had said to Margaret, if anything, about his current circumstances. "How about popcorn with lots of melted butter?"

He joined her, a smile lurking at the edges of his full mouth. His eyes were laughing, revealing his thoughts. He really did have wonderful eyes, and for a moment Shelly couldn't look away.

"I was thinking of something more like a triple-decker sandwich," he admitted.

"You know what your problem is, Garner?" It was obvious he didn't, so she took it upon herself to tell him. "No imagination."

"Because I prefer something meatier than popcorn?"

She pretended not to hear him—easy to do with her head buried in the open refrigerator. Without comment she brought out a variety of fixings and placed them on the tabletop.

She peeled off a slice of deli ham, tore it in two and gave Slade half. "How about a compromise?"

He looked dubious, as if he were sure she was about to suggest a popcorn sandwich. "I don't know…"

"How about if you bring in the tree while I fix us something to eat?"

"That's an offer I can't refuse."

Singing softly as she worked, Shelly concocted a meal neither of them was likely to forget. Sandwiches piled high with three different kinds of meat, sliced dill pickles and juicy green olives. In addition, she set out Christmas cookies and thick slices of fudge that she found sitting around the kitchen.

Slade set the tree in the holder, dragged it through the front door and stood it in the corner. "The snow's stopped," he told her when she carried in their meal.

"That's encouraging. I was beginning to think we'd be forced to stay until the spring thaw." Of course, she wouldn't have minded, and her smile was wistful.

Sitting Indian-style in front of the fireplace, their backs resting against the sofa, they dug into the sandwiches. But she found herself giving most of hers to Ol' Dan, having discovered that she had little appetite. Never had she been more aware of a man. They were so close that, when she lowered her sandwich to the plate, her upper arm brushed against his. But neither one of them made any effort to move, and she found that the contact, although impersonal, was soothing. She paused, trying to capture this moment of peacefulness.

"This has been a good day," he murmured, his gaze following hers as he stared out the living room window.

"It's certainly been crazy."

Without replying immediately, he reached for her

hand, entwining their fingers. "I don't know when I've enjoyed a day more." His dark gaze flickered over her and rested on her mouth. Abruptly he glanced away, his attention on the piano at the far side of the room. "Do you play?"

She sighed expressively. "A little. Dad claimed that my playing was what kept the mice out of the house."

He raised one dark brow with a touch of amusement. "That bad?"

"See for yourself." She rose and walked to the piano, lifted the lid of the bench seat and extracted some Christmas music.

When she pressed her fingers to the keys, the discordant notes were enough to make her wince, and cause Ol' Dan to lift his chin and cock his head curiously. He howled once.

"I told you I wasn't any good," she said with another dramatic sigh. Staring at the music, she squinted and sadly shook her head.

Slade joined her. Standing directly behind her, he laid his hands on her shoulders, leaning over to study the music.

"I think I may have found the problem," she stated seriously. Dimples formed in her cheeks as she tried not to smile. Turning the sheet music right side up, she leaned forward to study the notes a second time and tried again. This time a sweet melody flowed through the house.

Chuckling, Slade tightened his hands around her shoulders and spontaneously lowered his mouth to her cheek. "Have I told you how much fun you are?"

"No, but I'll accept that as a compliment."

"Good, because it was meant as one."

She continued to play, hitting a wrong note every once in a while and going back to repeat the bar until she got it right. Soon his rich voice blended with the melody. Her soprano tones mixed smoothly with his, although her playing faltered now and again.

Neither of them heard the front door open. "Merry Christmas Eve," Don announced.

Shelly froze with her hands above the keys and turned to look at him. "Welcome home. How's the Adlers' horse?"

Her father wiped a weary hand over his face. "She'll make it."

"What about you?" He was clearly exhausted. His pants were caked with mud and grit.

"Give me half an hour and I'll let you know."

"I can make you a sandwich if you're hungry."

"All I want right now is a hot shower." He paused to scratch Ol' Dan's ears. "Keep playing. You two sound good together."

"I thought we were scattering the mice to the barn," Slade teased.

Don scratched the side of his head with his index finger. "Say that again?"

"He's talking about my piano playing," she reminded her father.

"Oh, that. I don't suppose you play?"

"As a matter of fact, I do," Slade admitted.

"You do?" Shelly was stunned. "Why didn't you say something earlier? Here." She slid off the bench. "Trade places."

He claimed her position and ran his large, masculine hands over the keys with a familiarity that caused her heart to flutter. His fingers moved over the keys with reverence. Stroking, enticing the instrument, until the music practically had the room swaying. She felt tears gather in the corner of her eyes. Slade didn't play the piano; he made love to it.

When he'd finished, he rested his hands in his lap and slowly expelled his breath.

She sank into an easy chair. "Why didn't you tell me you could play like that?"

A smile brightened his eyes. "You didn't ask."

Even her father was awestruck and, for the first time in years, at a complete loss for words.

"You could play professionally. You're magnificent." Her soft voice cracked with the potency of her feelings.

"I briefly toyed with the idea at one time."

"Why didn't—"

"I play for enjoyment now." The light dimmed in his eyes, and the sharp edge of his words seemed to say that the decision hadn't come easy. And it clearly was not one he was willing to discuss, even with her.

"Will you play something else?" her father asked, his shower apparently on hold.

Judging by the look he shot her father, Slade appeared to regret admitting that he played the piano. She could tell that music was his real love, and he'd abandoned it. Coming this close again was probably pure torture for him. "Another time, perhaps."

Except that there wouldn't be another time, not for them. "Please," she whispered, rising to stand behind him, then placing her hands on his shoulders in a silent plea.

He covered her hand with his as he looked up into her imploring gaze. "All right, Shelly. For you."

For half an hour he played with such intensity that his shoulders sagged with exhaustion when he'd finished.

"God has given you a rare gift," her father said, his voice husky with appreciation. He glanced down at his mud-caked clothes. "Now, if you'll excuse me, I'll go take that shower before I start attracting flies."

As her father left the room, she moved to Slade's side, sitting on the bench beside him. Unable to find the words to express herself, she simply traced the sculptured line of his jaw as tears blurred her vision. The tightness in her chest made her breathing shallow and difficult.

He lifted a hand and stopped her, then brought her fingers to his lips and gently kissed her palm. She bit her bottom lip to hold back all the emotion stored in her heart.

A lone tear escaped and trickled down her pale cheek. Slade gently brushed it aside, his finger cool against her heated skin. He bent down and found her mouth with his. She realized that, without speaking a word, he was thanking her. With her, he'd allowed his facade to crumble. He'd opened his heart and revealed the deep, sensitive man inside. He was free now, with nothing more to hide.

Wrapping her arms around him, she kissed him in return, telling him in the only way she could how much she appreciated the gift of seeing his true self.

"Merry Christmas, Shortcake," her father greeted her on the tail end of a yawn.

Shelly stood in front of the picture window, cupping her coffee mug. Her gaze rested on the sunrise as it blanketed the morning with the bright hues of another day. She tried to force a smile when she turned to her father, but it refused to come. She felt chilled and empty inside.

"Where's Slade?" he asked.

"The snowplows came during the night," she whispered through the pain. "He's gone."

Eight

"Gone? Without saying goodbye?" A look of disbelief filled her father's eyes.

"He left a note." She withdrew it from her pocket and handed it to him. The message was only a few lines. He thanked them for their hospitality, and wished her and her father much happiness. And then said goodbye. Without regrets. Without second thoughts. Without looking back.

Her father looked up from the note and narrowed his eyes as he studied her. "Are you okay?"

"I'm fine."

He slowly shook his head. "I've never seen you look at a man the way you looked at Slade. You really liked him, didn't you?"

I love him! her heart cried. "He's a wonderful man. I only hope Margaret and that computer firm realize how lucky they are."

"They don't, you know," he whispered, slipping an arm around her shoulders and hugging her close. She offered him a feeble smile in return. "He might come back."

She knew differently. "No." He'd made his choice.

His future had been charted and defined as precisely as a road map. Slade Garner was a man of character and strength. He wouldn't abandon Margaret and all that was important to him for a two-day acquaintance and a few stolen kisses. He'd shared his deepest desires and secrets with her, opened his heart and trusted her. She shouldn't wish for more. But she did. She wanted Slade.

Christmas Day passed in a blur. Her brothers and their families were there, and somehow she managed to smile and talk and eat, with no one but her father any the wiser about her real feelings. She flew back to San Francisco the following afternoon, still numb, still aching, but holding her head up high and proud.

Her tiny apartment in the Garden District, although colorful and cheerfully decorated, did little to boost her drooping spirits.

Setting her suitcase on the polished hardwood floor, she kicked off her shoes and reached for the phone.

"Hi, Dad. I'm home." Taking the telephone with her, she sank into the overstuffed chair.

"How was the flight?"

"Went without a hitch."

"Just the way you like it." He chuckled, then grew serious. "I don't suppose…?"

"No, Dad." She knew what he was asking. He had thought that Slade would be in San Francisco waiting for her. She knew better. Slade wouldn't want to think of her. Already he'd banished any thought of her to the furthest corner of his mind. Perhaps what they'd shared was an embarrassment to him now.

She spoke to her father for a few minutes longer, then

claimed exhaustion and said goodbye. After she hung up she sat with the receiver cradled in her lap, staring blindly at the wallpaper.

Starting the next day she worked hard at putting her life back on an even keel. She went to work each day and did her utmost to forget the man who had touched her so profoundly.

Her one resolution for the New Year was simple: Find a man. For the first time since moving to San Francisco, she was lonely. Oh, she had friends and plenty of things to do, but nothing to take away the ache in her soul.

Two days before New Year's Eve, she stepped off the bus and on impulse bought flowers from a vendor on the street corner, then headed inside her building.

The elderly woman who lived across the hall opened her door as Shelly approached. "Good afternoon, Mrs. Lester," she said, pulling a red carnation from the bouquet and handing it to her neighbor.

"Now, isn't that a coincidence." Mrs. Lester chuckled. "I've got flowers for you."

Shelly's heart went still.

"The delivery boy asked me to give them to you." She stepped back inside, then stepped out and handed Shelly a narrow white box. "Roses, I suspect."

"Roses?" Shelly felt the blood drain from her face. She couldn't get inside her apartment fast enough. Closing the door with her foot, she walked across the room and set the box on a table. Inside she discovered a dozen of the most perfect roses she'd ever imagined. Each bud was identical to the others, their color brilliant.

Although she went through the box twice, she found no card. It was foolish to think Slade had sent them. Surely he wouldn't be so cruel as to say goodbye, only to invade her life again. Besides, he'd claimed roses were stupidly expensive, and she couldn't argue with that. They were, especially this time of year.

She was still puzzling over who could have sent them when the doorbell rang. She opened the door, and a deliveryman handed her a second long narrow box, identical to the first.

"Sign here." He offered her his pen.

Shelly scribbled her name across the bottom of the delivery order, then carried the second box to the kitchen table and opened it. Another dozen red roses, and again there was no card.

No sooner had she arranged all twenty-four flowers in her one and only tall vase when the doorbell chimed again. It was a deliveryman from another flower shop with another dozen roses.

"Are you sure you have the right address?" she asked.

"Shelly Griffin?" He read off her street address and apartment number, and raised expectant eyes to her.

"That's me," she conceded.

"Sign here."

She did. And for a third time discovered—with no surprise whatsoever at this point—that there was no card.

Without another vase to hold them, she emptied her tall jar of dill pickles into a bowl, rinsed out the jar and used that. With the first roses already brightening her living room, she left these to grace the kitchen.

Whoever was sending her so many flowers was either very rich or else extremely foolish, she thought.

Hands pressed against her hips, she surveyed the small apartment and couldn't decide if it resembled a flower shop or a funeral parlor.

When the doorbell chimed again, she sighed expressively. "Not again," she groaned aloud, turning the dead bolt and opening the door.

But instead of opening it to yet another delivery, she came face-to-face with Slade. He was so tall, so incredibly good-looking, that her breath became trapped in her lungs.

"Slade."

"Hello, Shelly." His eyes delved into hers, smiling and warm. "Can I come in?"

"Of…of course." Flustered, she stepped aside.

"Do you realize you only have on one shoe?"

"Why are you here?" she demanded. With her hands behind her back, she leaned against the closed front door, desperately wanting to believe everything she dared not even think about.

"I've missed you."

She closed her eyes to the tenderness in his voice. Words had never sounded sweeter. "Did you reschedule your meeting?" When he nodded, she asked, "How did it go?"

"Fine. Better than I expected."

"That's nice." She studied him, still unsure.

"I got a hefty bonus, but I may have offended a few friends."

"How did you do that?"

"They were hoping I'd accept a promotion."

"And you aren't?" A promotion sounded like something Margaret would love.

"No, I resigned this afternoon."

"Resigned? What did… Margaret have to say about that?"

"Well—" He took a step closer, stopping just short

of her but near enough to reach out and touch her if he wanted to. "—Margaret and I aren't exactly on speaking terms."

"Oh?" Her voice went incredibly weak.

"She didn't take kindly to some of my recent decisions."

I'll just bet, Shelly mused. "And what are those decisions…the most recent ones?"

"I decided to postpone the wedding."

She couldn't fault his fiancée for being upset about that. "Well, I can't say that I blame her. When—when's the new date?"

"Never."

"Never?" She swallowed tightly. "Why not?"

"Why not?" He smiled. "Because Margaret doesn't haul sourdough bread on an airplane or look forward to getting a horse blanket for Christmas or laugh at every opportunity or do any of the things that make life fun."

Speechless, she stared at him, love shining from her eyes.

"Nor does she believe I'll ever make a decent living as a pianist," he continued. "Hell, I'm nearly thirty now. It could be too late."

"But…?"

"But—" He smiled and reached for her, bringing her into the loving circle of his arms. "—I'm going to give it one whopper of a try. I'm no prize, Shelly Griffin. I don't have a job, and I'm not even sure the conservatory will renew the offer they made me once upon a time, but for the first time in too many years, I've got a dream."

"Oh, Slade," she whispered and pressed her face to

his broad chest. "I would consider it the greatest honor of my life to be a part of that dream."

"You couldn't help but be," he whispered, lifting her mouth to his. "You're the one who gave it to me."

* * * * *

1

From: Olivia Berg, Director, Christmas from the Heart
Date: 2-14-19
To: Ms. Marla Thompson, CSR Director, Hightower Enterprises
Subject: Holiday Joy

Dear Ms. Thompson,
Happy Valentine's Day to you! I'm following up our January newsletter with a special greeting as this is, of course, the month for love. Love for our sweethearts, our family and friends, and for those in need. As you could see from the newsletter, we put the money our loyal supporters donated to us to good use. So many families benefited from your generous donation to Christmas from the Heart last year and I just wanted to remind you that, even though the holidays seem far away they will be here before we know it. I hope we can count on Hightower Enterprises again this year. We have such a history together. Let's keep up the good work!
Warmly,
Olivia Berg

Christmas from the Heart
Giving from the heart makes all the difference

From: Marla Thompson, CSR Director, Hightower
Enterprises
Date: 2-14-19
To: Ms. Olivia Berg, Director, Christmas from the Heart
Subject: Holiday Joy

Dear Ms. Berg,
Thanks for reaching out. Our fiscal year is just ending
and I haven't yet received word as to how our chari-
table donations will be dispersed this year. I will keep
you apprised.
Best,
Marla Thompson
CSR Director, Hightower Enterprises

From: Olivia Berg, Director, Christmas from the Heart
Date: 2-14-19
To: Ms. Marla Thompson, CSR Director, Hightower
Enterprises
Subject: Holiday Joy

Thank you so much. Looking forward to hearing from
you!

From: Olivia Berg, Director, Christmas from the Heart
Date: 5-1-19
To: Ms. Marla Thompson, CSR Director, Hightower
Enterprises
Subject: Happy May Day!

Dear Ms. Thompson, just wanted to wish you a happy May Day. The flowers here in Pine River are now in full bloom, and our organization has been busy helping people make their dreams bloom as well. As you know, while our focus is primarily the holidays, Christmas from the Heart tries to help people all year round when needs arise. Of course, Christmas is our big thrust, and as there is no other organization working in this area, we are much needed. As are your kind contributions. I still haven't heard and I do hope we can count on you. Warmly,

Olivia Berg

Christmas from the Heart

Giving from the heart makes all the difference

From: Olivia Berg, Director, Christmas from the Heart
Date: 5-5-19
To: Ms. Marla Thompson
Subject: Just checking

Reaching out again in case my last email went astray. I'm wondering if you have any news for me regarding Hightower's involvement with our cause for this coming year.

Thanks!

Olivia Berg

Christmas from the Heart

Giving from the heart makes all the difference

From: Marla Thompson, CSR Director, Hightower Enterprises
Date: 5-5-19
To: Ms. Olivia Berg
Subject: Just checking

Ms. Berg, sorry I haven't been able to get back to you sooner. I'm afraid I have some bad news for you. It appears that the company is going to be scaling back on their charitable giving this year and funds have already been budgeted for other causes. I'm aware of the fact that in the past we've donated to your organization and I'm sorry I don't have better news for you. I do wish you all the best in your search for other funding.
Best,
Marla Thompson
CSR Director, Hightower Enterprises

From: Olivia Berg, Director, Christmas from the Heart
Date: 5-5-19
To: Ms. Marla Thompson
Subject: Just checking

There must be some sort of misunderstanding! Hightower has always donated to Christmas from the Heart. The company's founder, Elias Hightower, was my great-grandmother's first contributor, and he promised her that Hightower would always be there for this organization. This is a company tradition! Please speak to your director.
Hopefully,
Olivia Berg
Christmas from the Heart
Giving from the heart makes all the difference

From: Marla Thompson, CSR Director, Hightower Enterprises
Date: 5-5-19
To: Ms. Olivia Berg
Subject: Just checking

I'm sorry. The decision is out of my hands.
Marla Thompson
CSR Director, Hightower Enterprises

From: Olivia Berg, Director, Christmas from the Heart
Date: 5-5-19
To: Ms. Marla Thompson
Subject: Just checking

Then please tell me who I need to talk to. Who's your CFO?
Olivia Berg
Christmas from the Heart
Giving from the heart makes all the difference

From: Marla Thompson, CSR Director, Hightower Enterprises
Date: 5-5-19
Subject: Just checking

Our CFO is Guy Hightower, and his email is ghightower@hightowerenterprises.com
Good luck!
Marla Thompson
CSR Director, Hightower Enterprises

Olivia Berg, Director, Christmas from the Heart
Date: 5-5-19
To: Guy Hightower, CFO, Hightower Enterprises
Subject: Please reconsider

Dear Mr. Hightower, I understand from your corporate social resources director that Hightower isn't planning on making any donation to Christmas from the Heart this year. There must be some mistake! Surely you're aware of the long-standing relationship between your company and our organization. I'm sure I can count on you for some small amount.

Best,

Olivia Berg

Christmas from the Heart

Giving from the heart makes all the difference

Guy Hightower frowned when he saw the email from Olivia Berg in his in-box. Marla Thompson had been forwarding her emails to him, keeping him abreast of Olivia Berg's varied begging tactics, and had finally even come into his office, trying to dump the load of guilt the woman had laid on her from her shoulders to his.

"Don't open it," he told himself. He opened it anyway. Then he read it and swore.

Actually, he'd been swearing ever since meeting with his brothers to discuss the budget back in December. If either of them had listened to him three years ago, they wouldn't be having to pull the company belt so tight now. This was the problem with being the youngest. It didn't matter how many degrees you had, how smart you were or what your job title was. Big brothers never listened.

Hard to listen when you were going through your third divorce.

That was Mike's excuse. What was Bryan's? Oh yeah. He was a wuss. He always agreed with Mike, no matter what. And Mike hadn't wanted to change directions. Never mind that the company was struggling, keep on doing the same thing. The definition of insanity.

Sorry, little Miss Christmas. Times were tough all over. Hightower had kept its commitment to the more visible causes and turned the little fish loose. And that was how it worked in the corporate world.

He typed his reply.

Dear Ms. Berg, I regret that Hightower can't help you this year. We've had to reassess our commitments to various causes. I'm sure you'll understand.

Then he signed off with the time-honored adios: Respectfully, Guy Hightower.

And if she didn't understand, well, not his problem. He had his hands full trying to keep the family company afloat. Maybe now Mike would be ready to take his advice and diversify.

Olivia Berg—Livi to her family and friends—read the email from Guy Hightower a second time. Yes, the message was the same. Really? *Really?* Who was this man, Ebenezer Scrooge the Second?

She plowed her fingers through her hair, the birthstone ring Morris had given her for her birthday catching in the curls. She was so angry she barely noticed.

With a snarl, she began to type.

You should be ashamed. Your great grandfather is probably turning in his grave right now. What's the matter with you, anyway, you selfish bastard?

She pulled her fingers off the keyboard with a gasp. What was she thinking? Was this any way to get someone to contribute to her cause? And what kind of language was this? Her great-grandmother would be turning in her grave right now, along with Elias. Adelaide Brimwell had been a lady through and through. So had Livi's grandmother, Olivia, as well as Livi's mom.

The thought of her mother made her tear up. How she wished Mom was still around to advise her. They'd always planned that Livi would take over running the organization one day, but neither had dreamed that day would come so soon. Her mother's heart attack had struck like lightning. Livi's brother had left town, moving to Seattle, which was just far enough south to keep the memories at bay. Livi had stayed put, holding on to every single one, weaving them together into a lifeline to cling to as she kept Christmas from the Heart afloat.

Oh, Mom. What should I do?

Try again came the answer.

Yes, her mother never gave up. She'd chased one potential donor for two years before he finally came through. Livi still remembered the day her mom left the house, clad in a Mrs. Santa costume she'd created— requisite white wig along with a frilly white blouse and a red skirt topped with a red-striped apron. She'd taken with her a batch of home-baked cookies nestled in a red basket and returned home with a check for five hundred dollars. The man had been a loyal contributor ever since. Livi still took him cookies every year.

"Persistence pays," she told herself as she deleted what she'd typed.

She started over.

I'm asking you to reconsider. Your company is our major donor, and without you so many people will have little joy this Christmas. Any amount you can give will be greatly appreciated.

There. He'd have to be a heartless monster not to respond to that.

Guy trashed the guilt-inflicting email. What was he, Santa Claus? He had his hands full keeping his company solvent.

But then, people like Olivia Berg never considered the fact that a company might have needs of its own. What made them feel so entitled to sit at the edge of the salt mine while a man slaved away and then greet him with their hands out when he emerged broken and bruised? Maybe some of those people always begging for money should get out there and actually *earn* a living. Let them work their tails off, putting in seventy-hour weeks. *Sheesh.*

Anyway, the company had already met their good deed quota for the year. The only cause Guy was interested in now was Hightower Enterprises.

By the end of the workday, Guy Hightower still hadn't responded to Livi's last email. "You are a heartless monster," she grumbled, glaring at her empty email in-box.

"No word yet?" her part-time assistant, Bettina Thomas, asked as she shut down her computer.

Livi sighed and shook her head.

"That is so wrong," Bettina said in disgust.

It sure was. "They've been our major donor ever since my great-grandmother founded Christmas from the Heart. Without their contribution how will we put on the Christmas dinner at the community center? How many families won't have presents under the tree or Christmas stockings or a Christmas turkey?" There was no Salvation Army in Pine River, no Toys for Tots—none of the usual organizations serviced this area. There had been no need. Christmas from the Heart had it under control.

Until now.

"We've had to reassess our commitments," Livi quoted. The words left a bad taste in her mouth and she frowned. "It sounds like something your boyfriend says when he's dumping you."

"They are dumping us," Bettina pointed out. "But don't worry. We have time. We'll find someone else to come through."

"Not like Hightower. There must be something I can do," Livi mused.

"There is. Go home and eat chocolate."

And try not to think bad thoughts about Guy Hightower.

In all fairness, he probably didn't grasp the situation. She'd call him the next day and invite him to come to Pine River for a visit so she could let him see the need, show him a little of what Christmas from the Heart did for the community. She could take him to lunch, introduce him to some of the people in town, put a face—or better yet, several—to Christmas from the Heart. She'd top it all off by following in her mother's footsteps and baking him cookies. Then how could he help but catch the vision his great-great-grandfather and her great-great-grandmother had shared?

Yes, that would do it. Sometimes you had to be a little patient, give people a second chance.

2

Trying a more personal touch with Guy Hightower was the way to go, Olivia was sure of that, but getting past his secretary was proving to be a challenge. Maybe giving her name hadn't been such a good idea. The first time she called, Mr. Hightower was in a meeting. The second time she called, he was out. He was in another meeting on her third call, then unavailable on her fourth.

Finally, she asked, "Is there a good time to reach him?"

"I'm afraid Mr. Hightower is very busy," his secretary said evasively.

Livi suspected that Mr. Hightower was very busy avoiding her. "Tell him I'll only take a minute of his time," she pleaded.

"Can you hold please?"

"For as long as it takes," Olivia said sweetly.

Olivia Berg was never going to go away. She was going to keep on calling and calling, driving his secretary nuts, and Guy was beginning to suspect if he didn't talk to her she'd come to Seattle and camp out in the lobby of the Hightower Building until he would.

"Fine," he said irritably. "Put her through." *Get it over with.*

"Mr. Hightower, thank you so much for taking a moment to talk to me," she gushed as soon as he'd taken the call.

"I'm not sure we have much to talk about at this point, Ms. Berg," he said. "As I told you in my email—"

She cut him off, rushing on like a vacation time-share salesman. "I'm realizing that email isn't always the most effective way to communicate. I'd love to meet with you in person. I think if you could visit Pine River and see what Christmas from the Heart does—"

Like he had time to go charging up to her little town and get hassled in person. Now it was his turn to snip her off midsentence. "I'm sure you do a lot of good, but we can't help you this year."

"Mr. Hightower, we have such a history together."

He knew all about their history, probably more than she did.

"Surely you can manage something."

One thing Guy couldn't manage at this point was his temper. He'd just come from a very unpleasant meeting with his idiot brothers and he wanted to punch a wall. "Look—"

"Any amount would be helpful. People have so many needs during the holidays."

"I know they do but I can't help you."

"A big corporation like yours," she began.

Oh yeah. Play that card. *You're a big company so we'll hit you up and you should be proud that we are.*

"I don't know how many ways to say this politely but the answer is no."

"You can't mean that," she coaxed. "Your company's been so good to us all these years."

And here came here came the guilt card. Wrong card to play. "I'm afraid I can."

"Again, please consider the history we have together," she pleaded.

"I'm sorry, but things change."

"Change isn't always good," she snapped. "You have no idea how many people depend on Christmas from the Heart."

"I've got people depending on me, too. Okay?"

"Well, of course. But surely…"

"I can't give you anything." His voice was rising, right along with his blood pressure.

"There's no need to yell," she said stiffly. "I'd just hoped you'd reconsider. We're not asking a lot."

"It's a lot if you don't have it."

"Hightower Enterprises is a big company. Really, Mr. Hightower—"

Now she was going to lecture him on what his company could and couldn't afford to give? Okay, that was it. "What don't you understand about the word no? Look, lady, I've been as polite as I can, but I'm not getting through, so we're done here. We can't give to every leech that latches onto us and that's that."

"Leech!" she repeated, her voice vibrating with shock. "Well, of all the rude…"

"Hey, if you want to talk about rude, I'm not the one bugging people so they can't get their work done. I'm not the one who can't take no for an answer. But believe it or not, that's what it is. So cut it out with the high-pressure crap 'cause I'm not giving you squat. Got that?" He didn't give her time to say whether she got it or not. He ended the call.

And then he suffered a major guilt attack. That had been cold. Ebenezer Scrooge couldn't have said it better.

He rubbed his aching forehead. What was the matter with him, anyway? People had needs. They lost jobs and not always because they'd done anything wrong. Sometimes you worked your butt off and things didn't work out.

For all he knew, things might not work out for his company in spite of his long hours. But that was no excuse for being a jerk. Bad PR for the company, too.

He heaved a sigh and pulled his checkbook out of his desk drawer, then wrote a check for a couple hundred. There. Maybe that would make Olivia Christmas from the Heart happy.

Livi's heart soared when she went to the post office to collect the mail and saw the official Hightower Enterprises envelope. Yes! Guy Hightower had a heart after all. Or maybe he simply felt bad for the way he'd behaved over the phone. Either way, she'd happily take his company's contribution.

Of course, she thought as she slit open the envelope, it probably would be less this year. But, okay, they could make do with...

Two hundred dollars? She stared at the check. It wasn't a company check. It was a personal one, and this was it.

If any other person had donated a couple hundred

bucks, she'd have been delighted. Many of their donors gave small amounts of twenty-five or fifty dollars. But those were people on modest incomes, struggling to make ends meet, not well-heeled CFO's.

"You…cheapskate," she growled. "I hope you get what's coming to you this Christmas—poison in your eggnog and a lump of coal where the sun don't shine."

She stormed down the street back to her office, which was nothing more than a small suite in the second story of an old Victorian that housed Tillie's Teapot, a tearoom that was a draw for both locals and people from neighboring towns. Tillie Henderson owned both the tearoom and the house. She was pushing ninety, and her two daughters, Jean and Annette, did most of the work now—cooking and managing the place, serving high tea, offering elegant lunches and Sunday brunches you had to make a reservation for a month in advance. Tillie herself still acted as hostess on the weekdays though, and had the final say in the business decisions. She'd not only contributed to Christmas from the Heart over the years but had offered them office space at a bargain price. They shared the upper floor with an interior decorator and a writer who preferred to get out of the house to work. The interior decorator was rarely around, usually out staging houses for the local real estate companies, but the writer, Jillian George, was always in her office, and Livi could usually hear her in there toward the end of the day, reading aloud what she'd written earlier. Jillian wrote gory murder mysteries. If she was looking for someone to bump off Livi had just the man.

She marched upstairs to Christmas from the Heart

headquarters, sat down at her little desk and glared at her computer screen. Of course, she needed to acknowledge Guy Hightower's contribution. And she should be grateful. People gave to charities out of the goodness of their hearts and every gift helped the cause. But, in light of how much his company normally gave, this sure came off as stingy.

She opened her trusty refurbished laptop and began to type.

Dear Mr. Hightower. Thank you for your contribution.

No way was she going to call it generous.

We cheerfully accept all contributions, even small ones.

Heehee.

I do hope this Christmas you are blessed as generously as you've given.

Double heehee.

She hit Send with a smile.

"What are you looking so happy about?"

Livi looked up to see Kate Greer, her best friend and right-hand woman, leaning against the doorjamb. Kate was a genius with money, and when she wasn't doing accounting for local businesses like Tillie's, she could be found giving her time to Christmas from the Heart, watching over their finances.

Like Livi, she had hit the big 3-0, but she had more to show for it—a fat diamond on her left hand and a wedding planned for the next spring. She even had money in savings. Built like a Barbie doll, she did Pilates three times a week and had recently splurged for a Botox touch-up.

Livi didn't make enough to have extra money for savings, much less face fix-ups. New shoes were a splurge. Anyway, even if she had the money, she wasn't sure she could bring herself to spend it on such luxuries when Christmas from the Heart needed life support.

"I'm not happy," Livi informed her friend. "I'm just indulging in a moment of petty, evil glee." She went on to explain about the latest development with Guy Hightower and her tongue-in-cheek response to his token contribution.

Kate frowned disapprovingly and shook her head. "Was that one of your smarter moves?"

The evil glee disappeared faster than cookies for Santa. "Well."

"You don't want to burn bridges. I get that you're frustrated, but it's not like you to be so undiplomatic. That's my job," she added with a smile, softening the scold.

"I know. It's just that this jerk has got me so mad. And talk about undiplomatic. Leeches? Really?"

"He might feel like that. Maybe they get hit up a lot. They don't have to give you anything," Kate reminded her.

"But they gave to other nonprofits," Livi protested. "After supporting us for generations. It's like…breaking a treaty. And a lot of people are going to suffer because of it. And to put us off for so long and then unceremoniously dump us." She shook her head. "That was sick and wrong."

"Corporate finances are complicated. The company may be struggling to meet their payroll."

"We're all struggling," Livi said irritably. She held up the check. "A personal check. He's probably trying to ease his conscience."

"So, let him. What do you care?"

Of course, her friend was right. A donation was a donation. But Guy Hightower's words still stung. "A leech," she muttered.

"Yeah, that's you. Some leech. That pittance you take can hardly be called a salary."

"I don't need much," Olivia said. "I get by." To supplement her income, she cleaned house for one of the town's more well-off women and picked up an occasional pet-sitting job when someone got the itch to travel. So what if she didn't have a lot of money in savings? So what if she was still living at home? That was helping her make ends meet and helping her father, as well.

"You're running around in consignment clothes and at some point you're going to have to replace that beater of yours. Plus you've put nothing into your retirement fund in the last six months, Miss Live-on-fumes-so-you-can-help-the-whole-world." This was the downside of having her friend for her accountant.

"I'm not going to be helping very many people this year," Livi said miserably.

"Things will work out somehow," Kate assured her.

"Yeah, well, it's finding the *somehow* that I'm worried about."

"Come on. Let's go downstairs and have lunch. We can drown your sorrows in some Earl Grey and we'll brainstorm ways to make up the difference."

Livi currently had a whopping thirty-two dollars in her checking account and three dollars and some change in her wallet. Much as she liked Tillie and her daughters and loved to support their business, she'd as soon go home and make herself a PBJ sandwich and save the money.

"I'm paying," Kate added, "so don't give me any excuses."

"I hate when you pay for lunch," Liv said.

"I know. How many times have we had this conversation—about a million? I can afford lunch at Tillie's and every time I buy lunch it saves you money, which means you have more to pour back into Christmas with a Heart. So, really, when I buy lunch I'm doing a good deed."

"You already do enough good deeds around here."

"So do you. Come on, let's go. I'm starving."

Lunch at Tillie's Teapot always made Livi feel better when she was having a bad day. So what was different about today? The smells were as wonderful, the herbed scones were delicious, the homemade quiche to die for and Tillie's lemon pound cake was always incredible. But nothing tasted as good as it should have. Guilt made a poor seasoning. Kate was right. Livi shouldn't have sent that email. Instead she should have sent a gushy, suck-up, thank-you note. What was wrong with her, anyway?

That could be summed up in two words: Guy Hightower. The man was not bringing out the best in her. The sun was shining, the flowers were in bloom, people were coming and going, all smiling, and she wanted to jump in the river. She'd blown it. And when you were

dealing with big money and big egos you couldn't afford to blow it. Who knew what damage her lack of
graciousness had done?

Probably none, she finally decided. Guy Hightower
was a jerk.

Guy put in an extra two miles on the treadmill at
the gym, but it didn't help him run off his anger. Olivia
Berg was a snotty ingrate. Christmas from the Heart.
Yeah, right. She was all heart until you didn't come
through, then look out. They were well rid of her and
her tacky little charity. It would be a cold day in the
Caribbean before she ever saw another penny of Hightower money.

Of course, he'd matched her sarcastic tone, firing
back an email of his own:

And I hope you'll get just what you deserve. With your
great people skills, you'll have no problem finding more
sponsors for your cause.

As if he'd shown any great people skills in their encounter. He should have called her back and apologized,
explained that he was under a lot of pressure. But then
she'd have started in on him all over again.

He finished up at the gym, then went to his condo,
where he showered, pulled a microbrew from the fridge
and plopped onto his couch to glare at the killer view
from his tenth-floor window. He supposed Olivia Berg
would be scandalized if she saw where he lived. So he
had a nice place? So, sue him. He'd waited ten years to
buy this place, living with slob roommates and hoard-

ing his money. He worked his butt off, had rarely taken a vacation since he'd stepped in as CFO. This place and his Maserati Gran Turismo were his only extravagances, and he refused to feel guilty about either of them. Well, okay, so he and his brothers still had the place in Vail. But that was family owned so it didn't count. Not that anyone had any business to be counting.

A text came in from one of his old college buddies wanting to shoot some pool at their favorite sports bar.

"Oh yeah, now I remember. That's what you look like," teased Jackson when Guy walked up to him at the bar. "I was starting to forget."

Guy held up a hand. "I know, I know. Life's been crazy."

"Your life's been crazy ever since you put on the Hightower harness. Hale's Red Menace for my man," he said to the bartender, ordering Guy's favorite local amber ale. "On me." He gave Guy an assessing once-over. "You're already starting to look old."

"And you're starting to look like a loser," Guy shot back. "Forty hours a week. What's that gonna get you?"

"A life."

The bartender gave Guy his beer, and he and his friend clinked bottles. "Here's to having a life," Guy said. "Which I've got."

"Yeah, that's probably what Scrooge said," his friend scoffed.

Scrooge. Who'd invited him to this party? "He's my hero," Guy quipped, and then thought of Olivia Berg. She was convinced he was a Scrooge.

She was also a judgmental little pest. "Come on. I see a pool table calling our name," he said.

"Fifty bucks for a race to seven?" suggested Jackson.

"That all you can afford?" Guy taunted.

"Okay, a hundred. It'll be the easiest hundred I ever made. You're probably out of practice."

Jackson broke and Guy went next and a little voice at the back of his mind hissed, *You just wasted a hundred dollars betting on a pool game.*

I didn't waste it cuz I'm not gonna have to pay it, Guy hissed back, and missed his first shot.

"Yep, out of practice," teased Jackson.

No, just distracted.

And Guy remained distracted for the rest of the evening, missing shots he could normally make with his eyes closed. In the end he wound up forking over a hundred bucks to his pal.

You just wasted...the voice began.

Shut up!

Guy paid for one last round of beers, then scrammed. He'd had enough of pool for one night and he'd definitely had enough of the voice.

On Saturday, he had a date with a woman he'd been seeing off and on. Partway through dinner she began hinting about a vacation cruise. Like he had time to take a cruise? Like they were that serious? His lack of enthusiasm disappointed her and her disappointment irked him, and before the night was over they were done. "This relationship is going nowhere," she'd said.

That had been fine with him. The last serious relationship he'd had was in college and that had definitely gone somewhere. Somewhere bad. Oh yeah, Miss Perfect had loved him until she found someone with more money, then she'd dumped him like so much junk stock.

When Guy had demanded to know what was so special about the loser she was leaving him for—the guy she'd been sneaking into her life—she'd pretended her choice had nothing to do with greedy, grasping finger syndrome. "He's sweet."

He sure wasn't good-looking or very well liked. So, sweet? Really? Yeah, she'd been looking beneath the surface. Of his bank account.

"What? And I'm not?" Guy had demanded. He'd been sweet. Obviously, not sweet enough. Guy had only offered skiing at Vail while Mr. Sweet had offered a visit to Paris with his family.

"Come on, Jordan," Guy had argued. "The guy's a tool."

"And he's already a millionaire thanks to the app he created," she'd shot back, showing her true colors.

"I guess you have to think about the future," he'd said. His jaw had been clenched so tightly he'd barely been able to get the words out.

At least she'd had the grace to blush. But that was as far as her conscience was prepared to go. She left him in the coffee shop, bleeding internally.

Heart operation without anesthetic. Guy hadn't known which was worse, the pain of rejection or the humiliation. Just when he'd thought things were getting serious between them.

He should have seen the signs—the texts that went unanswered, the canceled dates. He'd been the world's smartest business major and the world's dumbest boyfriend.

"Lesson learned," his mother had said when she'd pried the whole ugly tale out of him. "There are givers in this world and there are takers. Spend enough time with someone and you'll eventually learn which one she is."

"I don't know why I didn't see it," he'd said miserably. He should have. A third of Jordan's sentences had seemed to start with "Buy me," or "Let's," which usually also amounted to "Buy me," only he got to be included.

"Don't be in a hurry. Take your time," his mom had advised. "The right woman will come along when she's supposed to."

Or not.

Ever since, he'd preferred to keep things light. He was in no hurry to get serious, and seeing the love mess his older brother's life was confirmed the wisdom of that. Women dated Hightower men for one thing only: their money. It was all they really wanted. Even the so-called altruistic ones like Olivia Berg. When it came to money, in the end, nobody was altruistic.

Christmas from the Heart
by Sheila Roberts
Available now from MIRA Books,
wherever books are sold.

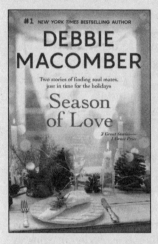

The countdown to Christmas begins now!
Keep track of all your Christmas reads.

September 24

☐ *A Coldwater Christmas* by Delores Fossen

☐ *A Country Christmas* by Debbie Macomber

☐ *A Haven Point Christmas* by RaeAnne Thayne

☐ *A MacGregor Christmas* by Nora Roberts

☐ *A Wedding in December* by Sarah Morgan

☐ *An Alaskan Christmas* by Jennifer Snow

☐ *Christmas at White Pines* by Sherryl Woods

☐ *Christmas from the Heart* by Sheila Roberts

☐ *Christmas in Winter Valley* by Jodi Thomas

☐ *Cowboy Christmas Redemption* by Maisey Yates

☐ *Kisses in the Snow* by Debbie Macomber

☐ *Low Country Christmas* by Lee Tobin McClain

☐ *Season of Wonder* by RaeAnne Thayne

☐ *The Christmas Sisters* by Sarah Morgan

☐ *Wyoming Heart* by Diana Palmer

October 22

☐ *Season of Love* by Debbie Macomber

October 29

☐ *Christmas in Silver Springs* by Brenda Novak

☐ *Christmas with You* by Nora Roberts

☐ *Stealing Kisses in the Snow* by Jo McNally

November 26

☐ *North to Alaska* by Debbie Macomber

☐ *Winter's Proposal* by Sherryl Woods

Harlequin.com

XMAS0319BPA

Get 4 FREE REWARDS!

We'll send you 2 FREE Books plus 2 FREE Mystery Gifts.

FREE
Value Over
$20

Both the **Romance** and **Suspense** collections feature compelling novels written by many of today's bestselling authors.